"Something about you here in my kitchen, in my space, freaks me out."

Darby wiped his mouth and contemplated Renny. "I'm not real comfortable being here myself, but it's got to be done."

She cocked her head. "Why? It's been years and we're both different people. Is there really a need to drag up old feelings? Can't we let it be what it was—two crazy kids looking to thumb their noses at authority then learning they weren't as smart as they thought they were? We were both to blame for what happened, so we don't need apologies."

"It's not about apologies, though I do think I owe you one. I had no idea you were injured so severely in the accident."

"You wouldn't have because you never bothered to come see me."

"What are you talking about? You refused to see me." Truth was evident in his gaze. He wasn't jerking her chain. The surprise in his reaction was honest.

"I never refused you anything. Ever." Renny sighed. "That was the problem."

Dear Reader,

Homecoming stories are a particularly satisfying read; in fact, they are my favorite type of story. There's something fulfilling about watching two people fall in love a second time around, so I couldn't wait to get my fingers on the keyboard to write Renny and Darby's story. After all, I'd been thinking about them from the very beginning of The Boys of Bayou Bridge series. I knew them and their past, so writing their story would be a snap, right?

Wrong. Like the Louisiana weather, Renny and Darby weren't easy to figure out, and as each chapter unfolded, they evolved into complex creatures who kept me guessing. See? Sometimes even an author is surprised by her own story.

And what a story it is—manipulative parents, a surprise marriage and whooping cranes. Yes, whooping cranes. Not to mention a little voodoo.

So grab a mint julep, or a mint tea, and give me your best Cajun accent. It's time to go back to Beau Soleil with its shadowed past and eccentric matriarch. It's time for gators, fishing and a piece of Lucille's pie…and most importantly, it's time for Darby Dufrene to walk the road back to Bayou Bridge.

I hope you enjoy this last book in The Boys of Bayou Bridge series. I love hearing from my readers—you can drop me a line at www.liztalleybooks.com or write to me at P.O. Box 5418, Bossier City, LA 71171.

Happy reading!

Liz Talley

P.S. Look for my next book coming in December 2012!

The Road to Bayou Bridge

LIZ TALLEY

HARLEQUIN®

entertain, enrich, inspire™

Recycling programs
for this product may
not exist in your area.

ISBN-13: 978-0-373-71800-9

THE ROAD TO BAYOU BRIDGE

www.Harlequin.com

Printed in U.S.A.

ABOUT THE AUTHOR

From devouring the Harlequin Superromance novels on the shelf of her aunt's used bookstore to swiping her grandmother's medical romances, Liz Talley has always loved a good romance. So it was no surprise to anyone when she started writing a book one day while her infant napped. She soon found writing more exciting than scrubbing hardened cereal off the love seat. Underneath Liz's baby-food-stained clothes, a dream stirred. She followed that dream, and after a foray into historical romance and a Golden Heart final, she started her first contemporary romance on the same day she met her editor. Coincidence? She prefers to call it fate.

Currently Liz lives in north Louisiana with her high-school sweetheart, two beautiful children and a passel of animals. Liz loves watching her boys play baseball, shopping for bargains and going out for lunch. When not writing contemporary romances for the Harlequin Superromance line, she can be found doing laundry, feeding kids or playing on Facebook.

Books by Liz Talley

HARLEQUIN SUPERROMANCE

1639—VEGAS TWO-STEP
1675—THE WAY TO TEXAS
1680—A LITTLE TEXAS
1705—A TASTE OF TEXAS
1738—A TOUCH OF SCARLET
1776—WATERS RUN DEEP*
1788—UNDER THE AUTUMN SKY*

*The Boys of Bayou Bridge

Other titles by this author available in ebook format.

For my grandmother Grace,
with her French temper, bayou roots and love of
a good bargain. No doubt you'd find kinship with
Bev…though you'd never admit to it.

You were a strong woman even if you
never filled up your own gas tank.
I miss you.

CHAPTER ONE

August 2012
Naval Station, Rota, Spain

THE PAPER ACTUALLY SHOOK in Darby Dufrene's hand—that's how shocked he was by the document he'd discovered in a box of old papers. He'd been looking for the grief book he'd made as a small child and instead had found something that made his gut lurch against his ribs.

"Dude, come on. The driver needs to go." Hal Severson's voice echoed in the half-full moving truck parked below the flat Darby had shared with the rotund navy chaplain for the past several years. His roommate had waited semi-good-naturedly while Darby climbed inside to grab the book before it was shipped to Seattle, but good humor had limits.

"Just a sec," Darby called, his eyes refusing to leave the elaborate font of the certificate he'd pulled from a clasped envelope trapped in the back of his Bayou Bridge Reveille yearbook. How in the hell had this escaped his attention? Albeit it had been buried in with some old school papers he'd tossed aside over ten years ago and vowed never to look at again, surely the state of Louisiana seal would have permeated his brain and screamed, *Open me!*

Yet, back then he'd been in a funk—a childish, rebellious huff of craptastic proportions. He probably hadn't thought about much else except the pity party he'd been throwing himself.

The moving truck's engine fired and a loud roar rumbled through the trailer, vibrating the wood floor. The driver was eager to pick up the rest of his load, presumably a navy family heading back to the States, and his patience with Darby climbing up and digging through boxes already packed was also at an end. Darby slid the certificate back into its manila envelope, tucked it into his jacket and emerged from the back end of the truck.

Hal's red hair glinted in the sunlight spilling over the tiled roof, and his expression had evoled to exasperation. The man was hungry. Had been hungry for hours while the movers slowly packed up Darby's personal effects and scant pieces of furniture, and no one stood between Hal and his last chance to dine in El Puerto de Santa Maria, the city near the Rota Naval Base, with his best comrade. "Let's go already. Saucy Terese and her crustacean friends await us."

"Not Il Caffe di Roma, Hal. I don't want to look into that woman's eyes and wonder if she might greet me with a filet knife."

"You ain't that good, brother," Hal said in a slow Oklahoma drawl. "She'll find someone else on which to ply her wiles when the new guy arrives."

"You mean the new guy whose name is Angela Dillard?"

"The new JAG officer's a girl?"

Darby smiled. "Actually she's a woman."

Hal jingled his keys. *"Entendido."*

"Your Spanish sucks."

"Whatever. Now get your butt in gear. There are some crabs and sherry with my name on them."

Darby tried to ignore the heat of the document pressing against his chest. Of course, it wasn't actually hot. Just burning a hole in his stomach with horrible dread. He was an attorney and the document he carried wasn't a prank, but he couldn't figure out how the license had been filed. His father had virtually screamed the implausibility at him nearly eleven years ago—the day he'd shipped Darby off to Virginia—so this didn't make sense. "Fine, but if Terese comes toward me with a blade, you must sacrifice yourself. If not, Picou will ply the sacrificial purifications of the Chickamauga on you. She's been waiting for five years to get me back home to Beau Soleil."

Hal rubbed his belly. "Did they perform human sacrifices?"

"Who? The Native Americans or Picou?"

"Either."

Darby grinned. "I don't know about the Chickamauga, but my mom will go psycho if I don't climb off that plane."

"Consider it done. No way I'm left to deal with your mother. She makes mine look like that woman from *Leave It to Beaver*."

"Your mom *is* June Cleaver all the way down to the apron and heels." Darby knew firsthand. Her weekly chocolate chips cookies had caused him to pack on a few pounds.

"I know. All women pale in comparison." Hal opened the door of his white convertible BMW, his one prideful sin, and slid in. He perched a pair of Ray-Bans on his nose and fired the engine.

"Except our housekeeper, Lucille. Can't wait to get my hands on her pecan pie." Darby took one last look at his beachfront flat before sliding onto the hot leather seats of Hal's car. He'd already shipped his motorcycle to the States weeks ago. He wanted it available when he got to Seattle and went in search of apartments, though he knew he'd likely have to sell it in favor of a respectable sedan. With all that Northwest rain, he'd have little chance to take as many mind-clearing drives as he had along the coast of Spain. Plus, Shelby hated it.

"Well, say goodbye, dude," Hal said, sweeping one arm over the sunbaked villa where Darby had spent the past two years, before pulling away and heading toward the motorway that would take them into the city.

"Goodbye, dude," Darby said, parroting his friend. He smiled as the wind hit his cheeks, but as soon as he remembered the document, his smile slipped away. Trouble brewed and this homecoming would be no cakewalk despite the pecan pie that waited.

"Are you sad? Thought you'd been ready to leave Rota since you got here, Louisiana boy."

How could Darby tell him his mood wasn't about leaving the base and his small adventure in Spain but about the marriage license he'd found in his high school trunk? He could, but there was no sense in ruining his last night with the man who'd become like a brother to him over the course of his deployment. With Hal being the base chaplain, most would think him an odd choice of roommate for a formerly degenerate bayou boy, but something about Hal clicked as soon as Darby met the man who'd been looking for a flatmate. Having Hal as a friend, guide and trusted mentor had made the move overseas tolerable. In fact, after a few months, Darby had downright enjoyed himself.

And he'd found Shelby through Hal.

And when he met the blonde teacher who taught at the American school on base, he knew he'd finally grown up, finally left his confusion and his past behind. Here was what he'd been looking for—a beautiful woman, a promising career, if the interview went well, and a clean slate in a new place—so he'd flung the dice and shipped his things to Seattle rather than home to Bayou Bridge.

He patted the inside pocket of his jacket.

But maybe he wouldn't be moving forward as soon as he'd planned.

Because he was fairly certain he was legally married to Renny Latioles.

RENNY LATIOLES ADJUSTED her reading glasses and stared at the computer screen. How did L9-10 get so far away from the Black Lake Reservoir? And even more disturbing, why was the damn crane on Beau Soleil property?

"She still there?" fellow biologist Carrie Dupuy asked, mindlessly sipping the bitter coffee that had been sitting in the urn all day long. Coffee stayed brewing at the Black Lake station where they worked side by side on the reintroduction of the whooping crane into South Louisiana.

"Yeah, and I don't get it. It's over sixty miles from the habitat you'd think she would prefer. No other crane has gone that far to the north. There isn't a lot of marsh in that parish even with the wetlands receding."

"It's been well over a week, Ren. Maybe you better head up and get a visual. Make sure she's not tangled up in something."

"But the bird is moving around in a fairly large perimeter. If you look at this satellite map, you can see the field it's inhabiting." Renny dragged a finger across the screen. "Look. Woodlands, bayou and one abandoned rice field."

Carrie frowned at the computer. "I agree. It doesn't make sense, but obviously L9-10 has found a little slice of heaven in St. Martin Parish. Maybe this is a good thing, this adapting and surviving in an atypical area, but we need to check this out in person, and since you live up that way…"

Renny pushed back from the screen, rolling toward the filing cabinet sitting a few yards away. She grabbed a fresh logbook.

"Why not just take your computer?"

Pushing tendrils of hair out of her eyes, Renny shook her head. "Nope. Going old-school. Especially since Stevo lost the tablet in the basin. I'll take handwritten notes and then add them to our files when I return. If L9-10 decides to stay in her new digs, I'll have to spend a bit more time close to Bayou Bridge."

"Easy for you because you live there."

Renny shook her head. "It actually worries me since you're heading to Virginia in a few weeks."

"I'll call Stevo in Baton Rouge and see if he can send Ruby back to work on field notes and mind the fledglings. The captive cranes seemed to like her. She even got L-3 to take walks with her."

Renny nodded. "She's a good grad assistant. Glad we got her instead of that smarmy ex-fraternity president."

As the project manager carrying out the reintroduction of the whooping crane into the wintering grounds of Southwest Louisiana, Renny had tremendous pressure to succeed on her shoulders. The federal and state grants only stretched so far, and after losing one of the released cranes to natural predators earlier that summer, she felt even more driven to prove all was going as planned. Private donors liked to see results—successful results—or they didn't open their wallets. And at the rate their funds were dwindling, they needed to tread carefully.

Renny felt something sink in her stomach. Ironically, L9-10 was on Beau Soleil property, which, come to think of it, wasn't so odd considering the Dufrenes owned lots of land in St. Martin Parish. No problem except there were far too many painful memories attached to anything named Dufrene—even an abandoned rice field.

Darby.

His image flashed in her mind. Long legged, brown from the sun, alligator smile. He'd been pure pleasure in a pair of worn jeans. God, she'd loved him so much. Loved the way he touched her, loved the way he made her feel. Wild, alive, made for him.

Of course that had all been a lie.

A young girl's dream of what love should be. And she wasn't a young girl anymore.

The real Darby hadn't looked back. He'd left Louisiana and the girl he supposedly loved behind. Left her behind broken both physically and spiritually. But his dismissal had made her stronger. Had made her who she now was, and she was damn proud of what she'd become.

She shook herself.

"Rat run over your grave?" Carrie asked.

"Yeah, something like that." Renny pulled off her reading glasses and tried not to think about the rat. Darby was behind her and she'd made peace with herself and what had happened…or rather what had not happened. They'd been eighteen, high school seniors and majorly naive. She'd long ago forgiven both herself and the wild Dufrene boy who'd talked her into loving him.

Besides, she was too old to worry about those feelings again, even if she would soon have to deal with his mother. And Picou was never easy to deal with. On the surface, Picou Dufrene seemed docile and enlightened in her yoga gear and caftans, but underneath the feathers and fluff was a woman of pure steel. A woman who always got her way.

Just like her youngest son.

"You heading out now?" Carrie wrinkled her nose at her coffee cup. "How long has this been sitting in the pot?"

"Long enough to grow hair on your chest," Renny said, sliding the journal into the beat-up leather tote she'd bought the day she got her master's in biology. "And, yeah, I'm going to head up and see what's going on with L9-10. She was always such a skittish bird. Should have known she'd settle down in some weird location. Damn storm."

Carrie set her mug down. "But a good opportunity for us to see how far they'll stretch the habitat. Go. Call me later and let me know what you find, and then go have yourself a good weekend. As in, go do something fun for a change."

"I have fun." Why was everyone pushing her to go out and lasso a man? Even her mother, who'd formerly harped on the evilness of the opposite sex, had started "suggesting" Renny go somewhere other than church for her social life. Renny was Bev's only shot at grandchildren. Forget biological clocks. Grandmother's clocks were wound tighter.

"If you call sitting in a pirogue watching herons mate fun, then I guess you do. Come on, it's Friday, Renny. Don't let your leg keep you from shaking it."

"Shaking it?"

"Your booty, girlfriend."

Renny pushed through the door leading to the lobby of the office. "Sure. I'll think about it."

But she wouldn't. Carrie had poked a soft spot in her psyche—one she tried to ignore. Renny didn't want to squirrel herself away like some disfigured misanthrope. No, she wanted to be that game gal who didn't mind the stares, whose zest for living and glowing smile chased away any thoughts of pity. A small part of her wanted to be the girl she used to be…but it was only a small part. The rest of her liked her life as it was. Simple. Driven.

Safe.

She dashed that last thought because what was wrong with living safe anyway? Having control was a good thing, considering she'd spent a good deal of time having no control over anything—even her body. Most of her doctors were convinced she'd never walk again. And here she was walking out of her office door.

Okay, the pitch in her step still bothered her. Vain, stupid and weak, sure, but walking into a bar, aka meat market, wasn't fun when a girl unintentionally lurched herself at men. So she didn't go to bars. Or singles mixers. Or on blind dates.

Renny angled across the gravel parking lot nestled into the grasslands of the Black Lake Conservation Area and slid into her crossover hatchback. The early fall sun shone overhead, spotlighting the small field office invading the natural landscape. The actual lake lay only fifty yards away and she could hear the low hum of a boat on the water as she cranked the engine.

Going to Beau Soleil would be hard. She hadn't been back in over ten years, and that had been only to meet Darby in the cloak of the night with a backpack holding her nightgown, a spare T-shirt and a toothbrush. So long ago. So utterly stupid.

So, no, it wasn't going to be much fun for her tripping down memory lane—all because L9-10 had an adventurer's soul.

The only consolation was Darby wouldn't be there.

In fact, other than the occasional holiday, he hadn't returned to Beau Soleil. Renny hadn't laid eyes on him since that horrible night, and she really hadn't wanted to see him again. Not since she'd woken up in the hospital and realized she'd meant less to him than his family, than his damn place in the not-so-grand society of Acadiana. The anger at him had burned hard and deep in her gut, fueling her desire to get well if only to prove to him she didn't need him anyway.

In one way, Darby's disinterest had given her life again. Had given her purpose, so finally after years of hating him, she'd let the hard kernel of pain go.

Now she felt nothing.

Or at least she'd convinced herself she felt nothing. Life was more tolerable that way.

RENNY PROWLED THROUGH the dense brush bordering the abandoned rice field sitting several acres off the Bayou Teche. L9-10 wasn't where the GPS tracker indicated.

Hmm. Had the bird somehow lost her tracking device? Or maybe some predator had eaten the bird, device and all? Improbable but not impossible.

Thorns tugged at the material encasing her legs. Luckily, she kept her protective costume and rubber boots in the trunk of her car for times such as this, so her jeans and T-shirt were protected by the white sheeting. A draped hat with a screen obscured her face so she resembled an odd-looking astronaut prowling through the prickly vines and brush rather than an everyday biologist.

"Ow," she muttered under her breath as she unlatched a nasty vine from the sheeting. She needed to be mindful of keeping a silent, remote figure in case she actually found her rogue crane. Handlers were always careful to erase any human aspect of their form when interacting with the cranes. The goal was to produce birds as wild as possible—birds that avoided human contact.

Where are you, L9-10?

She swiveled her head left and right, scanning the swaying marsh grass that was little more than five acres in scope. Then she raised her eyes and scoured the tree line across the wet grass bordering an inlet from the sluggish bayou to her right. A flash of white appeared before disappearing completely.

"Got ya," she whispered as she stepped over the barriers Mother Nature tossed in the way of all wetland biologists and conservationists. The hum of a boat on the bayou accompanied her muttered curses as she slogged through the grasses toward the area where she'd glimpsed the flash of white. L9-10 obviously had taken to roosting in one of the ginormous oaks dappling the remote landscape. Perhaps she was showing a creative way to adapt. Maybe she'd found something to eat in the wide-spread branches of the tree. Or maybe she'd taken to the thick limbs because an alligator sat below her.

Renny stopped walking and stared at the big gator on the sloping bank, tail halfway in the marsh water, basking beneath her poor L9-10.

"Damn it."

The huge prehistoric reptile lay sprawled with its baby claws spread looking like a socialite on a cocktail cruise. Wasn't in a hurry to go anywhere, especially since its next meal perched a few feet above, solemnly contemplating the marsh.

Perhaps the bird's tracking bands had snagged on something or perhaps it was already injured.

"And what are you doing here, big boy?" Renny whispered. Gators were notoriously shy and didn't frequent populated areas. But this little patch of St. Martin Parish was remote and near fresh water teeming with crawfish, snakes and frogs, along with the animals that fed on them. It was odd to see the gator away from a large body of water, but perhaps it was protecting hatchlings, since it was September. That would make her dangerous.

Rotten luck for L9-10.

Renny stood completely still many yards from the seven-foot gator and contemplated her course of action. She wanted to get the crane to safety, but where was safety? The purpose was to release the cranes into the wild. The wild had big teeth. The cranes had to learn how to adapt and live on their own. She didn't want to go all Darwin on L9-10, but it *was* about survival of the fittest.

But L9-10 wasn't just any bird. She was a very expensive endangered species like the American alligator below her had once been.

Nature couldn't win this round.

Renny would.

Even if it went against all she believed as a biologist. But how was she going to get L9-10 away from the gator?

A loud crack sent Renny ducking for cover.

She covered her ears and crouched down just as the

gator started thrashing, its long tail whiplashing the ground as it moved toward the tree line.

"Good Lord," Renny squealed as L9-10 took flight right over her and two hunters appeared to the left of her, heading for the gator that now moved toward the inlet hidden behind the trees. Three more gunshots followed, clouding the area with something invasive and foreign.

Renny unplugged her ears and looked frantically around for L9-10, but the crane had taken flight, which made her wonder why the silly bird hadn't taken to the skies in the first place to avoid being al fresco dining for the now-doomed gator.

Two hunters leaped from an ATV and moved quickly toward the place where the gator had disappeared. It had not been a boat she'd heard earlier, but rather a camouflaged, glorified golf cart favored by hunters. One of the men caught sight of her and stopped. He did a double take.

Well, she *was* an odd sight.

This man, clad also in camo, lowered his gun and moved toward her, his strides long and purposeful as he tramped through the lowland.

Renny tugged her draped hat off and started digging for her credentials. She'd already received permission from Picou to access the land, and these hunters themselves could be poaching on Dufrene property, though she was fairly certain the man who'd slipped through the tree line heading for the bayou was Nate, the oldest Dufrene brother.

"What the hell?" the man coming toward her muttered, shaking his head.

She lifted her eyes and her mind clicked and whirred as a horrible realization bloomed in her brain.

She blinked once before trying to school her features into something other than shock.

The man she hoped to never lay eyes on again was standing right in front of her, looking like a model for *The Great Outdoors Magazine*.

Darby Dufrene had come home to Beau Soleil.

CHAPTER TWO

DARBY DOUBLE-CHECKED the safety on his rifle and feasted his eyes on the woman who had always revved his blood and jacked with his mind. Renny had not changed much—still as rare and earthy as the Louisiana wetlands she now protected.

Oh, he knew she was a biologist, because his mother dropped in little asides about her during their rare conversations. But he'd not anticipated how her very presence, hell, her very scent, would affect him. Renny smelled exotic, like rainforest sunrises and Indian marketplaces.

Good Lord. What had he put in his coffee that morning? Or maybe all that weird music his mother had on when he left was making him loopy.

"Renny," he said, unable to keep the pleasure at seeing her out of his voice. He'd come to Beau Soleil to find her and here she was.

"What are *you* doing here?" The tension around her mouth spoke more than her words. Okay. Not very happy to see him.

"Home for a visit."

She swallowed and glanced over his shoulder. "You have a permit to shoot gators?"

"I'm not shooting gators. Nate is. *He* still has five tags left."

"But *you* have a gun in hand." She pointed toward his dad's old rifle.

"Only as a precaution. We were about to bait some hooks when Nate saw the gator." He gestured to the cold weapon. If she was this confrontational over his brother legally shooting at a gator, how would she react when he told her he was her legal husband? Wouldn't be good. Suddenly he was glad he held a gun. "I thought you were a biologist or something, not an agent."

She looked hard at him and her brown eyes narrowed. They were pretty brown eyes—eyes that could flash in anger as easily as they could widen then glaze over in pleasure. He remembered those eyes. "I am a biologist, but I also work for Wildlife and Fisheries, and we take violations seriously."

He smiled. "Good to know. I'll make sure I don't get out of line while I'm in town."

She frowned. "You always get out of line."

"Well, I'm pretty much an inside-the-lines kind of guy these days, Ren. Naval officer, attorney and all that."

"Right."

"You don't sound convinced," he said with a laugh. "Though I just got my separation papers. Guess I'm no longer in the navy, or rather no longer active duty."

Damn, he was rambling. Telling her things no one would have interest in. *Get control, Dufrene.*

Renny licked her lips, drawing his attention away from grumpy brown eyes to a part of her he'd always lavished attention upon. She was nervous, not flirting at all, but her tongue sliding between those plump lips had the same effect. He ripped his gaze away.

"Well, congratulations. Hope you enjoy your visit,"

she said, but he was almost certain she'd meant, *Hope you die a painful death.*

Her whole attitude puzzled him. She was the one who hadn't wanted him anymore—did she have to be so damn cold about it? But what did he care? Two weeks tops before he headed to Seattle, but there was work to do before he left, and part of that job stood right in front of him.

Renny twisted to glance behind her, and a piece of caramel hair tumbled against the white sheeting she'd draped herself in. When he'd first seen her, he'd had a flashback to those government guys in *E.T.* "Well, I've got a bird to track down."

"Yeah, I saw that. What was it? It was huge."

"Whooping crane. She's out of her natural habitat, or what we think to be her natural habitat. I think a storm a few weeks back blew her north, so that's why I'm here. I stopped by the house and cleared it with your mother before coming out." She paused a moment and then cleared her throat. "She didn't tell me you were home."

No, his mother wouldn't, would she? Picou had suggested this very area for setting a few baits for the gators. Not coincidental at all. "Who knows? She's been distracted lately with my sister and all."

"Yeah, I heard about Della. Amazing that y'all found her," Renny said, pushing her hair back from her face. The Louisiana heat had her flushed and tendrils of hair stuck to the curve of her cheek—something that made her undeniably attractive in a mussed-up, natural way. In a way that made him want to peel that white-drape crap off her and find out how her curves had filled out over the past eleven years.

"Yeah, that's the main reason I'm home," he said, wondering why he was giving her all the details about his twin sister, his job, what he was doing on his own family's property. Seemed natural to reveal his thoughts to Renny—just like in the past. He resisted the urge to scratch his neck. Mosquitos. Forgot how viscous they could be in South Louisiana.

"I've got to—"

"I need to talk—"

They both spoke at once before snapping their mouths closed. Pink bloomed on Renny's cheeks as she shifted uncomfortably. "Uh, sorry."

"No, I want to ask if maybe we can get together and talk? We have some things we need to work out, and I don't think this is the best place." He slapped another mosquito.

She shook her head. "Look, the past is the past. We don't have anything more to say to each other. We were young and stupid and—"

"Hey," Nate called from behind him. "Where'd you go? That was a big son of a gun, and I needed you to man the pole. Too late now. That gator sunk in the bayou like a stone."

Darby didn't turn toward his brother, but he could hear him getting closer. He couldn't take his eyes off his wife. Okay, not his wife, but, still, his wife. It had been so long and she looked as good as a piece of pecan pie and a cup of chicory coffee—the epitome of all things Southern and Louisianan. He hadn't expected to feel anything for her. He'd thought his feelings toward her childlike and gone in the wind like the world he'd left behind. But like a shadow, his past clung to him refusing to allow him to forget who he was, where he'd come from, and the girl he'd once loved.

Why was that so?

He didn't want to feel anything for Renny. Or for

this flooded field he stood in. Or the creaky boards squeaking beneath his feet as he climbed the stairs in the house in which he'd been raised.

He had to be done with Renny and Bayou Bridge. He had a new life waiting for him, and if all went as planned with Shelby and the job at her father's firm, it was a given the sophisticated blonde would one day wear his great-aunt Felicia's yellow diamond.

He just had to deal with the women of his past before that could happen, and unfortunately, both Della and Renny were like a backlash in his fishing reel. Not easy to untangle.

"Oh, hey, Renny," Nate said, halting beside him. "What're you doing out here? And what're you wearing?"

"A costume."

"Early for Halloween, isn't it?" Nate cracked. Darby glanced at his brother, who'd grown a hunting beard like so many guys did when mid-September rolled around. Nate's eyes crinkled and Darby almost didn't recognize the former sheriff's detective who'd nearly ground his nose off in an effort to solve cases. His wife, Annie, and son, Pax, had softened him, given him laugh lines and a lightness in his step.

Renny finally smiled and Darby felt as if someone had punched him in the gut. Good Lord. Obviously this was about more than the past. He had to dash a crazy impulse to grab Renny by the shoulders and kiss her. This wasn't good. He was no longer a horny, devil-take-it guy with no responsibilities and a flask of Crown in his back pocket.

"Required when we're approaching our cranes. Don't want them to trust humans, so I go around playing Casper." Renny shrugged with another guarded smile.

"Mom told me we had a crane on the property. She was pretty excited about it because the crane is a family symbol to her. She wanted to try and get a picture." Nate's gaze searched the tree line behind Renny. "Thought I saw it take off over there."

She turned around. "Yeah, she's likely in another tree. I need to a get a visual on her and then I'll go. I doubt she'll stick around too much longer because her natural habitat is the grasslands below here. But who knows, maybe the whooper likes the way your crawfish taste."

"Mmm, crawfish. Haven't had those in years," Darby said as the thought of five pounds of the fire-red mudbugs accompanying a bottle of locally brewed beer made his mouth literally water. Wasn't the season, but surely he could find some at the Crawfish Palace over in Henderson. But what would slake the old desire welling inside him for Renny?

Maybe a well-placed knee when he told her they were married? "Hey, Ren, I'll give you a call, okay?"

"No."

Nate made a whirring sound before balling his hands and flinging them apart. "Crash and burn."

"Shut up, Nate. Not a date. Just some stuff Renny and I need to clear up."

Renny shook her head, and he thought he glimpsed some flash of hurt. Or maybe it was regret. Something. "I don't think there's anything to catch up on, and I have plans this weekend with some friends, so…"

He could tell she was lying. He always could. Not a conniving, lying bone in Renny's hot body, and speaking of which, wasn't she burning up in all that white draping? She should take her costume off and show him what the good Lord had bestowed on her while he'd been doing push-ups in the mud and studying jurisprudence. "I get you may not want to spend any time with me, but there really is something we have to talk about. Like a must."

A wrinkle settled between Renny's dark eyebrows and he decided he didn't like that wrinkle much. She was too beautiful to scowl. "Okay. Fine. Your mother has my information including my cell number. Call me and we'll find a time to talk about whatever you're so hell-bent on saying to me. But right now I have to go."

She turned and started toward the place where the bird had disappeared, and that's when Darby noticed her limp. Rolling with a small lurch. Jesus.

"She limps," he whispered under his breath.

Nate's gaze jetted to his. "Yeah, the wreck nearly killed her, remember?"

He shook his head. "No. I knew she broke her leg, but I didn't know much about it. Her mother wouldn't even let me see her and then when—" No sense in bringing up what had happened after the accident with his father. "You know, doesn't matter anymore. I didn't know Renny had been affected to such a degree."

His eyes landed on the back of the slim woman moving through the grasses in her big, ugly white boots that came to her knees. The white drape covered the rest, but there was no disguising the pronounced limp. Something jabbed at his insides. Not pity because he could never pity anything as uniquely beautiful as Renny, but something sharp and bitter. Regret. Shame. Guilt. Something. Because he'd done that to her. He'd broken the girl he'd loved. And that stung. Even if no one had allowed him to make it right all those years ago.

Of course Renny hadn't wanted him or his apology. That much had been made absolutely clear that damp

May afternoon when he stood waiting for her in the obscene raucousness of Jackson Square and accepted there would be no more Darby and Renny.

"Come on. Let's set out bait. Annie said if I bring that slop in my bucket back to the house, I could sleep on the couch, and I like my bed." Nate headed for the ATV and the rotting chicken he had been marinating in his back shed for the past week in anticipation of alligator season.

With one last glance at the flash of white disappearing into the brush, Darby turned and followed his brother. "I'm in the mood for crawfish. Want to head over to Henderson?"

"Nah, Annie cooked something in the Crock-Pot. Take Renny and rehash all the good ol' days."

He would if he could, but he had a feeling getting Renny to go anywhere with him would be akin to Hercules facing his twelve feats. Almost impossible.

RENNY TRIED TO CONTROL her trembling hands, but the shaking that had originated deep inside her belly had spilled over. Even her teeth chattered—incredible since it was a blistering ninety-one degrees outside.

Darby Dufrene.

Here.

In Louisiana.

She closed her eyes, for a split second wondering if perhaps she'd fallen asleep in her office chair and had a horrible nightmare.

She opened her eyes and stared at the rough bark on the tree dead ahead. Nope. Still at Beau Soleil.

Could a girl ever prepare to run into her ex?

No, not totally. But she had been remarkably calm considering her sweaty hair was plastered to her neck and she was wrapped up in a white drape like an old couch hidden beneath a drop cloth. Plus, she wore not an ounce of makeup. Yeah, not prepared, but at least she hadn't shaken in front of him. She turned her thoughts to the task at hand. Put him out of sight. Put him out of mind.

She placed the hat that swathed her face back on and cautiously approached the crane, trying to make her steps as level as possible even though chances were good the bird would recognize her uneven gait and feel some measure of safety.

Up ahead L9-10 flapped its wings as it clung to the lowest branch of a scrubby tree where there wasn't much room for a five-foot crane. The tracking device was firmly affixed and the bird looked healthy, so other than gathering some water samples and making some notes on the general area the bird inhabited, there wasn't much left to do.

Why are you here? she mouthed as she looked up at the bird. The crane twisted its head, the black eyes alert to Renny below her, but it didn't do anything more than grow still. The encounter with the gator had spooked the bird, but the familiarity of the white costume had a marked effect.

Renny glanced across the field as the ATV rattled up the embankment, carrying Darby and his brother away from the field, and the separation was enough so her hands stopped trembling and her heart stopped thumping against her rib cage.

Dear God.

He'd looked so good. Different but good. His bearing was exact, no longer loose and rolling, and his carriage more erect. No lazy smile, no flirty blue eyes, no privileged fraternity boy blond hair flopping over his brow. Darby Dufrene had changed…and she hadn't expected that.

But why hadn't she? It had been over ten years since they'd last seen each other. Darby had moved on to military school, the Naval Academy and law school. This was no boy slinking among the oaks with a fake ID and a naughty promise for some grown-up fun. This was a man who'd served his country, broadened his shoulders and his horizons, and maybe forgotten the Louisiana girl he'd left behind.

Something zinged in her chest.

Renny shook her head, furious at herself for feeling any sort of hurt or regret over the man who'd ridden away and not looked back. She didn't need him—then or now.

What did he have to say that was so important? It was too late for an apology, but maybe he'd truly grown up and wanted some sort of closure crap like ex-lovers demanded in all the movies.

Fine. She'd give it to him.

But she'd make sure she wore some lipstick and washed her hair first. No sense in looking like a backwoods coonass.

Her cell phone vibrated in her pocket and she pulled it out and looked down. Her mother. So not the person she wanted to talk to at the moment, but if she didn't answer, Bev would call over and over again until she did. Her mother was nothing if not persistent.

She moved away from the crane moving through the trees skirting the bayou and answered it on round two.

"Hey, Mom."

"Darby Dufrene's in town. Just heard it from my hairdresser, and I wanted you to know."

"Well, I'll try not to tear his clothes off and impregnate myself when I see him."

Bev huffed. "Don't get smart with me."

"I've already seen him, and my clothes are buttoned up tight. You can stop panicking."

"Where did you see him? Aren't you still at work?"

Renny walked to a viable spot, bent down and filled a vial with water from the flooded field. "Technically, yes. But one of our cranes got blown north and has found a home at Beau Soleil."

Silence sat for a moment. "Beau Soleil? You're joking, right?"

"I wish I were."

"I worry about you, you know," her mother said, her voice slightly softer than normal. Bev Latioles made no bones about loving her daughter, even if at times that love felt like a blanket thrown over her head. Renny was always covered. In fact, Bev had even had a friend run a background check on a guy she'd dated a few years back.

"I know, but I'm a big girl and don't need you worrying about me. Especially about an old high school boyfriend. We were kids, Mom. He doesn't have the same effect on me that he once did." Renny took one last look at the bird and started making her way back the way she came, hoping that the words she'd uttered were indeed true.

"Good because that boy was nothing but trouble, and I happen to know leopards don't change their spots. Your father taught me that hard lesson."

"So you've said time and again, Mom." Renny didn't want to talk about her father. Or Darby Dufrene. Or any man for that matter.

Not that she'd completely given up hope on finding a special someone, but her social life lay gasping for air on the side of the road. She'd been cursed in the guy department lately and had become a bit too settled in her own protective bubble of work and renovating her house.

"You know I'm not trying to stop you from finding a good man, honey, but I don't want you to go off track again because I know how charming Darby can be."

"You don't have to worry about that, okay? Darby and I are ancient history. Besides, he's in town visiting his family."

"But I heard he's out of the service and looking to join a law firm. Jackie said Helen Hammond told her that Picou said she was trying to get him to stay around here and practice. So this might not be only a visit. Just be careful around that boy. He's hurt you enough, sweetheart."

Renny shook her head and tried to tamp down the aggravation welling inside her. Bev meant well—she always meant well—but Renny was too old to have to explain herself to her mother. "I appreciate your caring enough to call me and warn me, but the last thing I want is anything to do with Darby Dufrene. There's nothing between us but some faded memories."

Renny heard her mother blow out a breath as she wove in between the trees, heading back toward the utility thruway where she'd parked her car. "Good, honey. Well, I suppose I'll see you Sunday for my birthday? Aaron is taking us to lunch."

"I'll be there." Renny clicked off the phone and tried not to growl at the blank screen.

Mothers.

Did they ever let go or was hers just abnormally leechy?

Probably just hers.

The hum of the ATV broke her from thoughts of being smothered to thoughts of the very man her mother had warned her about moments ago. The man her mother loved to hate almost as much as Renny's own father. She'd never understood why her mother had hung on so long to her anger at both, especially since Bev seemed relatively happy with her boyfriend, Aaron, a passive, bald chiropractor she'd met a few years ago.

But Bev didn't have to worry about Renny.

She wanted nothing to do with Darby.

No ties bound them.

CHAPTER THREE

"You DIDN'T BOTHER TO mention Renny Latioles was out on the land today," Darby said as he poured a glass of ice-cold milk into one of the tall tumblers that had occupied the kitchen for as long as he could remember.

"No, I didn't," Picou said, stirring something on the huge Viking stove. It smelled like feet, but Darby wasn't going to say as much. Maybe he'd head over to the house Nate and Annie had built a mere mile away and check out Annie's Crock-Pot dinner.

He took a sip. "Why?"

His mother shrugged. "No real reason. Figured it wouldn't really make a difference, though I suppose I should have told her you and your brother were out toting guns. Oversight on my part."

Darby narrowed his eyes at her erect form, covered from head to toe in black spandex. A long silver braid parted her shoulder blades, the only color on a palette of black. Odd choice in outfit even for his kooky mother, but her clothes didn't matter. Only the fact she'd already started manipulating situations for her own reasons. What they were, he couldn't guess.

"Yeah. So, I've been meaning to talk to you."

"Yeah?"

"About Seattle."

"I don't want to hear about it, Darby."

"I know you don't, but it's where I'll be calling home for the near future."

The spoon clinked against the pot. She turned and met his gaze with eyes the same color as his own. "Why would you want to live there? It rains all the time. How is that interesting?"

"I'm not concerned with interesting. I'm ready to start a new chapter in my life and that city fits the bill, and besides, I told you I met somebody. Right now it's not serious, but if things go as planned, I'm thinking she's the one."

Picou snorted. "The one? How long have you known her? Two months? That's not nearly long enough to know the color of her toothbrush much less if you'll suit for the rest of your life."

"It's blue, and I haven't made any decisions regarding Shelby, but you're the only parent I have, so I'd appreciate some support." He wasn't going to tell her the only reason he knew Shelby's toothbrush was blue was because he'd watched her pick it out at the commissary. He and Shelby hadn't been intimate yet because he didn't want to rush their relationship. They'd both agreed to allow things to build as they got to know each other better.

His mother looked away, spun and turned down the fire under the saucepan. "That figures."

"What?"

"Blue toothbrush. Sounds boring."

He almost laughed. "Mom, come on. You haven't even met her and you're writing her off. Besides, Nate only knew Annie for three weeks before he promised happily ever after."

"You're not your brother, and I'm not writing her off. I'm sure she's perfectly lovely. I just can't imagine you living on the West Coast. This place has always been such a part of you. Never figured you wouldn't come home once you were done roaming."

"I'm home now, and there are these things called airplanes. You climb inside, buckle up and they get you where you need to go pretty quickly."

His mother frowned. "And cost an arm and a leg. I happen to be fond of my appendages."

Darby closed his eyes for a moment. Dealing with his mother had never been easy. They brushed against each other like earth along a fault line. Many said their butting heads were a result of being too much alike, but Darby knew it was because his mother tried to control every aspect of life surrounding her, including his own. Only he and his siblings saw it. Everyone else thought her harmless and loving.

Picou had been avoiding the topic of his heading to Seattle since he'd arrived home a day before. Any time he mentioned his intent of interviewing for the position with Mackey and Associates, she snorted, sniffed or blatantly ignored him. At times she resembled his boyhood pony Marigold, but somehow he doubted feeding her an apple would appease her.

She turned back around to face him, her face softening into the woman who'd wiped his brow when he'd vomited or blown on his boo-boos after applying antiseptic. "I understand it's your life to live, sweetheart, but I think you should give considerable thought before making such a drastic decision. You haven't been home in years. The distance has distorted your image of this place."

He blinked. "Mom, I'm not moving back to Bayou Bridge. I'm not moving into Beau Soleil. I'm nearly thirty years old, and I've been on my own for a long time now. I can't go back in time."

"I know how old you are, and I'm not pulling out your old *Star Wars* sheets to put on your bed. All I'm asking, even if it sounds unreasonable, is for you to spend some time thinking about what moving to Seattle to pursue a career and wife there means in the long run." He could see his mother tried to say the right things, the things he wanted to hear, but he knew her. On the surface she said one thing, but underneath she plotted something quite different. She wanted her baby home. She wanted him to be part of the family—a family that was finally complete with the discovery of his twin sister, Della.

Everyone but he and Picou had believed Della to be dead. Picou proclaimed some spiritual knowledge about her children, but Darby had known. Like in his bones. When he was young, he'd dream about his sister, wake crying, asking why no one would go and get her.

And he'd been right.

Della had been living two hours southeast of Beau Soleil in the backwaters off Bayou Lafourche, raised by a tough old bayou woman named Enola Cheramie. Even Enola hadn't known the girl she called Sally was the long-lost Della, for the child had been hidden there by her kidnapper, Enola's grandson, whose body had been discovered in the waters not far from Bayou Bridge. That Della had been found was a fluke, one started when Sally discovered by accident that she wasn't related to Enola. One thing led to another and her file had landed on Nate's desk. His older brother said it had taken one glance to know the young teacher was a Dufrene—Della had looked almost exactly like the young

Picou Dufrene in the wedding photograph sitting in the formal living room.

So, yeah, Picou wanted to gather her brood together so she might tend them all without any interference from a husband whose will was as strong as hers. But like Martin, she'd had a hand in making Darby feel as he did. Picou had not made waves when his father sent him away. She couldn't undo what she'd done easily.

Picou wanted him to live the life she'd built in her head for him—living down the street, eating at her dinner table every Sunday, fishing with his brothers, basically just being at hand. But Darby had not been part of life at Beau Soleil for some time. He didn't feel comfortable here, didn't know what doors stuck or where Lucille hid the cookies she baked. Even hunting with Nate that afternoon had felt forced.

Darby sighed. "I'm considering all things, Mom, but I can't imagine a life here in Bayou Bridge. If I stayed in Louisiana, I'd be looking at New Orleans or Baton Rouge. I'm different now, and I won't go back to being the boy I was."

"Whoever said you were so awful as a child? I hope the past is not keeping you away from the present," she said, her voice soft as the velvet hanging in the windows in the front parlor.

"Seriously? You and Dad sent me away. Remember?"

His mother shook her head as tears gathered in her eyes. "To grow up, not become like—"

"That's what I did," he interrupted. "I grew up and I became a man who recognizes responsibility and doesn't shirk it. A man who doesn't want to come back to a place that is finished for him. I like where I'm headed."

Picou bit her lip and said nothing.

He didn't understand why his mother was so disappointed. His parents had sent him away, hoping military school would break him. It had. Broken him down then built him up. The navy had taken over and done the rest, and he'd emerged a skilled, reliable attorney and naval officer. "I'm here, aren't I? This was what you wanted—for me to come home, meet Della, and sew things up for the family. But I'm not staying."

Picou stared at him for a full minute before shaking her head. "I don't expect you to fix anything, Darby. I only wanted you to meet your sister and help her if you can. Just be part of this family, and don't be afraid of finding a piece of the boy you left behind. You don't have to live here, but you shouldn't close your mind off and dust your hands of who you are."

Darby shrugged. "I'll try."

He didn't want to admit part of that boy he'd left behind had showed up that afternoon at first sight of Renny. Sheer lust had lurched through his body, stirring him, waking him, making him want to do irrational things.

Which was a bad idea.

Renny might be his legal wife, but that title meant little. In fact, before he'd come to Beau Soleil, he'd stopped in Lafayette to talk with Sid Platt, his father's former college roommate and long-time legal advisor to the Dufrene family, and had him discreetly initiate divorce proceedings. Since neither he nor Renny would contest and neither had cohabited, the case should move through the cogwheels without difficulty. Six months easily, but if Sid could work some magic, maybe even sooner.

"There is no try, only do."

Darby rolled his eyes. "Yoda?"

Picou gave a small smile and turned back to whatever brew she was concocting as he slipped out the swinging door and headed up to his former room for a quick shower. Maybe he could stop by Renny's place and break the news they were married. Didn't know how he'd do it, but the longer he waited, the more the secret burned inside him.

She needed to know.

Of course, he had no clue where she lived or if she had plans for the evening, but once he cleared the air, he'd feel better. Maybe.

Then he could focus on meeting Della and getting his ass to Seattle to start a new life.

Seattle. He'd been kicking around the possibilities of where to settle as his time in the service wound down and the Pacific Coast city was high on his list. Then when he met Shelby at an officer mixer and struck up a conversation with her, things fell into place. She was from Seattle, leaving to return to her home in mere weeks, and her father was looking for a new associate for his firm situated in the heart of the city. At that moment, standing there holding a gin and tonic, he'd felt destiny tap him on the shoulder and ask him to dance the pretty teacher all the way to a new life.

So he'd taken Shelby's hand and vowed to listen to reason. To fate. To what the stars had lined up for him. It was as if life had laid all the pieces out in front of him and said, *Here you go, Darby.*

Seattle and Shelby sounded good. There he wasn't known and could be whoever he wanted to be without any preconceived notions. Without a family name. Without whispers of his past or a meddling mother trying to dredge up history so she could spackle it with plaster and make it all better.

Onward and upward.

Or maybe backward and downward.

He wasn't sure.

But before he could move anywhere, he had to divorce Renny.

RENNY GLARED AT THE MAN standing on her front porch holding two take-out boxes and a bottle of wine.

What in the hell did he think he was doing?

She gripped the French door and tried not to let her bad leg buckle. "What do you think you're—"

"I've got to talk to you," he said, shouldering past her into her house. "Better to do this in private."

She spun around. "Get out."

"You don't want the neighbors to hear this. I brought food." He walked through her living area to the adjoining dining area and set the boxes on her newly restored antique drop-leaf table, looking as if he had every right to stalk into her world and tilt it on its side. Typical Darby. It was how he'd always been. Presumptuous and entitled. A true Dufrene.

"I didn't invite you in, and I really don't want to hear what you have to say to me. Nor do I want any food. So get the hell out before I call the police." She waved toward the open door. Her body trembled with rage and something unidentifiable. She didn't have time to worry about what that was. She needed him to take his larger-than-life body and remove it from the intimacy of her living room.

"Give me a few minutes, okay? You need to hear me out. Trust me."

"Trust you? I don't even know you anymore. You're a memory. That's it."

He turned around and waved the wine bottle. "Do

you have an opener? Trust or not, you'll need a drink for this conversation."

"I don't want a drink. I want you to leave. Don't be an asshole, Darby. If you need closure, fine. I forgive you for getting drunk, hitting a tree, nearly killing me and then forgetting about me while you went off to the East Coast. There. Done. Now get out." Her knee did that buckle thing and the scar on her thigh ached. She wanted to sit down, but didn't dare show weakness in front of this man.

"I didn't forget you," he said, his brow crinkling in confusion. "I don't even know what you're talking about."

Realizing he wasn't going to leave without her actually calling the sheriff, she slammed the door. "Fine. You want to talk. Bring it on. I'll get the damn bottle opener."

Renny moved toward the kitchen, more aware of her limp than normal. She didn't want him to watch her. Didn't want his pity or his guilt, but even so, she felt it with every step. "Stop looking at me."

She swallowed unshed emotion that had appeared out of nowhere and entered the kitchen, yanking open a drawer and ignoring the fact her cat, Chauncey, had leaped onto the counter and drank milk from the cereal bowl she'd left in the sink that morning.

She turned and jabbed the opener toward the man who'd followed her into the kitchen. "Here."

"Why wouldn't I look at you? You're still so beautiful it takes my breath away."

His words slammed her and she flinched. "Oh, God, Darby. Are you serious? That's what you're going to say. I'm beautiful?"

He shrugged in a matter-of-fact manner that was so achingly familiar it made her heart hurt.

"Look, I know what I am, so don't give me your pity. At least show me that courtesy." She waggled the opener before thrusting it at him once again.

His blue eyes darkened and his mouth softened. She wished she hadn't noticed, but she had. The man was abnormally good-looking with that golden hair and tan skin. Probably had a six-pack, too. He was too good to be true…like most things were. She wasn't biting whatever worm he wriggled at her. She knew what trusting Darby had gotten her. "Lord, Renny, I don't pity you."

She rolled her eyes. "Okay, sure. No one pities me. I don't have a complex. I swear. Something about you here in my kitchen, in my space, freaks me out. Let's go back into the living room."

He reached out and brushed a piece of hair from her cheek and she flinched again. Not because she didn't want his touch, but because the heat in that simple gesture seared her. It was as if a match had been struck and the air thickened with something dangerous. "I don't want to freak you out. I'm sorry about that, but don't ever think I would pity something as rare as you."

His words plucked a chord in her and she didn't like where her heart and head were sliding. She needed to get it together. Fast. "Lay that manure on someone else, Darby."

She jerked away from him and headed back to the dining room. As she pulled out a chair, she begged her body to obey the dictates of her mind. Stay away. Keep the wall up. Don't allow Darby access to anything he could use to drag the past forward. Be polite and aloof. *Be the woman you are today, Renny.* "So, you brought dinner. At least I'll get something out of this."

"Your cat is drinking something out of your sink. Is that okay?"

"You implying that I'm a lonely cat woman?"

The sound of the wine bottle being uncorked accompanied his question. "Well, if you're a cat woman, I wanna see you in that black leather costume and not that weird white furniture cover."

Renny stifled a smile. Here was the charm that bled out of Darby as easily as the sun shone. It played havoc with a girl's intent. "In your dreams, Officer."

He emerged from around the corner. "How did you know one of my fantasies is you in a catsuit?"

"You were always a degenerate."

At that, his eyes shuttered and she felt his mood shift. "I was many things, wasn't I?"

She didn't answer because suddenly it felt a little like swimming into the unknown, so she stalled by prying open the nearest take-out box. Steam rose off the crawfish fettuccini inside and made her mouth water.

He set the bottle on the table. "I know you get lots of home cooking, but it's been a while for me, so I stopped at Jacqueline's."

"Good choice. Her food's the best, so I guess I'll have to force myself." She tempered her words with a small smile, determined to throw a speed bump in front of their forthcoming conversation so she could enjoy the meal. No sense in letting good food go to waste, even if it was with a man she'd hoped never to lay eyes on again. Darby had obviously snagged two wineglasses from her cabinet while in the kitchen. He poured a healthy portion into each glass and handed one to her.

"Please don't toast," she warned, taking the glass from him, careful not to touch his hand. She wanted no more flares of awareness. Couldn't handle them.

"I wouldn't dare," he muttered, taking a big gulp of the chardonnay. He opened his own box, revealing another serving of crawfish pasta, and dug in. A semi-comfortable silence settled in as they ate.

After several minutes, Renny looked up. "I don't like being forced into something, but I do appreciate dinner. The wine's not bad, either."

He wiped his mouth. "I'm not real comfortable being here myself, but it's got to be done."

Renny cocked her head. "Why? It's been years and we're both different people. Is there really a need to drag up old feelings? I've moved on. You've moved on. Can't we let it be what it was—two crazy kids looking to thumb their noses at authority then learning they weren't as smart as they thought they were? We were both to blame for what happened, so we don't need apologies."

Darby took another swallow of the crisp wine and leveled his blue eyes at her. "It's not about apologies though I do think I owe you one. I had no idea you were injured so severely."

The sorrow in his gaze melted something and for the first time in a long time a familiar longing wormed its way along the tunnels of her soul, convincing her the misery she'd suffered after the accident hadn't been so awful after all. She dashed that devil of a feeling against the stone-hard resolve built long ago in the recesses of her heart. "You wouldn't have, because you never bothered to come see me."

"What are you talking about? You refused to see me." Truth sat in his gaze. He wasn't jerking her chain. The reaction was honest.

"I never refused you anything. Ever. That was the problem."

For a moment, they held each other's gaze. Dawning descended and in that moment, they both seemed to understand something—they had not been the only players that moonlit night. There had been others involved, each with his or her own motives.

"No, you never did, did you?" His words were almost a whisper and the tone in those words made Renny swallow hard.

"But that's the past," she muttered, reaching for her wineglass so quickly she knocked it over. The liquid splashed across the buffed cypress table she'd found in an old warehouse outside Lake Charles and ran off onto the carpet.

"I'll get it," Darby said, leaping to his feet, jogging toward the kitchen and reemerging with a dish towel. Chauncey shot out behind him as he knelt to wipe up the spill. Renny sat glued to her chair, mostly because she didn't trust her legs, especially the one that had been broken in several places and gouged by the splintered fence…but that wasn't the true reason she couldn't manage to rise. No, the true reason hummed inside her.

Most of what she'd believed about the man stooping at her feet had been a lie—a lie perpetuated by her mother. The Dufrenes. Hell, even the hospital staff.

He hadn't denied her.

Why hadn't she known that?

Darby tossed the cloth on the table and looked up. His eyes were so blue and the chin that had once been smooth to the touch was scruffy and manly.

It was a face she knew well.

It was a stranger's face.

"You know why I came tonight?"

She licked her lips and shook her head. "I guess I don't."

He eased forward and lifted one of the hands she'd curled in her lap. The warmth of his touch and the heady smell of the spilled wine kick-started something slithery and dangerous in her belly.

"It's not about apologies." He shook his head. "Man, this isn't easy. I don't know how to do this."

"What?" She looked down at him on his knees and for an instant her mind flitted back to an eighteen-year-old Darby on his knees outside the Bayou Bridge high school football stadium. The flash of a simple gold band—one still lying at the bottom of her jewelry box. The flash of his smile. The hope and possibility of young love under a February moon.

"Renny, I'd like to ask you to unmarry me."

She pulled her hand away. "What? Unmarry you? We're not—"

"You remember what happened that afternoon before we guzzled two bottles of champagne?" Darby interrupted, wiping his hand on the thigh of his jeans. Now her mind flashed to champagne dripping down her neck and Darby licking it off before his head went lower and lower still. Before they spread the blanket he'd packed in the back of his pickup and made love beneath the arms of the live oak in the center of the property his grandfather had left him. "Before the car accident?"

Renny shook her head as something much heavier replaced the desire brewing inside her. It felt like she'd reached the zenith of the world's highest roller coaster and the track tilted south. "Oh, God, we got married."

CHAPTER FOUR

DARBY WATCHED THE EMOTIONS dance across Renny's face—dawning, incredulity, anger, and then confusion. All the same things he felt nearly two weeks ago when he'd found the marriage certificate among his old papers.

"How? It wasn't legal."

Her question was the simplest of questions, but he didn't have a good answer. "I don't know. Somehow the license was filed. I'm checking into that, but hold on a sec—"

He went back to where he'd laid the boxes, picked up a manila envelope she hadn't seen earlier and gave it to her.

Renny pulled the document from its sheath and studied it with a little crinkle in her forehead. He sank back into the chair he'd abandoned and waited.

"This is official? Not a joke?"

"Who would have forged a marriage certificate and mailed it to me at Winston Prep?"

She shrugged. "I don't understand. That boat captain was drunk and there wasn't really anything official about it. I don't even remember signing this."

"But it's my signature, and if I'm remembering correctly, that's yours. Whatever may have happened, somehow we ended up married."

Renny slumped back in her chair, fork abandoned

in the half-eaten pasta, and rubbed her face. "This is crazy."

"Yeah. More than a little."

She sat up straight. "Oh, my God! What if one of us had gotten married…had kids?"

"That would have been…awkward. Guess that's a silver lining in all this. We both stayed single…or rather secretly married."

The sound of the chair scraping against the floor jarred him. Renny launched herself from the table, whipping up his empty container along with her empty wineglass, and headed toward the kitchen. "I can't deal with this right now. This is nuts."

He didn't move, because he knew she needed time to process. Likely she was in the kitchen trying not to hyperventilate. Maybe he should go check on her, but that didn't feel like the thing to do. She needed space—from him. Her cat curled in and out through his outstretched legs and purred. Any other time, he'd have reached down and given it a pat, but he didn't feel friendly toward any creature at the moment, so he jerked his legs away and shooed the long-haired cat away.

The sound of glass breaking in the kitchen made him leap to his feet.

"Damn it." Her words sounded tinged in tears. Or hysteria. He wasn't sure which but neither was good.

He nearly tripped over the cat as he hurried to the kitchen. A yowl later, he found Renny standing at the sink with a broken wineglass in one hand, her other under the faucet.

"You okay?"

"No." She held up a hand and studied the blood streaming down her finger and dropping into the ceramic sink. "I cut my finger."

"Here," he said, taking her wrist in his hand and studying the gash on her pointer finger. No slivers of glass and no need for stitches. "Don't think we'll have to go to the hospital. Let's put pressure on it."

He grabbed a clean white towel from the half-open drawer next to the sink and wrapped her finger in it, holding it firmly to stop the bleeding. Renny studied his hand curled around hers, reverting to careful observation like any good scientist. He followed her gaze and noticed their two left hands were linked together and wondered about her thoughts.

"Better?" he asked, dropping his voice to a lower, softer register.

Renny shrugged and lifted her brown eyes to meet his gaze. The emotions pooling within the depths socked him hard in the solar plexus and sucked him back in time. How many times had he looked into those eyes? How many times had he smelled that scent that was hers alone? How many times had he bent his head to hers? Too many to name. Déjà vu blanketed him, covering him in memories, forcing him to remember how much he'd once loved this woman.

"Renny," he breathed, exhaling her name like a prayer. He didn't want to want her with such intensity. But he did.

"Don't," she whispered, stepping back.

But he couldn't help himself.

Old feelings had tumbled down, slamming into them both. He could see the same in her eyes—the want, the confusion, the desire.

He lowered his head and caught her lips as he'd done so many times before. Her slight intake of breath only invited him further.

Ah, sweet, sweet Renny.

"Darby," she whispered, before closing her eyes and surrendering. He needed no further invitation. He slid his free arm around her waist, trapping her between him and the sink, and deepened the kiss.

Something slammed him for a second time. Raw desire. The kind with hooks that latched tight and refused any rational thought. Damn. She tasted so good. Like Louisiana spice. Like all things good, sweet and bitter. She tasted like home and he couldn't get enough of her.

"Mmm," he groaned as he slid his free hand up to cup her jaw, angling her head so he could draw in more of her essence, more of some elixir he couldn't name but was so good it made him forget the man he'd become.

Renny's hand fisted in his shirt and she gave as good as she got. He felt her hand relax and then the brush of her fingertips on his jaw and something more ignited in him. He wanted her beneath him, naked, open to him. He wanted—

She broke the kiss. "Stop. This is—"

Her eyes closed and she shook her head, sliding to the side, tugging her injured hand from his grasp. Her shallow breaths accompanied his as he inwardly shook himself.

What had he done?

Never should have gone down that path. Her taste had struck a match in him, undoing what years of repression had given him—some kind of closure or peace with how they'd left things.

All that had been destroyed with one little kiss.

Her eyes opened and her gaze met his. "We shouldn't have done that."

"No, we shouldn't have," he said, moving away from her, resting his backside against her oven range. "Guess old feelings came back and I got carried away. Won't happen again."

Something flickered in her eyes, but he didn't want to acknowledge exactly what that was. He wasn't living in the past. He was very much in the future with a new path set out before him. A path that included a prestigious law firm, rain-soaked Saturdays in out-of-the-way cafés, and a teacher with soft blond hair and a weakness for chocolate.

Not a golden-skinned biologist with hair the color of café au lait and kisses addictive as caramel candy. Not Louisiana with its curling bayous, graceful oaks and soulful vibrations wrapping around him like the roots hidden beneath the fertile soils. He was done with Renny and Louisiana.

Something he needed to remember before he went planting his lips where they didn't belong.

"Good," she said, dragging her wrist across her lips as if she could wipe the taste of him away. He didn't fail to notice her hands trembled. She'd been more affected than she wanted to admit.

But so had he.

"So what do we do now?" Her words were cold water down his back.

"About the kiss?"

She shook her head. "No. This crazy marriage."

"Oh," he pushed off from the stove. "I'm working on that. Put in a call to Baton Rouge to check on the filing, and I've already talked to Sid Platt. He'll draw up papers so we can proceed with a divorce and bring by the petition by the end of next week. It'll be filed ASAP."

She nodded. "Anything I need to do?"

"We haven't lived together and neither one of us has any issues with division of community property since we've had none together. If you're willing to waive papers being served, then we can shorten it even further."

"So it should be cut-and-dried."

"Should. Six months at tops."

"I still can't believe this." She scooped up the cat that had started yowling in displeasure, opened the back door and deposited it on the back stoop—all with one hand.

"Yeah, it's a little hard to wrap the mind around."

Renny held up her injured finger. "I need to put something on this and grab a bandage. Are we through?"

He shook his head. "Not really."

She cocked her head. "Is there something else left to say?"

Wasn't there? Perhaps he should ignore the unanswered questions, but he'd wondered for so long why Renny had given up on them. "Maybe. Yeah. There are some things."

Her mouth thinned. "You're talking about the accident?"

"I'm talking about what happened after the accident. About why you wanted to skewer me when you first saw me this afternoon."

Renny pushed back her hair. "Okay, but can I deal with my finger first? I don't want blood all over my furniture. Make yourself useful—put on some coffee—and we'll try to get that closure you seem to need." She turned and disappeared.

"So you don't need closure?" he called as he searched the white-tiled counters for the coffeepot.

"No. I got past *us* a long time ago," she yelled from the back of the house.

"Yeah? Well, I don't think so," he muttered as he pulled out the carafe and walked to the sink. "You think you're over me, but your body didn't get the memo, sweetheart."

And obviously neither had his.

Which could end up being a big problem if he wasn't careful.

RENNY TRIED TO CONTROL her trembling hands as she pulled the backing off the bandage. Shaking was becoming a habit ever since Darby had stalked across that rice field and back into her life. Her body felt not her own. Obviously. She'd just about tossed her clothes to the floor of the kitchen and climbed on top of Darby moments ago. Yeah, control might be an issue.

Her words to her mother earlier that afternoon rang in her ears. Okay, she hadn't actually jumped his bones upon first sight. Did second sight count?

"Coffee's ready," Darby called, his voice echoing through her bedroom into her restored turn-of-the-twentieth-century bathroom. She closed the mirrored cabinet and glanced at herself.

Good gravy. Her lips were swollen from his kiss. And her hair swirled around her wantonly, making her look like some sexed-up wild woman. She grabbed a ponytail holder and a brush. After taming her hair and tucking her T-shirt into her well-worn jeans, she felt stronger. She even shoved her bare feet into the sheepskin mules sitting beside her closet.

There.

Ready for closure.

She walked back into the living room and found Darby sitting on her pink sofa stroking Chauncey. Something about his very masculine hands stroking the back of her cat made her mouth grow dry.

"He was meowing, so I let him in," he said, crossing

his legs casually and picking up a steaming mug of coffee. "I fixed yours the way you like it. One sweetener and a dollop of cream."

"I drink it black now."

Darby gave her a smile that would make a less stable gal drop her panties. "Grown-up girl, aren't you?"

"Mmm," Renny said, scooping Chauncey up for the second time and carrying him toward the door. "He's spoiled, but he's going outside no matter how much he cries."

"Not just grown-up, but tough."

She turned around, closing the door with a definitive click. "You have no idea."

He stared at her as she walked back, picking up the mug from the old trunk that served as her coffee table. For a few seconds, neither of them said anything.

"I didn't leave you, you know."

Renny averted her gaze and took a sip. Sweet and creamy. A cup of coffee for a naive girl—the girl she'd once been. "Well, I thought you had. When I woke up, you weren't there. You were in Virginia."

"Not by choice."

"It didn't feel that way, Darby," she said, all those old feelings flooding back, hurting her all over again. "Come on. We were in our senior year. You were eighteen. A man. You had the choice to stay with me, but you didn't. When the going got tough, you got going... in the wrong direction."

"So you would think, but that's not what happened. Not when faced with my father's wrath. Not when faced with an ultimatum."

She sank into the reupholstered armchair that wasn't so much comfortable as it was beautiful. "Ultimatum?"

"After the doctor released me from the emergency

room, the sheriff put me in his car and took me to the parish jail where my father waited. He'd already made some kind of deal with Ed Bergeron, the D.A. Dad dragged me to the car, took me home and told me to pack my camp trunk. He said one way or the other I was leaving Beau Soleil."

"He kicked you out?"

"Not exactly. He gave me the choice—hit the streets with nothing but the clothes on my back or go to Winston Prep in Virginia where he'd already bought me late admission."

Renny took another sip, accustoming herself to the taste of the sweeter brew. Martin Dufrene had always been something of a bastard. Hard-nosed businessman who controlled all aspects of his life with an iron fist. When the one thing he couldn't control spiraled away from him—the kidnapping and presumed murder of his daughter—he'd become even more intolerable. His crushing dictates and forcing of his will on his remaining children had had varied effects. In Darby it had manifested itself as rebellion. Darby had been as wild as the creatures that crept along the bayous and prowled the Louisiana woods. And he had taken her along for the ride.

"So you just did what he wanted?"

Darby frowned. "I didn't see it that way. I thought of it as buying us some time. If I went to Virginia, graduated and saved enough money, I could find us a place in Baton Rouge. I wrote all of that in the letters I sent. I thought you'd understand I went to Virginia because it would be better for us in the long run."

"I never got any letters."

"I mailed one a day for a month and a half." His

words sounded almost accusatory, as if he thought she lied.

She didn't say anything because her mind reeled, trying to pull out fact from the fiction painted so long ago. She was married. Darby hadn't abandoned her. Her mother had lied. Her brain was at full capacity on what it could deal with and Renny felt on the verge of hysteria.

She took a deep breath and exhaled. "So you're saying you didn't 'leave' me. Just went to Virginia to buy time? You're saying everything I believed was a lie? And you're saying our parents sabotaged us? But you didn't know this until…?"

"Tonight?" His steady gaze said it all, and she knew it was so. Betrayal stabbed, an echo of the cut to her finger. "Honestly."

Silence crouched between them as the past came winging back, knocking down grudges held for too long. She'd sat with this man so many times. Knew what it meant when he stroked his chin, when he rotated his ankles, cracking them in the silence. Relief tinged her uncertainty.

He'd not abandoned her.

Darby folded his arms across his chest and stretched his legs. "I didn't realize you thought I'd abandoned you. All these years I believed you hated me because I had hurt you. It sounded pretty damn convincing when you told me you never wanted to see me again, and it felt pretty damn final when you chose something other than us."

"What?" Renny shook her head. "I don't—"

"You do remember the last time you spoke to me?"

Closing her eyes, Renny wished she didn't remember

her cold words, the pain that spurred her to tell him to leave her the hell alone. Forever.

"I called the hospital every chance I got, and finally, your mother let me talk to you. You said those words."

She wanted to tell him she'd never meant it, but that would be another lie, and it seemed fairly obvious there were far too many lies to deal with at present. "I was hurt and angry. Two months had gone by without word from you."

He arched an eyebrow and it made him even more handsome.

She leaned forward onto her knees. "Okay, I know. You sent letters, but I never received even one of them. The only certainty I knew was the four gray striped walls of my hospital room and the unceasing pain in my leg and head. I knew only what my mother told me. What your parents told me. You were gone and not coming back for me, and it felt like the worst betrayal."

"Renny, why would you think that? You knew me. You knew what we had was real. Am I right? Was I the only one who wanted us on a forever kind of basis?"

His words made her bleed. She *had* thought what they had was real but hadn't held on to that conviction. She could blame the drugs and her mother, but maybe her love for Darby hadn't been strong enough to weather what happened. Perhaps, he'd been the one to face the world, chin out, daring someone to separate them…and Renny had been the one to fold.

Or maybe she'd folded because she'd believe his father's words when he'd come to see her.

Darby wanted to marry you because it defied me. You understand this, don't you, Renny? It wouldn't have worked out, because that boy has never faced any per-

son or thing he couldn't have or manipulate...including you.

And there had been truth in Martin Dufrene's words.

Whether she'd given up or had her love ripped from her, her dream of being with Darby had died. And either way, she knew they wouldn't have lasted. With Darby, she'd always felt like the other shoe was about to drop.

She'd never been good enough for a Dufrene.

Her voice sounded froglike when she said, "I thought I wanted forever. I did. But things were so skewed... so backwards. I needed to be strong, but my body and my heart were broken. You weren't there. It was easy to believe you'd abandoned me and moved on. It was easy to believe our running away was another way for you to poke sticks at your father. I always felt I was into you way more than you were into me."

He raked a hand through his honey hair, making it stick up, and his Paul Newman blue eyes met her gaze. "You know, I could ask why you thought that, but I already know the answer."

She wished he would tell her. She didn't know why she'd believed everyone else rather than her own heart. Why she hadn't had faith in Darby. "I don't know what to say."

"Maybe there isn't anything left to say now," he said, leaning forward, pressing his elbows to his knees, a mirror pose to hers. His shoulders were much broader, the jaw bristled with golden scruff was more pronounced, the hands clasped were no longer a boy's.

Even though tears seemed precariously close, her internal thermometer rose a few degrees, but she couldn't give credence to desire. She'd already made that mistake in the kitchen moments ago. "Maybe not, but we still have to deal with our future."

"When I get the paperwork, I'll come by." He rose and looked around her house. "I'm sorry to disrupt the life you've built, Ren. Seems like a nice one. We'll get through this. Now go on back to your Friday night."

She followed his gaze about her room. She had built a nice life for herself, even if it was a bit lonely. At that moment, she really wished she were dating someone if only so she didn't look quite so pathetic with her cat and polished antiques. Maybe she should call Carrie and go out. Pick up a dude to try and forget the trouble that had landed on her door. But would that make her an adulterer? Dear Lord. She couldn't believe she was married. "Yeah, it was a little disruptive—helluva curve ball."

"So let's turn on it and hit it out of the park," Darby smiled, moving toward the door. His demeanor had shifted again and he was back to being light and charming. How could he accomplish that so quickly? She felt pressed down by an unbearable weight with the news he'd delivered, with the falsehoods uncovered. She needed time to process. Time to grieve. Time to confront. Time to…drink enough wine to forget what had transpired over the course of the past two hours.

"Yeah, hit it out of the park," she echoed, following him to the door, trying not to wince at the ache in her leg. It was always worse at the end of the week, which was another reason she usually spent Friday nights with Chauncey, a glass of white and three hours of Lifetime TV.

Darby opened the door and Chauncey shot inside. "He seems pretty attached to you."

"Or his food bowl."

He turned and brushed a lock of hair that had escaped her ponytail behind her ear. "I think it's you. You have a way of growing on people…and cats."

Her heart flopped over at his touch. At his words. "God, Darby, you say things that make me want to—"

"Kiss me?"

She shook her head and smiled. "Make me want to forgive you."

"And you have to forgive me for…what? Loving you once?"

"I really don't know."

CHAPTER FIVE

DARBY WATCHED ANNIE ROLL a ball across the hardwood floor to Paxton, who immediately picked it up and shoved it in his mouth.

"No, Pax. Dirty," Annie said, wrestling the soft ball from her ten-month-old son's mouth. The kid cranked up like a siren.

"Get used to women denying you, kid," Darby said, clinking a beer bottle to the one in his brother's hand. They sat in double recliners centered in front of a bigscreen in Nate's den. For the first time since he'd hit land in New Orleans, Darby felt at home. Odd, since he'd never even glimpsed the new house Nate had built nor met the tenacious Annie.

"Yeah, Nate's living a hard life sitting back in that leather recliner drinking Abita. Denial is the man's middle name." Annie scooped up the wailing kid and plopped a pacifier in his mouth. Pax's super-suction made the car or train or whatever was on the end of it bob like a cork on a fishing line, but it appeased. Darby wished he had one of those for hard times, then he looked at the amber bottle in his hand. Guess he kind of had a little something to soothe him.

Nate belched. "Yeah, life's tough."

Annie rolled her eyes, settled the kid on her hip and regarded her husband. "It's your turn to change Pax."

"Come on, hon, I'm hanging with my little brother."

"And that gives you reason to shirk your duty? This is an equal partnership, bud." Annie's gray eyes were sort of shardlike. He could see former FBI agent written all over her.

Darby struggled up from the depths of the recliner. "Give him here. I'll do it. Been wanting to spend some time with my nephew anyway."

His new sister-in-law raised her eyebrows. "You know this is a poopy diaper, don't you? Might ruin the relationship before it's out of the gate."

Darby set his beer on the table. "How hard can it be? I've had plenty of practice."

Nate's bark of laughter startled Pax, who started fussing again. "On who?"

"Myself."

Nate rose and shook his head. "Totally not the same thing. Trust me."

His brother held out his hands and Pax sort of fell into them with a drooling grin behind his enormous pacifier…and that's when Darby got a whiff.

Dear God.

His nephew smelled dead.

"Um, on second thought, I'll keep Annie company. Haven't had the opportunity to spend much time with her, either."

His brother frowned but dropped a kiss atop the baby's head. Yeah, Nate knew when he'd been suckered, but he didn't say anything more as he left the den, noxious fumes trailing behind him.

"You're good." Annie smiled as she sank onto the couch adjacent from the recliners and propped her bare feet on the ottoman. "Almost as good as me."

Darby shrugged. "I'm the baby of the family—we're born knowing how to manipulate the oldest."

"So does the wife. It wasn't even his turn to change the baby."

Darby laughed. He liked this new addition to the Dufrene clan. Spunky might have been Annie's middle name, something she'd need when up against his head-strong, set-in-his-ways brother. "Nate's happy finally."

Her eyes darkened. "Yeah, so am I."

"I'm sorry I couldn't come to the wedding." Darby had felt guilty about missing his brother tie the knot, but could do nothing except send a nice gift since he hadn't had enough leave to head stateside.

"He missed having you there, but he understands. That's the good thing about Nate. He's reasonable, otherwise, he wouldn't be here at Beau Soleil."

"Mother?"

Annie laughed. "She's hard to live next door to at times, but we love her. She's a good mother even if a bit, um, managing."

"You mean Attila the Hun tries to control your life?" Darby shook his head. "Give her an inch of rope, she'll take a mile, truss you up and drag you screaming and kicking behind her."

"She's not that bad. Just always at war with herself. She professes to allow life to take its course, but like those engineers who control the Mississippi River levee, she wears herself out trying to steer it to come out the way she wishes."

Darby shifted in the recliner and took another slug of beer. His brother's wife had Picou pegged, but she seemed remarkably tolerant of the interfering woman. He glanced at his sister-in-law and she stared back, an almost odd probing in her gaze. She shoved a brown curl behind her ear and sighed. "You're her logjam in that river."

"Huh?"

Annie shook her head. "Nothing. Never mind. Tell me about Spain. Did you enjoy living there?"

He didn't want to talk about Spain. He wanted to talk about what Annie meant, but she'd closed that chapter. Something told him not to try and go backward with this woman. So he didn't. Instead he chatted about the country he'd left behind—the food, the culture, the really bad drivers.

Nate walked back into the room during a story about getting lost when out on his motorcycle. He was Pax-free.

"Where's the kid?" Annie interrupted.

"Left him in his crib gumming that toy you bought him. Turned on music to stimulate him."

"Classical?"

Nate smiled. "Classic rock."

Darby vaguely heard Eddie Van Halen's infamous guitar licks coming from the hallway. "Nice."

"We want a well-rounded kid," Annie said, patting the spot next to her. Like a spaniel, Nate went to her. Bet she scratched his belly regularly. Of course, Darby understood the appeal of belly-scratching from a woman who had a vibe like Annie—that sort of vibe would have a man happily doing as bidden.

It made him think of Renny.

She had that vibe. Or she had at one time. Beautiful golden skin, tumbling caramel hair and a soft laugh that made a man twitch thinking about her hands on him. But she'd changed. Her laugh wasn't easy, her disposition more guarded…even if some remnant of the past lurked in her eyes, in her voice. It was like a promised resurgence.

He wanted to make her laugh again. To watch her

glow in the light of the sun sinking over the Atchafa-laya. To tangle his hands in that hair and make love to her under the full moon just as he'd done so many times.

Hunger clawed at him.

"Darby?"

He blinked. "Huh?"

"Want another beer?"

"Sure."

Nate stared blankly at him. "Grab me one, too, when you come back."

Checkmate. Older brothers always had the last laugh. Darby huffed and got to his feet, heading toward the kitchen. "Annie?"

"Me, too." She nodded. Nate hooked her around her neck and kissed the side of her mouth. Darby made a face but smiled as he turned toward the kitchen. Seeing his brother happy satisfied him on a lot of levels. Nate had suffered through so much guilt regarding Della and had shouldered much of the burden of dealing with the estate and their mother that Darby figured the man deserved some peace with his woman.

The kitchen was clean and modern with the smell of rich wood and laundry soap, and it had a specialty fridge built in for beer and wine. He grabbed three Abita Turbodogs and started back toward the den, wondering if he should confide in Annie and Nate about his strange marriage and ensuing divorce.

Nice to share a burden, but did he want the drama?

Because Picou would find out.

Maybe.

If he could keep it under wraps that would be best. Picou wanted a reason to keep him in Louisiana under her thumb. What better way to chain him here than to encourage some sort of romance between him and Renny?

He knew that's what she'd do.

And there was a tiny part of him that wanted it, too.

But the grown-up part of him knew he needed to forget his past and move toward a future. In Seattle. With Shelby.

Damn it.

He couldn't summon Shelby's face. She had blond hair, a nice pair of blue eyes to match a nice pair of breasts that filled out tight sweaters, but her face escaped him at the moment. His thoughts were full of sun-kissed skin and golden-flecked eyes. God, he had to stop thinking of her.

"Lucille said you went to see Renny. Did you get to have that talk you wanted to have?" Nate held out an expectant hand.

Ah, there it was. The best reason to head to Seattle— nosy kinfolk. "Yeah, just some things from the past. An apology and all that."

"For what?" Annie asked, accepting the cold bottle from him. "And we're talking about Renny Latioles? The woman who lives in that restored gatehouse on the outskirts of town?"

"Yeah. Darby and Renny were an item in high school. In fact, they tried to run off and get married when they turned eighteen. They were seniors and Dad blew a gasket. Only thing that saved Darby's ass was that wreck. Of course it screwed him, too, since he got sent to military school."

"You tried to get married? At eighteen?"

Darby shrugged. "We were young and in love. When you're eighteen you think anything is possible...even getting out of being sent away."

"I thought I was in love with Lily Bamburg. We were going to get married and then breed and train lab puppies for hunters." Nate ignored the bitterness in Darby's voice, obviously not wanting to travel down that path of discord.

"The waitress at Marmalades?" Annie's eyebrows arched into her bangs.

Nate laughed. "Two hundred pounds ago and before she had five kids, Lily was a looker. Plus she had an eye for a good retriever."

Darby didn't like the direction the conversation took. He didn't want to talk about his father, marriage or past loves—it was all too close for comfort. "So tell me about Della. What's the deal?"

Nate shrugged as Annie shifted her eyes away for a moment, growing contemplative as the conversation took a serious turn. "She's scared…and she's still grieving for Enola Cheramie."

Nate nodded. "It's been more difficult than I thought it would be to reconcile her to this family, and some of that might be because your twin sister is a Dufrene through and through. Nothing done the easy way." Nate took another pull on his beer and curled his arm around his wife again. Annie settled against him, but not in a girlish way, merely in a comfortable way. Nothing girlish about Annie except for her size. She was barely five foot two.

Darby knew the MO of his family. They weren't an easy lot. Fiercely loyal, insufferably headstrong and irrevocably passionate, the children of Martin and Picou Dufrene got their temperament honestly. Though his sister had been kidnapped and raised by an old bayou woman, she'd be no different. It was in her blood. "I guess I'm not good with understanding women, so I don't know what help I can be. I—"

"This is not about gender," Annie said, a furrow between those serious gray eyes. "This is about being part of a family that is, uh, difficult at times. She's been thrust into this culture, this name, and that's a hard thing. Trust me."

Nate looked sharply at his wife. "What do you mean by that?"

"You know who your family is. Been here longer than any other family in the region. Your great-grandfather was mayor, your uncle ran the bank, streets are named after your great-grandmothers and there's a statue of your cousin in front of the city hall. About forty percent of the lands surrounding Bayou Bridge bear the name Laborde or Dufrene. It's unsettling at times."

Darby's gaze crashed into his brother's. "Well, put like that…"

"And your mother is a most determined woman." Annie propped her chin on her hand and leaned forward. "That's been the hardest thing for Sally."

"Is she still calling herself 'Sally'?" Darby asked.

"Why wouldn't she? That's what she's been called since she was a baby. It's what she knows and right now she's clinging to everything she's ever been and running from who she's likely to become. She doesn't feel comfortable in her skin, so she damn sure doesn't feel comfortable here at Beau Soleil."

Darby sank back into the chair, knowing exactly how his sister felt, but even that might not be enough to put him on even keel with her. After all, he hadn't seen Della since his parents had driven away that morning over twenty-six years ago to take him to town to see the doctor. He couldn't remember that day without thinking about his mother's face. It was all he could recall in his feverish state. His mother collapsing on the floor that night, holding the ransom letter left nailed to a tree in the garden. Something like that made an impression even on a three-year-old child.

He didn't know the woman his sister had grown into, raised in the backwaters of Bayou Lafourche with a woman who made her living from the land and waters of South Louisiana. She would be a stranger to him, so he doubted anything he said to her would change the way she felt about the Dufrenes or Beau Soleil. He told his mother he would try, and he would. That was the reason he'd dug out that old book the therapist had him make. The grief book that was to have helped him cope with losing his twin—the book that had led him to the marriage certificate.

"I told Mom I would go down to Galliano and try to talk to her. I don't know how she'll react, but your insights help." Darby rose from the cushioned leather depths of the chair and stretched. "I guess I should head back to the big house."

"I'd recommend you don't alert our sister that you're coming," Nate said.

"You don't think?"

Annie nodded. "I agree. May be a little unfair, but you don't want her prepared to meet you. She's hiding…and that means she's hiding her emotions. And what this family needs, what your mother needs, is for your sister to let go and feel. Until she does that, she's never going to heal from Enola's death and she's never going to open her heart to our family."

Nate smiled. "You said 'our' family."

"And I meant it." Annie reached over and rubbed her husband's shoulders.

"If y'all start canoodling again, I may vomit." Darby pulled on his boots and stood up, trying to ignore the warm, fuzzy vibes coming from the couch. "But thanks for the beers. I'll let you know how it goes with Della. Sally. Whatever her name is."

"How about *sister* because that's what she is," Annie said, rising and grabbing a magazine. "And all you can do is try, right?"

"Right."

Nate rose also, glancing at the clock. "I'll catch up with you later. Annie and I will be in Baton Rouge tomorrow on a case so you'll have to call on my cell."

"I think I might wait until Sunday afternoon. Maybe wait and catch her after Mass. And I didn't know you worked on Saturdays. What do you do with the kid?"

A glint hit Annie's eyes. "Why? You wanna babysit?"

"Um, after getting a whiff of that diaper, not really."

"He has a sitter who comes most days, and we work every day. Crime doesn't take a break, so neither can we. Got an interview with a woman who may have witnessed an abduction and murder. She's off tomorrow so we're on the case."

"You see why I love her?" Nate smiled at his brother.

"She was made for you," Darby said, heading to the front door. For some reason those words conjured up the image of Renny. Made for him. How many times had he told her that, whispering it into her ear as they made out in the back of his truck? Plenty.

But that was then and this was now. He was a different person, so Renny wasn't made for him any more than Lily Bamburg had been made for Nate. Those had been the thoughts of an irresponsible boy. The hopes of a naive bayou girl. The dreams of two eighteen-year-olds who didn't know the way the world worked. That dream was gone, cold ashes on a grate.

But as Darby pushed out the front door into the cloak of the Louisiana night, sticky even in September, he knew he lied to himself.

Because there was a spark smoldering beneath those ashes, awaiting a slight stirring, and Darby knew he needed to stay away from them.

Needed to stay away from Renny or he'd be sucked into his past. And that might leave little room for the future he wanted.

Far away from Beau Soleil.

CHAPTER SIX

RENNY WATCHED HER MOTHER'S Pomeranian hop about her feet before begrudgingly bending down and petting Hopscotch. The yipping dog squirmed, a stark contrast to Chauncey with his lazy swoop about the feet or aloof stare from across the room. Hopscotch was as in-your-face annoying as she was cute.

"Come here, Hop-Hop, and leave your sister alone," Beverly Latioles crowed in a voice reserved for babies and fluffy dogs.

Renny refrained from rolling her eyes since the little apricot dog was her mother's pride and joy. Hopscotch pranced over to Bev, licked her hand and then leaped into her lap. The dog turned her brown eyes on Renny and lolled out her tongue as if to say *mine*.

"Isn't she the sweetest little thing? I got her a new sweater at Target yesterday but it's too warm to put it on her yet. Won't she look adorable?"

"Mmm-hmm," Renny said, moving two of the brocade pillows off the toile couch so she could sit down. *Good Housekeeping* and *Better Homes and Gardens* sat in piles on the tufted matching ottoman that also held an antique platter for tea. A steaming cup of chai tea waited in a Royal Doulton Blue Versailles cup. For a few moments she sat in her mother's precise world wondering how in the devil to bring up the fact the woman had been lying for eleven years.

"You're awfully quiet, honey. Not that you're overly talkative any other day. Is everything okay at work? Or is this little visit about that Dufrene boy showing back up? We're having lunch tomorrow..."

Renny jerked her head. "Why would this visit be about him?"

Her mother spread her hands and a new polished turquoise ring drew attention to her long nails. Beverly's silver hair fell in long loping curls past her ears, almost to the gold lamé blouse. Her mother was Lafayette's version of a Jersey Shore socialite replete with large sunglasses, glittering jewelry and over-the-top taste. "Anytime that boy was in the vicinity, your brain turned to mush and your panties hit the floor."

"Well, I'm wearing panties, Mother."

"Are you, dear?" Her mother smiled and extended a tray of sugar and cream. "Thinking with your head has led to good decisions in your life. Look at what it's gotten you—you're under thirty and a project manager for a huge reintroduction. But with that Dufrene boy you never thought with your head."

"You think it's good I don't have a social life? You think I can't handle Darby?"

Bev gave her a deprecating smile. "That's not what I meant. As you know, I've actually found you some nice guys, men who will suit your nature."

"You can't design a guy for me, Mom."

"I can try," Bev said, a twinkle in her eye. "After all, I do want grandchildren one day."

Renny couldn't figure her mother out, but didn't have to at the moment. She had more pressing issues. "Actually, this *is* about Darby."

Her mother's drawn-on left eyebrow kicked up. "So I was right? I had hoped you'd move past that whole sordid affair. I, for one, would like to forget I ever wore clothes from the Salvation Army and recycled aluminum foil. It wasn't a good thing being so far beneath the Dufrenes. You were always a small, beautiful flower crushed beneath his boot heel. Why would you go backward, honey? I've vowed to forget about Bayou Bridge and those bad, bad memories. You should, too."

Her mother spooned sugar into her own cup and lifted it to her lips with a frown. Beverly Latioles had spent many years scrubbing spaghetti sauce from the tiled floors of many a home in Bayou Bridge. She'd also cleaned their toilets, dusted their ceiling fans and folded their undies before saving up enough money, getting a loan from a bank and starting a small cleaning business that had grown into a fairly large company centered in Lafayette and surrounding small towns. Of course, being a cleaning lady's daughter hadn't been a walk in the park for Renny, either. Neither one of them savored much about poverty and desperation. So, yeah, she had plenty she wanted to forget about Bayou Bridge.

"But you lied to me."

Bev lifted her dark eyes and studied her daughter. A few seconds ticked off the cuckoo clock. "About what? About that boy's intentions? About how he almost killed you?"

"You know exactly what I'm talking about."

Her mother took another sip of tea, and Renny noted her hands quivered. For another long moment, her mother stared out the window at the crepe myrtles still staggered in blooms on the trees. Finally, her gaze returned to Renny's. "You mean the letters."

"Yeah, the letters he sent me. The phone calls he made. Those little things that said the opposite of what you told me. He didn't abandon me. He didn't leave me behind like you wanted me to believe."

"But, yet, you believed it. Pretty easily if I remember."

Renny flinched and the hot tea she balanced on her knee spilled on her jeans. "Only because I trusted you. I was hurt and it was easy to believe he'd washed his hands of me, of Bayou Bridge. You said you'd heard him say as much with your own two ears."

Her mother sighed. "You didn't trust him for good reason. He wasn't reliable. He was a boy—an irresponsible, spoiled boy who didn't have any of your best interests at heart. He wanted you like you were a thing to be owned. Like something he could collect and place on his shelf next to a signed baseball or a rock he once picked up down at the bayou. I know exactly who he was, and I knew he'd take everything you were and smother it beneath his ego. Men like that don't care for anyone but themselves. I couldn't allow him or the Dufrene family do that to you."

"Do what to me?"

"What was done to me." Her mother thunked the saucer and cup onto the tray. "I wasn't going to let you be duped and then tossed aside like trash in a gutter."

"You projected what happened to you with my father onto me, and that's not fair, Mom. Darby loved me and you lied about that." Renny sat her tea beside her mother's with a careful hand. Her heart raced against her ribs and she felt trembly. Dealing with her mother was never easy, but the bill was past due when it came to Darby Dufrene.

"You're damn right I lied. I'm your mother and my job is to protect you. I won't apologize for that." Her mother's declaration sounded final, scratch-a-line-in-the-sand final, but Renny wasn't finished. She needed to understand what had happened while she'd been in deep sedation, but even more, she wanted to understand what had happened when she'd woken. Understand why she had believed her mother over her boyfriend. Wait. Her husband.

Strange to acknowledge Darby as her husband, but until the divorce papers were signed, that's legally who he was.

"Look, I'm not itching for a fight, Mom. You've always been a good parent to me, but I need to understand what happened all those years ago. Why did you tell Darby I wanted nothing to do with him? Why did you tell me he never came to see me? That he never called?"

Her mother stood. "I don't have anything left to say on this matter, Renny Eva. I did what was best for you, just as the Dufrenes did what was best for their son."

"Please, Mom. I'm an adult now, and what's done is done. But you owe me an explanation. Surely, you can manage that much."

Her mother closed her eyes and mouthed something, but said nothing aloud. After several seconds she gave a tremendous sigh. "Why do we have to do this? The Dufrenes are in the past, and that's where they should stay. I knew this would happen. I knew when that boy showed up, the pot would get stirred. I've been having bad dreams all week. Premonitions of trouble."

"Mom," Renny said, allowing that one word to show her exasperation, her need, her love.

Bev scooped up her dog and stalked toward the open doorway, her kitten heels silent on the thick nearly white carpet. Renny watched with her mouth open, amazed she couldn't budge her mother on the subject. Bev was tough, but she usually gave Renny what she asked for.

Anger boiled inside her veins. How dare her mother refuse to give an explanation? The woman had played God with her life, setting up a scam to keep two crazy-in-love kids from being together—and she'd had help from the Dufrenes. Renny didn't know why she hadn't seen this all along. She knew her mother disliked Darby and the effect he had on her. How many times had she been lectured about her grades, about breaking curfew, about using birth control and taking precautions from getting knocked up? And how many times had Renny ditched classes, stayed out all night drinking and carousing, and practicing safe and unsafe sex in the back of Darby's truck?

That she hadn't guessed her mother and Darby's parents had plotted against them made her feel more than dumb.

Almost moronic.

Almost like one of those blinking lollipops on those retro cartoons.

Sucker.

Hopscotch came zipping back into the room and hopped onto the couch, placing a paw on Renny's thigh. The fur ball yipped twice then took off back toward where Beverly had disappeared.

"What is it, girl? Has Timmy fallen down a well?" Renny joked to a silent room. She shoved herself off the couch with a huff and followed "Lassie" toward her mother's bedroom where she heard several thumps and a pretty naughty word from a prayer group leader.

She walked into Bev's bedroom where the walls were a soft Pepto and the carpet the same ecru as the sitting room. French blue silk swags swooped across the floor-length windows, giving contrast to the assorted shades of pink and cream. It was a powder-puff room for a strong-willed woman.

For a liar.

And that liar was in the huge walk-in closet standing on a step stool, shoving boxes around on the top shelf.

"We weren't through talking," Renny said, bracing her hands on the closet doorjamb.

Her mother didn't look away from her rummaging— merely held up a pointer finger. Her attention lit on an old boot box that she slid her way, yanking the worn cardboard lid upward. She clasped a ragtag manila envelope and held it up. "This is it."

"What are you doing?"

Beverly turned toward her, teetering in shoes too fussy for a woman who carried as many pounds as she did. She jabbed the envelope at Renny. "Here."

Renny took the parcel. "What's this?"

"Those damn letters he sent."

Her mother climbed down, folded the step stool and stuck it in a corner. She didn't glance toward where Renny stood holding the envelope.

"You kept them?" Renny looked down at the innocuous-looking envelope that had been stuffed so full the clasp threatened to tear.

"Mmm-hmm, though I wish to hell I'd burned them long ago. Don't know why I kept them. I never wanted you to see them. Never wanted you to think Darby Dufrene was any kind of option for you."

Renny looked down at the envelope then back at her mother. "We're married."

Beverly froze. "Who's married?"

"Me and Darby."

She could feel her mother's shock. "What?"

"The night we ran off, before the accident, we got married."

Her mother sank against the built-in shoe racks, her painted nails searching for the cushion on the built-in bench. "How? Martin said your marriage wasn't legal. Getting married by a boat captain doesn't hold up in a court of law, so you can't be married. Darby's lying to you."

Renny shook her head. "No. I saw the marriage certificate. We were loaded on champagne, and I don't remember much because of the accident, but it's my signature on the license. The boat captain must have filed it in the parish court. Not sure how it worked, but according to the State of Louisiana, I'm Renny Latioles Dufrene."

Her mother grabbed the bench with both hands, looking as if she might slide to the carpet below her. "You mean he's known all this time and didn't tell you? I don't buy it. This is some kind of hoax. Some kind of way he can get back at you."

"You're a piece of work, Mom."

Her mother glanced up. "What?"

"Why do you hate Darby so much? Why do you always think the worst of him?"

"Because he wanted to ruin you. He made you forget who you were, forget where you were going in life. We had a plan, remember? Valedictorian, full-ride scholarship, doctorate by the time you were thirty. But all that went away when you met him. Suddenly, I didn't know you anymore. You failed tests, you shirked your time at the church, and you snuck out all the time, getting into trouble, drinking, screwing around, and to make it worse, you thought he was the answer to your life…but he wasn't."

"You took that choice away from me. You didn't think about me, about what I wanted. You stole that from me." The memories of her mother stifling her came roaring back. Being with Darby had felt good... free. She'd loved Darby because he never expected anything but love from her, and her mother had done exactly what she accused Darby of—she'd crushed Renny under her ridiculous stilettos, refusing to allow Renny any control of her life.

Her mother rose. "All I thought about was you. Renny. My girl. The girl who had a future that didn't rely on marrying a Dufrene. I didn't want him to save you because you could damn well save yourself. And he never would have amounted to anything had he stayed. I could see the future for him clear as daybreak. He'd go to LSU, pledge some fraternity, and come back here to live on his name. He'd drag you with him, and then where would you be? You were bad for each other."

"No, we weren't, and it was *my* life. *My* choice. Not yours. Not Martin or Picou's. Mine and Darby's mistake to make on our own." Renny couldn't stop the tears forming in her voice. She was so incredulous she didn't know whether to cuss or cry. So much of her past had been determined by others—and she hadn't even realized it. What had her mother thought—she was too stupid to make good choices? Or too horny to see reason? Everyone tried to save Renny from herself, never bothering to think about whether it was right or wrong. Never seeing what they'd wrought in their own motivations—a woman who never felt good enough. "I can't believe this. What did y'all do? Get together in some kind of secret meeting and make a deal?"

She didn't have to wait for an answer—she saw the guilt in her mother's eyes.

"You did. Oh, God, please tell me you didn't take money or anything. Please don't tell me they bribed me out of Darby's life."

"I didn't take money."

"You took something from the mighty Dufrenes. I can see it in your eyes, Mother."

Beverly knit her lips together and averted her gaze. She said nothing.

"No need to hold back. Let's get this all out. Tell me what the deal was." Renny shoved a hand through her unbound hair and waited while her mother swallowed the tears that had welled in her eyes. Lacking anything else to do with her hands, she folded them across her chest, clasping the envelope over her heart, hearing the crunch of the letters within.

Everything had been a lie.

Beverly finally lifted her eyes—brown eyes filled with regret and tears. "I wanted to do what was best for you. Until I started my business, you were the only thing keeping me going. You were my sun and my moon, and when you started dating Darby, I lost you. You listened to him. You dreamed about a future with him. And when he nearly took your life, I went a little crazy."

Renny sank onto her knees, settling in front of her mother, surrounded by the smell of Estée Lauder Beautiful and a garish arrangement of bright colors and animal prints. "But that wreck was an accident. I could have been the one driving and the results would be the same."

"I warned you from the beginning your relationship with Darby would end badly, but that never stopped you. You did what Darby wanted you to do. You hid your acceptance letters to colleges because you wanted to go to LSU with him. You drank and smoked pot, and you became some wild creature I didn't know. Basically, you became me at seventeen, and I wasn't going to let history repeat itself."

"Mom, I didn't smoke pot. Well, once, but I wasn't out of control." Renny paused a moment before glancing at the envelope she'd laid beside her. "I loved him, don't you understand?"

"All too well. It's how I felt about your father. I rebelled against my folks and followed him from Alexandria to down here. He left me pregnant with no options, and my daddy wouldn't let me back through their front door. He told me I was dead to him. So I couldn't go home, and then your father took off to California with some other woman he'd met in Texas. Left me here in a crappy, roach-infested apartment with a baby and no job. Do you think I wanted that for you, Ren?"

Renny shook her head. "I know you didn't, but that still didn't give you the right to take away my choice."

"Well, I thought it did when I saw you lying in that bed fighting for your life. Your leg was so badly damaged they said you'd never walk again, and that you'd be lucky to survive the next few days. Do you know what that feels like? To know he nearly destroyed you both mentally and physically? I didn't really care what you thought was best for you. And I damn sure didn't care what the Dufrenes thought. All I wanted was that boy away from you."

Her mother stopped and caught Renny's gaze. "Turns out the Dufrenes wanted the same thing."

Renny felt the sting of tears in her eyes. The Dufrenes had always been so kind to her, but deep down she'd seen their concern over their son dating a housekeeper's daughter. After all, Darby was a Dufrene, and their family owned half of Bayou Bridge and likely had the governor on speed dial…though in Louisiana that wasn't always a good thing. "You're saying they thought I wasn't good enough?"

Her mother shrugged. "I'd hate to think that about Picou, but I wouldn't put it past Martin. He was, after all, a social climber himself. His people were from New Iberia and not nearly as influential as the Labordes. But, honestly, I think it had more to do with Darby selling himself short, not with you, but on life in general. He was heading for disaster. Everyone saw it but Darby."

Renny sat back on her heels and tried to wrap her mind around what her mother had revealed, and she couldn't help but feel a renewed sense of betrayal. She'd trusted her mother and Darby's parents, but her trust had been misplaced. Her feelings for Darby should have superseded all the doubts that had been planted, but there was truth in some of what Bev said. Besides, Renny had always wondered about Darby's intentions. His chief desire in life at seventeen was to rankle his father. As a housekeeper's daughter, Renny had always felt she'd been a tool in that process of vexing Martin Dufrene. "Darby *could* be destructive just to prove a point."

"Two wrecked trucks in one year, a drunk and disorderly charge and a nearly dead girlfriend all seemed to point in that direction."

"So what did they give you for keeping me away from their son?"

Her mother's face shuttered. "I didn't take Dufrene money if that's what you're implying. I have some pride."

"Oh, I know you do, but you're also not an idiot. Darby was drunk and that meant possible legal problems."

"True. I was pissed and I let Martin know exactly what I wanted. His son to leave you alone, but I also wanted you taken care of. I didn't need his money. I had insurance, thanks to the company I worked for, but I did need his influence. I wasn't going to turn up my nose at a pointed word to the bank president or a phone call to college scholarship committees." Beverly shrugged as if it were a most natural thing to blackmail a man for what she wanted, and though Renny didn't approve, she guessed her mother had been forged by the fires of injustice. She knew how to survive and thrive.

"So not money, but it might as well have been." Renny pushed herself off the plush carpet, snatching up the envelope she'd set beside her on the floor.

"Where are you going?" her mother asked, also rising.

"Home. I need time to think about this."

"But tomorrow's my birthday. We're having lunch."

"Seriously, Mom? You lay this on me, and that's what your concern is? Your birthday?"

"Honey, I'm your mama. I did my job. What's hard to understand about that? You were a girl, and it was a silly infatuation that would have withered."

"I was a grown woman. Old enough to vote. Old as you were when you got pregnant with me, so you can't justify that decision."

Her mother grabbed her arm as she turned. "One day, if you are lucky, you will have a child of your own, and you will know what it feels like to love someone more than you do yourself. You'll look down at that baby sleeping in its crib and vow to do whatever it takes to keep her safe. Then, you call me and tell me what a bad mother I was for wanting to protect you."

Renny pulled her mother's hand from her forearm.

"I've never doubted your love, Mother, but love doesn't give you the right to erase what I felt. And that's what you did. You took my love for Darby and scrubbed it out. That will never be okay."

Her mother shook her head. "One day you'll see why I did what I did. But first you'll have to love with every fiber of your being."

"Maybe I already did."

Renny walked out of her mother's closet, carrying words written long ago by a boy who loved her, by a man she was still tied to through marriage. She didn't know if she could forgive her mother for taking him away, but she didn't think she could hate her for it, either.

Much had been done in the name of love.

And somehow Renny knew she'd only scratched the surface of its power.

Hopscotch dragged a ragged stuffed bunny to the door, dropped it and barked at Renny as she walked out of her mother's suite.

"Go see your mama, Hopscotch. She needs a friend."

Then Renny left, wiping away silent tears streaming down her face, leaving her mother sobbing quietly in the closet.

CHAPTER SEVEN

RENNY TOOK ANOTHER SIP of the sweet chardonnay and wiped the dampness from her cheeks with a napkin. Scattered around her on the sofa were dozens of letters from Darby.

She sniffled and tore open another envelope addressed to her old house in Bayou Bridge. Even his slanted handwriting seemed desperate.

More of the same met her eyes.

I'm so worried about you.
Why won't you talk to me?
I still want us to be together.
Please forgive me for jerking the wheel so hard—
I didn't see that tree.
Be okay, Renny. Please say you're okay.
I love you.

"God," Renny croaked, tossing the letter on top of the one she'd just read. Her poor heart ached for the past, for the boy who'd been sent away to a new school, a new state, midterm…a boy who thought she wanted nothing more to do with him. How alone he must have felt all those miles away.

She'd gone through all the letters and found the last one to be the most devastating. In his flowing script, he'd begged her to meet him in New Orleans at the statue of Andrew Jackson in the middle of the square at noon, so they could begin a new life. He had saved enough money to get them through the summer and had already applied for grants and housing at LSU.

Had he gone that June afternoon? Had he stood there, hands in his Levi's pockets, scanning the crowd between the huge banana plants, sidestepping tourists posing in front of St. Louis Cathedral? Had he sat near a palm reader contemplating a future without her?

And what would that future have looked like? They'd shared dreams. Darby's career had always been sketchy—he'd go from doctor to baseball player to attorney, but Renny had always wanted to work with animals. They'd finish school, build their dream house on the land Darby's grandfather had left him, and raise a family. They'd kiss each other good-night every night and pay all their bills on time. Church, family and friends. Happy ever after.

Their shattered dreams broke her heart all over again.

"Oh, Darby, I'm so sorry I didn't know." She stroked a purring Chauncey as she slumped against the sofa and looked for the crumpled napkin so she could blow her nose, but it was missing. She looked under her crossed legs and beneath the sofa before giving up with a sigh. "Darn it."

She struggled to her feet and spun around just as the doorbell sounded.

"Great," she muttered, sniffing and using her sleeve to mop up her face. She wasn't a pretty crier, so she knew her face was blotchy and her eyes swollen. Whoever was at the door might get an early Halloween scare. She looked at the letters around her before gathering them up and hurriedly shoving them under the sofa cushion. No need for anyone to see her private business.

She peeped through the window.

Darby.

"Oh, crap," she whispered, tucking her hair behind her ears and giving an extra sniff. She'd come home from her mother's house, drawn a hot bath, and put on an old sweatshirt and a pair of gym shorts. Her toenails weren't even polished.

What was he doing here?

The irony didn't miss her. It kinda smacked her in the head.

"Ren," he called, knocking once again, and glancing toward her car parked in the driveway. The early evening shadows had fallen, casting burnished fingers of light across the stoop, making Darby's hair flame golden, making her swallow hard before pulling open the door.

"Oh," he said, stepping back, "there you are."

She nodded and gave him a quizzical look, hoping to play off the fact she looked soggy, slouchy and sad by looking put out.

"You okay? Something happen?" He stepped forward, all golden and yummy in the waning sunlight. The same sunlight that probably showcased the start of crow's feet in the corner of her eyes.

Yeah, something happened.

She'd learned the absolute truth from the woman who had long ago sabotaged their love.

"Nothing. The ragweed must be kicking up." She pushed her hair back and squinted against the sun. "What are you doing here? Again."

His eyes darkened, or at least she thought they did. The sun was damn bright. "Sid couriered over the divorce petition."

"Okay."

"So I brought you a copy."

"Okay."

Darby's forehead crinkled. Her one-word responses were peeving him, but she didn't care. She didn't want him there. After having read those plaintive words he'd written so long ago, she knew how vulnerable she was. Knew he wouldn't have to push hard to get her to... God, she couldn't even think what the man could do to her if he so wanted.

"Sid said he could draw up a waiver of service that would shave a couple of weeks off the process. But regardless, we'll be good to go in 180 days."

She held out a hand, wondering his true motive. He'd basically repeated the same info he'd given her the night before.

After a look around the darkening neighborhood, Darby turned back to her. "Think I could come in for a minute?"

Her mind flashed to the letters stuffed beneath the cushions. Had she hidden them well enough? Did it matter if he found them? For some reason it made her feel naked, bare to him, and she wasn't ready to feel that way with Darby.

"Sure, I guess. Come on in." She stepped back, allowing him to pass, hoping he'd avoid her living room and go straight to the dining table, but like every other man she'd ever known, he didn't do as she hoped. He headed straight for where Chauncey lay curled up and purring on a fluffy throw pillow.

"Hey, Chaunce," Darby said, stroking a hand down the cat's back and getting a loud purr in return.

"Why are you really here?" she asked, shutting the door and leaning against it.

He looked up at her. "To give you the papers, and then I thought we could—"

"You could have given them to me later, Darby. You want something more. I know you."

"No, you don't."

"Better than you know yourself. I can feel what's going on between us. I know it's not what we expected."

"You've changed," he said, his voice like a snowflake—soft in appearance but landing with a sting.

"Of course I have. It's been over eleven years. The accident and losing you affected me. I had to learn how to eat, talk and walk again, all the while believing you didn't want me. That makes a person tough."

Darby shook his head and leaned against the cushion with a sigh.

She heard the crackle of the paper from her position at the door. Her eyes widened as his hand found the crumpled letter and lifted it from where it had been wedged between the cushions. "What's thi—"

His words died as his eyes moved over the words.

She wanted to tell him to put it down, stop nosing through her house and get out, but she didn't. When she'd let him in the door, she'd committed to letting him into her pain. Watching realization dawn on his face as his eyes scanned the handwritten letter was akin to watching a car wreck. No looking away. No turning back.

He lowered the letter. "So you had these all along? You lied?"

"No. I had no reason to lie to you. I went to my mom's today to confront her about what really happened in those days following the accident. After we argued, she handed me a big envelope crammed full of the letters she'd hidden from me but, for whatever reason, kept."

"You read them?" he asked, placing the letter in his hand on the coffee table. "That's why you've been crying?"

She didn't answer because he knew she had.

"Ren?"

Crossing her arms, she finally lifted her eyes to meet his gaze. "They made me sad. So?"

For a moment neither one of them said anything. Just stood apart, holding each other's gaze. Unspoken words filled the space between them, but those words felt too raw to acknowledge. The past separating them felt like a raging river. And she wondered if she'd laid groundwork in crossing that bridge as she'd read those words he'd penned years before.

Or maybe there was no need to bridge the space between them.

"So, you said you had the papers for me?" Renny broke the silence and walked toward the small dining area, separated from the living room by only a change in flooring, and flipped the light switch. Sinking into a chair, she grabbed a pen from the cup on the bookshelf and clicked it expectantly.

Darby pulled out the chair across from her and laid a folder on the table. "Sid Platt sent me the petition, but not the waiver. There's nothing to sign yet."

"Oh. Okay. When you get it, I'll sign it."

"Okay." Darby didn't look like he wanted to leave anytime soon. Why? Was this just an excuse to see her? She was nearly certain it was, and it both excited and scared her to know they'd broken past the barrier of resentment they'd each carried for so long. But what would that mean? "So you're certain this union was legitimate in the first place? I read online being married by a boat or ship captain isn't upheld in the court of law."

Darby nodded. "That's right. It's become urban legend that it's legitimate, but Sid did some digging around on this boat captain and found the reason why the license was filed and *is* legal."

She arched an eyebrow.

"The captain who married us was an ordained minister."

"That drunk?"

"Well, he wasn't practicing as a minister at the time, but that's the reason his deck hands called him 'Rev' instead of captain…and the reason he was listed in the yellow pages under 'Red Snapper, Amberjack and Leg Shacklin'."

"You've got to be kidding. Any other boat captain and we wouldn't be in this mess?"

"Pretty much."

She opened the folder, glanced at the legalese within and then closed it. "Okay, I'll read through this."

"Good, and if you have any questions, I'll be happy to answer them or explain any of the legal terminology."

"Okay."

Silence hung over them. Renny averted her gaze and wondered what she could say to one's soon-to-be ex-husband, especially when she wanted to touch him, wanted to forget those years between them if only for a few hours. Didn't matter that her rational thoughts screamed the opposite. Whenever he was near, she felt some primeval urge to possess him, mark him, something.

She sighed.

His gaze jerked to her. "Why were you so quick to

believe our parents? Why didn't you have any faith in me?" His words might as well have been bullets. They punctured her heart much the same way.

"Darby, aren't we water under the bridge? Do we really have to do this? The past twenty-four hours have been almost traumatizing, so let's not make it even harder by trying to find the root of what went wrong. We never would have worked even if you'd have stayed on the road that night."

"Why do you think that?"

"Because we weren't meant to be. The stars were crossed for good reason."

"How do you know?"

Renny covered her face with her hands if only to avoid looking into his seductive blue eyes. In those depths she could see her past, could see the sorrow for what they'd lost, and it pulled her to him. "I don't want to talk about the past anymore, Darby. Doesn't do any good. What we had between us is over—"

"Is it? Because something doesn't feel over. After that kiss in the kitchen—"

"—which won't happen again. We forgot we're two different people, two people who have different paths. You're here visiting before going off to God only knows where, and I've built a life here. Neither one of us has reason to think about kisses…or the relationship we once shared. So, please, stop." Renny pushed back the chair and rose, hoping to close the conversation on that note.

"You're running from me," he said, flinging out words like a challenge.

Renny stopped her retreat. "I'm not running, because there is nothing to run away from. What I felt for you was a young girl's infatuation. It wasn't love,

Darby, or it would have conquered. It didn't because it wasn't real. That stupid kiss doesn't change anything, because we're not who we once were. Let's consider it a goodbye, not a hello."

His chair scraped the polished wood as he stood abruptly. His body crowded her space, but she refused to step back even an inch. "*Stupid* kiss? I thought it was way better than that."

She could smell his cologne, something manly and spicy, and his T-shirt hugged his body enough for her to see his lanky youthful chest and shoulders had grown into masculine splendor. Not Arnold Schwarzenegger, but definitely something worthy of good, long contemplation. She raised her eyes to meet his gaze. A spark of something dangerous flashed within the depths. "You would. You always overrated your abilities."

At this he gave a clipped laugh and suddenly he was the man she didn't know. A naval officer, calm, confident and oozing something she wanted to grab hold of.

"You were always such a challenge, Renny. Ever since I first met you, you've kept me on my toes, blackberry girl."

Shrugging a shoulder and trying to ignore his old nickname for her, she twisted her lips. "I'm a Southern girl. We don't take crap off—"

She couldn't finish her sentence...not when his lips were covering hers.

"Darby," she murmured against his mouth as one hand crept through her hair to cup the back of her head as the other wound round her waist, drawing her to him.

"Shut up," he whispered, silencing her with his kiss, a sweet, erotic delving that made her bare toes curl into the carpet. And like the night before, she felt her defenses weaken and her blood sing with a new desire, something she'd never felt with the man holding her—a woman's need.

It bloomed in her blood, rare and strong.

She deserved more than a kiss.

More than the goodbye she never got.

His hand glided up her back, like a flame licking her spine, while his tongue traced her lower lip before plunging within her mouth. She wanted to forget all she was and get lost in Darby.

But she couldn't forget who she was.

"Darby," she said as she pulled back.

He blinked at her with sexy bedroom eyes. "Yeah?"

"We shouldn't be doing this."

"Why not?"

"Because it will complicate matters. Sex does that."

He dropped the hand threaded through her hair and it ripped through a tangle, giving her added clarity. "Sex?"

She rubbed her lips together, but didn't step away. "Sorry, I shouldn't make assumptions based on incomplete data."

"What?"

"Oh, I... Never mind." But the word "sex" sat there, goading her. She wanted him. So why not? Why not take some pleasure for just this one night? She was a big girl. She could control her world. Hadn't she proved that for the past ten-and-a-half years?

Darby jerked his gaze to hers. "How was that incomplete data? I'm pretty certain it was explicit. Concrete. Rock-hard concrete evidence."

"I felt it." She met his eyes, met the challenge. "But if we go there, we're opening up a whole new can of worms. Can you handle that? 'Cause I don't know if I can."

Yeah, that was the enormous question in her mind. Making love with Darby would be good—it always had been—but could she handle the fallout if her heart got involved?

The trick was to keep her heart out of it.

Sex and friendship—she'd had it before with several other guys. Never had to even dip the slightest bit of her heart into those treacherous waters. But could she do that with the only man she'd ever loved?

If they went there.

Not a given that both of them could handle sex at this point, even if her own body nagged her to give it the ol' Harvard try.

He quirked an eyebrow and his lips curled at the corners. "I'm fairly certain I can handle anything you throw at me, Renny. I know I want to handle every piece of you in the most loving and delightful of ways."

"You can't jump in just because you're horny."

He laughed again, but this time he tugged her to him, his hands sliding up her back, causing her stomach to dip, hot molten need to stir in her pelvis and her breasts to feel tingly and heavy. "I'm jumping in *because* I'm horny."

"Not a good enough reason. You can't take back sex. Once it happens, it's done."

"Okay, it's more than being horny. Being with you doesn't scare me, Renny. Quite the opposite. I can't seem to stop wanting you. It's about a man and a woman. Me and you. Living in the moment, taking a little pleasure from this messed-up load of crap we've been handed."

"Bet you say that to all the girls."

He ducked his head and kissed her again, doing it so well she could hardly catch her breath. Then his mouth moved to her jaw, sliding around to her ear, sucking in her earlobe, before he whispered, "We've always been good together in bed. Give me what I want."

She snapped her head up, pushing him back. "No, you give me what I want."

At that moment, Renny felt a little crazy, a little out of control. She'd spent every day since the accident safeguarding her world. How long had it been since she'd lost herself in the magic of lovemaking? Way too long.

This time nothing inside her wavered.

After all, they *were* consenting adults—adults not involved in a relationship with someone else. Adults who wanted each other, who needed something more right at this moment.

What would it hurt?

People hooked up with exes all the time, didn't they?

Tonight she wanted what was taken away from her. Darby.

She didn't need to keep him forever. Just for right now. This night. It wasn't about love, sorrow or tenderness. It was about grabbing hold of this man and driving out all the pain he'd given her. She needed very adultlike, self-serving, healing sex.

Darby's blue eyes flared as she jerked the hem of his shirt up, revealing a taut stomach and a broad chest lightly sprinkled with golden hair.

"Nice," she breathed, sliding her hands up his hard stomach, savoring the feel of him beneath her fingertips. She looked up, pleased at the incredulity on his face.

"You *have* changed," he said, with a devilish grin.

"Can you handle that, too?"

Darby's gaze slid from hers to her body, undressing her with his eyes. Those blue eyes lingered on the racing pulse at her throat, then at the way her nipples stood out against the cotton of her shirt and finally at her bare thighs. "I'll risk the danger if I can taste you, touch you, make you moan, make you shudder against me."

Damn, he wasn't even freaking touching her, but she felt her temperature ratchet up a degree or two.

Yeah, she needed Darby with a big girl's hunger.

So Renny took a dive over the cliff and reached for the hem of her own shirt. "Ironically, having hot, *dirty* sex with you feels sort of safe to me. Like I don't have to worry about second dates or phone calls. It's an end."

The shirt cleared her head and she tossed it behind her. His breath quickened, probably because she wasn't wearing anything underneath, and suddenly she was grateful she still did yoga and ran three miles a day—in a good support bra.

Darby reached for her, but she backed away, hooking her thumbs in the waistband of the ratty gym shorts and sliding them down her thighs, allowing them to fall in a pool on the floor. Finally, she stood, placing her hands lightly on her hips, really glad she'd done laundry last night and wore her new yellow lace hipsters.

"Jumping Jehoshaphat," Darby breathed, taking her in. "You are the most beautiful woman I've ever had the pleasure of—"

"Doing?" She smiled, swaying her hips flirtatiously. She hadn't felt this powerful, this free in such a long time. With Darby she didn't feel the least self-conscious about her limp or the jagged scar that fell below her hip and extended to the top of her knee, mostly because the man was not looking at her scar.

"Come here," he breathed, motioning her with one hand.

She shook her head. "Not yet."

"Please."

"Part of the pleasure generated in sexual intercourse is the building of anticipation. It's a scientific fact, and as a scientist, I like testing subject matter."

"Fire," he said, coming toward her.

"Beg your pardon?"

He reached for her, but she shimmied away. "That's what you're playing with, darling."

"No, I'm conducting a field test," she said, loving every second of making Darby want her again. It was a powerful elixir to drive a man to the edge of reason. She wanted that feeling to last. Wanted him to drown in wanting her. She had no clue why, but she needed it. Needed to feel in control of her decision, and slightly in control of him.

"So you want an experiment, huh? So this is what happens when you get a degree in birds?" He moved toward her and this time she didn't move away.

"A degree in birds?" She quirked an eyebrow.

"My, oh my, how Renny Latioles has nerded up." With a glint in his eye, he traced a finger over her collarbone.

Two could play at this game, so she ran a hand across his stomach, delighting at the way his muscles contracted. "Let's see. Scientifically, what do you feel when I do this?"

His eyes flashed molten blue and her temperature went up another degree. "I think you know."

She smiled and dropped her hand lower. "Attraction, arousal, mating."

He caught her hand and moved it up to his chest. She felt his heart galloping beneath her fingers. "We're not animals. There's emotion."

"True. Emotion can play a major role. For example, I'm emotionally exhausted, steeped in sentimentalism, and as always, very attracted to you. It's a combination allowing me to unhook my bra rather than slam the door in your face. In my not-so-scientific opinion, emotion and alcohol are equally responsible for insuring the survival of the species."

He slid a hand beneath her rib cage, warm flesh against warm flesh as his hand traveled up to cup her breast. She literally hissed. "You're not wearing a bra, Dr. Latioles, and I think I could dig this kind of scientific study."

Renny closed her eyes as his thumb found her nipple. "Okay, let's get the experiment underway."

His lips brushed hers as he gathered her against him. "Where's your bedroom?"

She lifted her head and smiled. "You mean my lab? Uh, behind you to the left."

"I love it when you talk geeky."

Renny disengaged from Darby's grasp and wiggled out of her lace undies before turning toward the direction she indicated.

"Holy test tube," Darby breathed, "I don't think I've ever loved science as much as I do right now."

CHAPTER EIGHT

SHADOWS PLAYED HIDE-AND-SEEK on the floor near the closed door as Renny snuggled into Darby's chest and exhaled.

He twirled a piece of her hair around his finger and wondered how in the hell he'd gotten himself back into Renny's bed. Oh, the answer was fairly obvious. Desire still coiled between them like a serpent—like a dangerous, bewitching serpent.

He shouldn't have allowed his body to override his intent.

But then again he couldn't have stopped it. Seemed as if explosive sex had to happen between them before they could move forward. And he'd enjoyed every minute of every kiss, every stroke of her hand, every taste of her body. What had just taken place in her comfortable brass bed had been epically satisfying—and utterly stupid.

He felt like he'd screwed more than the sweet woman in his arms. On some level, he'd screwed his future. Renny had been right. Once they'd committed to such an intimate act, it was out there between them. Again.

Renny lifted her head and squinted at him. "Guess we allowed our bodies to overtake good reason. Probably wasn't a good idea."

He dropped the strand of honeyed hair. "Maybe not, but it was the most pleasurable one I've had in a while."

"I couldn't seem to help myself. It was like being marooned in the desert and happening upon a pool of water."

"Like the last cookie."

She gave a wry smile. "I thought it was better than a cookie."

"No one ever said I was good with analogies. Um, like a bag full of money sitting before a bank robber?"

She shook her head. "You do suck at euphemisms."

"Not a euphemism. I couldn't downplay what just happened between us. It blew my mind. And that ain't no lie, lady."

Her brown eyes studied him in the faint light of the early evening and he loved the delicious feeling of her naked, warm body next to his. He may have effed up on a huge level but he could take the memory of her wrapped round him mewling his name when the Seattle nights were cold and lonely.

Seattle.

Shelby.

Shame slid hard and cold into the pit of his stomach. How had he forgotten her so easily? If she were the woman for him, wouldn't he have turned and walked away from Renny's little experiment? Wouldn't he have not shown up on his ex's front doorstep with a flimsy reason for seeing her again?

He knew the answer, but was stubborn enough to ignore it.

No use feeling guilty because he and Shelby weren't exclusive—they'd been batting around taking a step toward something more than dating. That was it. No promises. No framework for anything other than a possibility. But he knew Shelby expected more. Hell, he expected more. That was the whole reason he was moving to Seattle. Maybe not the whole, but a good chuck of it.

Yet, what had happened between him and Renny was a wake-up call. Maybe this was nature's way of telling him Shelby wasn't the woman for him. Or maybe nature didn't give a flip. Maybe it was his slimy conscience trying to make what he'd done okay.

Should he have told Renny he'd been seeing someone?

No. He and Renny were just sex and memories. Not a future. What had just occurred was extraordinary, marked by need, reminiscence and fondness for one another.

"Yeah," she said, drawing circles on his chest. "It was good, but it has to be what it is, right? We both got wrapped up in the past and it sucked us back in time. So, I don't see us—"

"Having a future?" How did she always know what he was thinking?

She swallowed and her fingers stilled. "How could we? We're too different now, both of us on different paths. This is like getting stuck in the elevator. Like time slows down and you're hyperaware of who you are at that moment, but when the doors open the world sucks you back into who you were before. You know?" Her fingers resumed the tracing of circles on his chest.

Her touch caused funny triggers of desire to shoot to his pelvis and he felt interest stir down below. He usually needed a good hour or two refractory before he could even think about round two, but not with this woman. He caught her hand. "I know, but we're still in the elevator. My hyperawareness is hyperaware…very hyperaware."

Renny smiled and her gaze slid down to where the

sheet rested at his waist. "So I see. Guess I feel a little awkward since I don't usually engage in consenting adult sex much."

"Oh, so you're into the nonconsenting bondage stuff, huh?" He couldn't help but tease her because he didn't like where they were going. He, too, felt it had been an unwise decision, but he didn't want to overanalyze. It was what it was. He wanted to leave it at that.

She tweaked his nipple.

"Ow!"

"You know what I mean. I don't do this often. I'm not casual about sex."

He inched from beneath her head and sat up. Renny fell on her back onto the pink cotton sheet, clutching the top sheet to her chest. He rolled over and looked down at her. "Ren, let's not end this badly. This wasn't casual and I didn't do it lightly. I don't know why it happened. It just did. Okay?"

The crinkle in her forehead didn't disappear, but she nodded. "Okay."

He didn't know what to do next. He wanted to unwrap her out of the sheet and explore the beautiful curves that filled his hands so nicely. He wanted to press the stop button on the elevator again so he could have a few more hours to memorize her scent, her taste, the sound of her panting in his ear as she wrapped her legs around him and surged against him, taking him over the sweetest ledge a man could fall from.

But maybe it was time to let the doors open.

Renny lifted herself on her elbows, allowing the sheet to slide down, revealing breasts that were rounded and perfect.

"You opening the doors?" he asked.

She shook her head, and her beautiful eyes mirrored

the passion that had stirred within him seconds ago. "All good scientists repeat the experiment to test the results against the first outcome. We probably should follow the scientific method, you know, to make sure our first experiment in sexual desire was valid. For example, is your response the same if I do this?" Her hand glanced his stomach and slipped beneath the covers.

He groaned and closed his eyes. "Are you trying to kill me?"

Renny crept up on all fours and placed her lips over his. He passively allowed her to work her own magic, to deepen the kiss. She broke the kiss and looked up. "Is that what you think? 'Cause if so, I doubt you understand what's about to happen. It's not about expiring. It's about inspiring. Let me show you."

Her fingers started some magical sort of symphony on him and he collapsed back onto the feathered pillows crammed into the crease between the mattress and brass rails. "I kinda got the idea you wanted this to be a one-time thing."

"I did." She gave a throaty laugh as she peppered kisses down his chest. "But, Darby, let's make our closure damn good."

He shoved his hands in her hair, framing her face and tilting it up so he could see her expression. In her eyes he saw a determined, turned-on woman, and what man could stop that?

Not any man he knew.

He certainly would leave Louisiana, but he knew he'd never regret making love to the woman drawing circles around his belly button. No, Renny had always been the sweetest of gifts, surprising, rewarding and rich like dessert. She was right—they'd deserved a better ending than what they'd got years ago.

Her kisses peppered his belly and her hands did wild, wicked things—things that made it impossible to turn back. She paused and glanced up at him. "I've hurt too much over what didn't happen between us to miss a chance to say goodbye to what we once were."

He slid his hands down to her armpits and dragged her up his body. His erection settled right where it should.

"Oh," she breathed.

He cupped her head and brought her lips to his as she allowed her knees to fall to either side of his thighs. She was open to him and, if his powers of detection were working, very ready for him. "Condom?"

She didn't stop kissing him. Finally, she lifted her head. "I dropped one on the floor a little bit ago. Let me get it."

She leaned over and he groaned at the slick heat nearly enveloping him. "Fire, madam."

Her head went over the side of the bed for a moment before she popped back up. "I love playing with fire. Why do you think I chose science? Bunsen burners, remember?"

She held the wrapped condom aloft before ripping it open with her teeth. Dropping down, she kissed him and placed the condom in his hand. The warm sweetness of her mouth complimented the heat of her body, and Darby couldn't wait much longer. He lifted himself up, spun her over, and made short work of being a responsible partner. "I remember, Renny. Oh, how I remember."

And then he let his inhibitions, thoughts and recriminations fade away as he lost himself in the age-old rhythm that would take them to a place of delight.

The last thought as he slid inside Renny was how good the past felt sometimes.

MAKING LOVE TO DARBY three times in one night left a girl tired. It also left a girl with plenty of shame, doubt and a sort of soft glow in her cheeks that people commented upon. Which is why she knew it was true when Picou told her she looked well that morning.

Of course, Picou had snuck up on her as she stood in the abandoned rice field checking on the whooping crane. She'd seen a group of marsh birds take flight and knew someone else was there. Sure enough, she'd turned to find Picou pulling up in the ATV vehicle.

"Renny!" Picou called across the field, making L9-10 skulk back into some reeds along the edge of the woods. "What are you doing here so early on a Sunday morning?"

Renny pressed the air with her hands, hoping Picou got the message to be quiet, then slogged toward the older woman. As soon as she was close enough she yell-whispered, "How did you know it was me?"

Picou closed the lid on the plastic bin on the seat next to her and climbed from the mule. "Who else would it be? And who goes around dressed like that?"

Renny wore the costume she'd been wearing days before. Had it only been Friday? So much had happened within that span of time. Seemed longer.

She watched as the older woman, clad in jeans and a pair of dark rubber boots, started toward her. Renny shouldn't have come that morning. But work had seemed attractive—even on her day off—because work was the one normal thing in her life at that moment. All else had tipped over and scattered her emotions everywhere. Work she could handle.

The woman stopping in front of her, shading her eyes against the early morning sun, she could not.

"Morning, Picou," Renny said. She might have said, *Morning, traitor.* Same thing. Now she knew the woman she'd once trusted had been Judas in the dissolution of Renny and Darby. Jeez. It sounded like a play title. The Dissolution of Teenage Love.

"What are you doing out here?" Picou blinked nervously, like a kid caught filching the cake pulled out of the oven, which was odd.

"You already asked that and I think it's obvious—I'm doing my job."

Picou's gaze shuffled away and she scanned the area behind them. "So where's this bird you're so concerned with?"

Renny jerked her head toward the reeds where the bird hid and motioned Picou back toward the higher ground where the ATV sat. Birds were smart, and Renny didn't want to remove any part of her costume until she was well away from the crane.

The morning sun stabbed through the scrubby shrubbery and tall hardwoods marking the wooded area of Beau Soleil property. Even that brightness couldn't penetrate the mystery of the lowland. Once she was out of sight of the crane, she removed her face shield. "The crane is not accustomed to humans, Mrs. Dufrene, so if you see her, I'd appreciate your moving away and not getting too close. We want these birds wholly dependent on their habitat for survival."

"But I'm her habitat. This is our land." Picou's gaze was earnest. She wasn't being a smart-ass.

"True, but still it would be best if the bird does not have much human contact. We already worry about them being too familiar with our scent and the way we move."

"Oh," Picou said, her eyes moving along the tree line where the crane had disappeared. "I'll be sure to look out for her and stay away."

"Good."

"You look awfully pretty this morning."

Did she? Renny pushed her hair back and averted her eyes.

"Did you see Darby last night?"

She jerked her gaze back to Picou as alarm uncoiled. "Why would you ask me?"

"Well, he went out last night and didn't show up till nearly dawn. I assumed he was with you."

"Why?"

Picou blinked. "Because you are you."

"What does that mean?" Renny asked.

The older woman's brow wrinkled and for a moment she didn't answer. "Well, things were left unfinished between you."

You think? Irritation snuck up on her again. In front of her was one of the people responsible for keeping her and Darby apart years ago. "Well, you would know."

This time Picou's brows rose. "I guess that little cat is out of the bag?"

"Yeah, and it's pissed." Renny shaded her eyes and tried to allow the anger between her shoulder blades to slide away. *Water under the bridge, Ren.* But she couldn't shake the disappointment. Picou had always seemed like the kind of woman who wouldn't stop love. More like the kind of person who would pitch a tent, pull up a chair and train binoculars on love so she could watch it unfold.

"As well it should be. But—"

"There are no buts. You knew how Darby and I felt better than anyone else. I shared those hopes and desires with you, and you let my mom and your husband stomp all over them until they were nothing but rubble and dust. You may not have robbed the bank, but you drove the getaway car. Same difference. And I expected more from you."

"Ah, I suppose you did. And I'm sure you've heard your mother's platitudes about doing what was best for both of you, so I won't offer those."

And she didn't. Picou merely stood there, hands latched behind her back, observing the fluttering leaves overhead and the sound of nature surrounding them.

"So that's it?"

"What, dear?"

"All you have to say?"

Picou shrugged. "What more do you want me to say? I *am* sorry, but given the circumstances, perhaps I would have done the same. I can't say. At the time it made a great deal of sense. Both you and Darby were out of control, minds set on a path that would never have worked."

"So you thought."

"Mmm." Picou's gaze met hers. "Every person has things in life he or she regrets, and I am no exception."

And that was it. As close as Renny would get to an apology. "Yeah, we all have regrets."

"Mmm," Picou said again.

"Well, I should get back to work."

"You never answered my question. Were you with Darby last night?"

Renny looked away from Picou. "If I were, why would you need to know? Kinda nosy considering he's nearly thirty years old."

"I'm not being nosy."

And the sun wasn't shining. "You should talk to him. Not me."

Renny started back toward the abandoned rice field, intent on noting L9-10's appearance along with additional notes on the habitat. She'd forgotten her camera, so a detailed description would have to do until she could get back. The bird seemed remarkably well so it had to be finding adequate food in the area, though Renny couldn't figure out the bird's propensity to cling to this particular patch of earth.

She was about to put her headgear on when Picou's voice caught her. "Do you believe in prophecy?"

"Huh?" Renny turned toward the older woman.

"I have lived a long time with hurt. My daughter taken from me, my husband's oppressive manner, his death—so much has brought tears and bitterness. Seeking out some higher power, some understanding of the world, has been some solace to me."

Renny had no idea where the woman was heading, and she didn't really want to listen—too much to do this morning. Much of it aimed at trying to make sense of what she and Darby had done last night...or maybe she shouldn't think too hard about that. She couldn't let it mean too much to her because that could lead to trouble.

"Finally, not too long ago, I was able to procure a visit with the most powerful mambo in all of Louisiana. Zelda Trosclair retreated into the drawing room of Beau Soleil in the dead of night. My house smelled of her candles for days after, but what she left behind still lingers. A prophecy."

"You hired a mambo to tell you your future?"

Picou looked hard at Renny. "What more could I lose? For many years I had asked after the woman, and for years, she refused me. But then one day a note arrived, pinned to my back door. Scared Lucille half to death."

"Why?"

"It was written in red, like blood, and Lucille knows the power of voodoo, the way the black or white magic can summon spirits, make mischief, and bring heartache. She begged me not to invite the mambo to Beau Soleil, but what choice did I have? How else was I to bring Della back?"

Renny shivered despite the warmth of the morning. "You could rely on science—on Nate. After all, he found her."

Picou shook her head. "No, things were set in motion by the prophecy. Two weeks after the mambo revealed her prophecy, Nate got the folder on Sally Cheramie."

"Coincidence."

"You would think, but I don't. I know what it was. I know what I felt in that room when Zelda talked to darkness, when she prayed to the light. Hair stood on my nape."

"You're kind of scaring me, Picou. You know voodoo is hocus-pocus." Renny clutched the hat in her hand and tried to ward off the hair standing on the back of her own neck. The woman's words were so impassioned by her belief that magic had something to do with bringing her daughter back.

"Yes, Della was found but that wasn't all Zelda told me. She told me the sun wouldn't set on Beau Soleil until the past was rectified, until old hurts were healed, and until the great bird returned to the land that gave it life. When all was as it should be, the bird would leave again." The older woman looked past her to where the crane stalked some smaller creature in the soggy wetland at the edge of the field.

Renny glanced from the bird to the crazy loon. "You're telling me you think this crane is part of an old mambo's prophecy? Seriously?"

Picou didn't say anything, merely stared at the bird.

"Okay, then. I guess the bird is here for you. Maybe I can get it to fly away and you can have a pretty sunset and get on with life." Sarcasm may have been lost on Picou because she wasn't paying attention to Renny. Her Darby-like eyes had grown misty and she'd gone far away to some other land. "Mrs. Dufrene?"

She straightened. "Yes? And it's Picou, please."

"I'm going now."

"I wanted you to know, because you are part of righting old wrongs. What happened between you and my son was a mistake, a mistake I want to put right."

Renny stepped back because that's how startling the woman's words were. Picou wanted her and Darby back together? Or was it some kind of closure she wished upon them? "Uh, I'm not sure you can do that. Darby and I don't have anything left between us."

Liar.

The voice in her head sounded almost gleeful. Damn it.

"Now who is being untruthful, dear?" Picou smiled a slow cat-just-wounding-the-poor-field-mouse smile.

"You can put your efforts to do anything for me or Darby aside, Mrs. Dufrene. If, and that's so not even likely, but if Darby and I move toward anything other than acceptance over our past, it won't have anything to do with you, sunsets or that crane out there."

Picou laughed. "Okay, dear. I understand. But I got

the answer I needed. Have a good day, Renny, and if you see your mother, send her my regards."

The older woman spun on a rubber boot and climbed into the ATV, firing it so quickly, Renny didn't have time to ask what the woman was talking about. With a brisk wave, Picou backed around and swung toward the big yellow house holding the name that glorified the sun.

"What's the question?" Renny asked the trees before donning the hat and arranging the netting around her face.

The trees whispered their answer.

Possibility.

Or maybe it was wishful thinking on Renny's part. She wanted to pretend what she'd created with Darby in the sweet darkness of her bedroom had been two adults doing something that adults were wont to do— have good sex that didn't mean anything in the light of day. But she knew deep down in her heart, she wanted it to be something more. Something scary and lasting. Something dark and wonderful. Something similar to the magic Picou clung to. Something not of this earth, but of the eternal.

Yeah, she wanted more.

She wanted Darby…and always had.

And that had nothing to do with magic.

But her life was a life of reality. One where the sun rose and the sun set. Beau Soleil and prophecies be damned.

She wasn't angling to reconcile with Darby, because she knew they weren't meant for one another. They were too different and Darby wanted a new life away from Louisiana and away from her. And Renny wasn't about to toss her heart out into a game that would leave her broken. Not again. Dreams of her and Darby were just that—dreams.

So there was only one good question that morning.

What the heck was Picou doing out so early wearing rubber boots and acting secretive?

Yeah, that was the better question.

DARBY GRIPPED THE STEERING wheel as the organ music rose, indicating the closing of the church service. Soon the church doors would open and chattering people would pour out onto the covered walkway. He had parked in the side lot, trying to cover his bases. With a front entrance and a back, he was certain to catch sight of his twin sister as long as he stopped daydreaming about Renny and the way she'd looked asleep in the soft light streaming into her bedroom.

Dear Lord, she'd been everything he'd dreamed over the years, in the wee hours of the morning, when the heart overrides the mind, when real desires blanket truth. Oh, yes, there had been many early hours spent thinking of the golden skin, the brandy eyes, the sweet taste of the girl he thought he'd forgotten.

Even now he could still smell her on his skin. Her taste lingered on his tongue. His hands had memorized her body, the silken shoulders and smooth stomach.

Okay, he had to stop. His body hardened, his blood rushed.

Jeez. He was in the parking lot of the Golden Meadow First United Methodist Church.

Get a grip, Darby. Find your sister.

He glanced down at the cell phone sitting in the cup holder of the console. Shelby still hadn't returned his call, and he really needed to talk to her after what had happened between him and Renny. Wasn't fair to keep

Shelby hoping for something that may never happen. He had too much to sort out before he could move forward.

After all, he wasn't some ass who would keep a woman on a string while he explored his feelings. Cripes, he sounded like a therapist.

The doors opened, drawing his attention back to where it should be—on finding his sister. His eyes scanned the crowd, skipping over little girls with helicopter bows, exuberant boys jumping on one another's' backs, and parents helping the elderly shuffle down the ramp while keeping an eagle eye on their scattering children. Typical Sunday scene unfolding all over the South.

Then he saw her.

His twin sister.

Della wore a conservative navy dress that belted at the waist and flowed over slender tan legs. Her hair lay on her shoulders and she talked animatedly to a chubby older woman who wore an old-fashioned pantsuit and carried a cake holder.

He climbed out of the rental and pocketed the keys, moving at a good clip so he could catch her before she followed the crowd into the large building behind the church. He must have moved too fast because when he reached them, Della gasped and pulled away, placing a hand over her heart.

"Darby!"

She recognized him and that made him smile. "Hi."

"I didn't— Um." She looked around kind of desperately, as if she wanted to escape. He knew this wouldn't be easy but the woman looked like a dog cornered by animal control. Something inside him pinged with hurt. He'd expected something more favorable than the reaction he got.

The woman standing next to his sister looked expectantly at Della as if awaiting introduction. She didn't get one, so finally she stuck out her free hand. "Hi, I'm Laura Spitzer, the associate pastor."

He shook her hand, glancing at Della, who looked as if a semi were bearing down on her. "I'm Darby."

The woman again waited expectantly for Della to clarify the situation, but his twin sister seemed to have lost words.

"I'm Della's brother."

Laura nodded. "Oh. Who's Della?"

"Uh, Laura, can you excuse us for a moment?" Della tugged on the sleeve of his shirt and jerked her head toward the small playground hunkered between the two buildings.

"Sure," Laura said, her gaze following them as they moved toward the big plastic green slide. He'd seen the questions lingering there and the pastor didn't seem to want to move away, but another member of the congregation caught her and moved her along toward wherever everyone else headed.

"What are you doing here?" Della whispered.

"Nice to see you, too. It's only been almost twenty-six years since you last saw me. That's my greeting?"

Della swallowed. "I—I— Why are you here?"

"I wanted to see you."

"Okay, you've seen me. Now you can go."

He sank down on the foot of the slide and stared up at her. Lord, she was cagey, glancing around like she was about to be caught talking to the very devil. Of course, many back in Bayou Bridge would have said that was nearly true. Della was so pretty, prettier than he'd expected. And she looked so much like his mother. A gushing, squishy feeling invaded his heart as he looked up at her. "So that's it?"

She bit her lip and looked down at him, and that's when he saw it. The fear. The pain. The hope. "I don't know what you want me to say. What you people want me to be. I want to be left alone to live my life."

He didn't say anything, because her words hurt more than her earlier reaction. He hadn't considered this moment, hadn't guessed he'd feel so betrayed by her admonition. He felt as if he stood in quicksand, and it was not often he felt off solid ground. "Oh."

"Oh?" She cocked her head. "So you don't care?"

"Care about what?"

"That I don't want to be part of your family."

"Don't you mean our family?"

She shook her head. "It's not my family. Not really. I told Picou I couldn't do it. I'm grateful to know who I am, but I want my life to be here. I just can't be Della."

He sat staring ahead, trying to understand why she didn't want to love them. Wasn't she alone since the death of her grandmother? Wasn't she...

Scared?

Yes, he'd seen it in her eyes—those eyes that were the exact shade of his, of his mother's. But how was he supposed to reach her? He hadn't a clue.

His hand seemed to move on its own volition, reaching up, grabbing Della's elbow and tugging her hard. Just like a real brother would have done...if he'd have been five years old.

"Agh!" She lost her balance, tilted over and fell hard onto her butt, right at his feet. "What in the hell do you think—"

He couldn't help it. He laughed.

Her mouth snapped closed and her eyes shot poison

arrows at him. Elegant fingers grasped the wood chips beneath her. "Are you crazy?"

He blinked a couple of times, grinning like an idiot, not having any idea why he'd knocked his sister down. She stared at him, a small furrow growing deeper on her brow, her eyes narrowing, mouth setting.

Then the wood chips hit him right in the face.

"What?" He spit out the grit. "Pfff. Yuck."

A fistful of woodchips were in his hand before he could think better of it. He grabbed her neckline, pulled and dumped a fistful down her back.

"Oh, yeah?" she said, scrabbling to her knees, tossing more his way. Harder. Stinging his neck. Then she punched him in the chest.

And he pushed her back onto her butt again.

He found himself slammed backward.

And then it was on.

Full-on wrestling match on the playground of the Golden Meadow First United Methodist Church.

Della grabbed his hair and pulled. Hard. "Ow!"

Darby flipped her over, pinning her to the ground. She kicked and cursed in his ear, landing a blow on the side of his head. "You fight dirty."

Her leg hooked around his and she flipped him like a pro wrestler. The skirt of her dress bunched around her waist and she kicked like a damn yearling he'd once tried to ride…but harder. He lifted her and tried to toss her, but she had him by his shirt. The fabric ripped and that's when he heard the intake of breath and a shout of alarm.

"Oh, my God! Help! Help Sally!"

The voice came from over his right shoulder.

Della panted and released his shirt, staring up at him with eyes that looked just like his. She threw a hand up to her mouth and then she started laughing. Not pretty female giggling, but full-out donkey guffawing.

And something broke inside him, some dam he'd built very long ago, made of sorrow, loss and anger. Made of little-boy tears for the sister who'd been taken from him. For the little girl who sucked her thumb and curled beside him every night despite being put in her own room at bedtime. For the one who'd grown in the womb beside him. That dam cracked and broke to pieces as he lay there beside a laughing Della with her skirt flipped up, wood chips embedded in her dark hair and tears streaming down her cheeks.

There was nothing else to be done but join her.

So they lay there, laughing, crying, and becoming quite the spectacle for the congregation who looked to be pouring out the doors of the back building.

CHAPTER NINE

"OH, MY DEAR LORD! SALLY? Are you okay?" This came from Laura, who stood on the covered walkway along with half the congregation, still holding the cake carrier, looking ready to brain Darby if he harmed one hair on her friend's head.

But the woman should have been more worried about him. His sister fought like an inmate. It was a wonder he hadn't been shanked.

Della sat up and nodded while brushing the random bits of wood from her hair and wiping the dampness from her cheeks. "Uh, yeah. It's not what it looks like. Sorry."

"What in tarnation is going on?" asked an older man in a dark blue suit. Darby presumed the man to be the pastor of the church by the gold cross pin on his lapel and the fact several of the congregation looked at him rather than the pair sprawled on the playground after having wrestled like naughty puppies.

"Uh, just a little, uh—" Della twisted her mouth and peered at the man with contrite eyes.

Darby stood and brushed his pants off. He was almost certain the collar of his polo shirt had partially detached, but he ignored his untucked shirt and the grit in his mouth and offered a hand to his sister. She took it and he hauled her to her feet. "What she's trying to say is, uh—"

Everyone waited, eyes wide, one poor woman with her mouth open looking like a gawping trout.

Della smoothed her skirt and tucked her hair behind her ears. "What we're trying to say is this is my twin brother, Darby."

A couple of people drew in sharp breaths.

"I didn't know you had a brother," the man said.

"I have three." His sister cast a glance at him before refocusing on the man. "Actually, I have a mother, too."

The man's eyes narrowed and it was as if he saw something neither one of them could vocalize. "Okay, then. So shall we all go back inside and leave Sally to her relation?"

Several of the people shuffled toward the door.

"Wait. Reverend Howard?"

The graying man turned back at the sound of Della's voice. "Yes?"

"My name isn't Sally. It's Della. Della Dufrene. And I'm not a Cheramie."

He raised an eyebrow. "You're not?"

"No. I'm not. I wanted you to know. All of you to know because you're like my family and I've been hiding from who I am for a long time." She looked back at Darby. "But I guess I'm done with hiding. Seems my brother won't let me just slide away again."

A smile flirted with the stern Rev. Howard's mouth as he seemed to think about her words. Finally he nodded. "You've been running and hiding, huh? Well, many great men and women of the Bible tried to hide from God. Tried to deny who they were meant to be. I don't know the particulars, and I'm sure you will tell me, but I sense this is something the Good Lord meant you to experience, Sally. I mean Della. We'll leave you to your brother. Come on, everyone. My stomach's growling."

The people standing on the walkway made their way back into the building, leaving Darby and Della alone again on the playground.

"Why did you do that?" Darby asked.

"What?" She turned back to him with a lift of an elegant eyebrow, looking so much like his mother it was freaky.

"Tell everyone about who you are like that."

She shrugged. "I don't know."

Silence sat between them for a few seconds.

"I think it's been a long time coming. These past few months I've felt like a criminal hiding in the midst of normalcy, praying I'm not discovered, but scared I won't be, afraid nobody would bother to look for me."

He shoved his hands in his pockets and walked to the small iron bench situated in the corner, benefiting from the shade of a thick crepe myrtle tree. Sinking down, he patted the spot beside him. Della walked over and sat down. "I'm happy to see you."

Her eyes jerked up and her gaze measured him. For a moment she merely took him in. "It's good to see you, too."

He inched his hand over to hers, linking his pinky with hers. Her finger curled around his as natural as breathing.

"Why'd you tell Mom you didn't want anything to do with us?"

She shrugged. "I know I've been a pain in the ass. I do. I couldn't seem to help running. I—I think maybe I need a psychiatrist or someone to talk to, to help me deal with the way I feel. Each of my feet are in a different world and straddling them has been—" She threw her head back and contemplated the pale blue sky. Her hair was silky and black, her jaw square and her skin tanned from the sun. His heart swelled with pride. Della. Here beside him. Something inside him squeezed hard and that lost piece of himself that had swirled like a cyclone inside him year after year since she went missing clicked into place. Peace settled deep inside his soul. "Exhausting."

For a moment he'd forgotten what she'd been talking about. Straddling two worlds. Wasn't that what he'd been doing ever since he'd left Bayou Bridge? Existing in one world while knowing a part of him remained elsewhere?

Remained in the dark bayou soil, the graceful trees, and the foundation of that old house built long ago by his forefathers. Remained in the heart of a girl who'd loved him, unknowingly married him, and then survived without him.

Straddling two worlds… He knew what that felt like. "I understand."

She turned toward him. "Maybe, but I doubt it. I've spent twenty-six years being someone else. Picou wanted me to toss that away. I can't."

He shook his head. "No, but you can't cheat yourself out of a family who would love you. You can't pretend us away."

She cast her gaze across the playground and grew still. "What if I'm less than all of you expect? What if you wish you'd never found me? I'm not a Dufrene no matter who my parents are. I grew up on the bayou. I'm rough. I don't know how to set a table or decorate a mansion. I don't know fine materials from cheap ones. I don't even like wine. I wouldn't know a good pair of shoes from ones I'd bought at Dollar Darla's. I can bait a hook, clean a deer and skin a gator. I'm not one of you."

Darby started laughing. "Who do you think we are?

Mom is about as far as you can get from the Queen of England. Have you seen what she wears?"

Della chuckled. "Yeah."

Darby wrapped his arms around his sister and kissed the side of her head. "You are ours, Della. That's all that really matters, darlin'."

He expected her to feel uncomfortable with his affection. Actually, he wasn't sure why he felt such comfort around her other than the fact he just did. Della didn't pull away, she merely sighed. "Okay."

"Okay what?"

She pulled back and looked at him. "Okay, I'm willing to try again. I can't make any promises, but I think I've finally grieved for my *grand-mère* and all that I lost long ago. I just didn't know it until you pushed me on my ass and—why did you do that anyway?"

"Haven't the foggiest. Guess I was mad at you for being such a little shit."

"Shh—we're at church."

Darby stifled a smile. "Sorry. It hurt that you weren't happy to see me. Guess I reverted back to where we left off?"

His sister laughed. "It felt kinda good. I was mad, too. And I've never wrestled with a boy."

He arched a brow.

"Oh, my gosh, that's sick." But she laughed again.

"I know what you mean. I've beaten the sh—mess out of Nate and Abram, but I never got the chance to fight with you. Guess we're making up for lost time?"

She nodded. "Lots to make up."

He slung a brotherly arm around her shoulders. "So let's start with lunch. Y'all having a potluck or something? I'm starving."

"Just like that? We're starting over right here, right now?"

Darby nodded. "No better time."

Della shrugged. "All right. Let's start with lunch. Tongues are already wagging, I'm sure."

They rose together. Together again for the first time in twenty-six years, and somehow rather than feeling awkward like wearing shoes on the wrong feet, it felt natural and right.

Maybe, finally, Della had come home—miles away from Beau Soleil.

RENNY STUDIED THE WILTED flowers in the beds surrounding her back stoop and wondered whether it was still too hot for pansies. Well, she'd have to do something. All her summer flowers looked faded and gasping for breath.

Plus she needed a better reason for missing her mother's birthday lunch than she was still pissed about what had happened years ago. Bev would be hurt, and some part of Renny felt really lousy at disappointing her mother. The other part of her felt validated.

Would doing yard work count as an excuse?

No, but she'd give it anyway. Funny how having Darby back in her life had her already blurring the lines again. She was nearly certain it was further proof that Darby wasn't good for her. Or maybe it was something she made up to keep her heart at arm's length. What did Darby have to do with her not going to her mother's birthday lunch?

Maybe something like she hoped he'd come by or call.

Stop being a fool, Renny.

So she stopped thinking about her mother, Darby and

the past, and started pulling the dead marigolds out of the bed, knowing it'd be better to have bare beds than ones that looked as if the owner didn't care about her home and yard. She'd start in the back and move around to the front before going into Lafayette sometime this week and visiting the home improvement store.

Pride in ownership—it was definitely something she had for the small gatehouse that had outlived Guthrie House, a large plantation that had burned to the ground over forty years before. The small gatekeeper's cottage had stayed intact, nestled beneath the three-hundred-year-old oaks, holding vigil over the still-visible foundation nearly half a mile behind it. Renny had bought the cottage three years ago, making the move from Lafayette back to her old stomping grounds when she'd seen the For Sale sign on the road as she passed one random afternoon. She'd never planned on coming back to Bayou Bridge, but after one showing of the house, Renny had fallen in love.

The place had been in disrepair, but she'd seen the potential in restoring the Creole-style cottage. Luckily the previous owner had needed to get out from under the mortgage, so Renny had made real estate history in St. Martin Parish getting a dirt-cheap price, leaving her with enough money to strip and restore the cypress floors and repaint the entire place a shipshape white, accenting with colors that were period accurate.

Dirt sprayed all over her as she yanked the dying flowers from their home and thought about Picou's words earlier that morning.

Words about prophecies. Words about questions. And then that knowing little smirk.

"So what did those flowers ever do to you?"

Renny jumped. "Ahh!"

She spun around too fast and nearly ended up on her rump. Darby stood silhouetted by the sinking sun. "What is it with you and your entrances? Can't you toot your horn or something? You scared the pants off me."

His eyes dropped to her legs.

"It's a saying," she grumped, struggling to gain a better footing on the stone path, silently cursing her bad leg—a bad leg Darby had kissed his way down, and up, the night before. A blush seared her cheeks at the thought.

"I know. Just bemoaning the fact it's merely a saying and not an actual happening."

"What're you doing here?"

He shrugged. "Standing."

She rolled her eyes.

"I wanted to see you again."

She tried to suppress the way her heart leaped at those words. *Stupid, Renny, stupid. He's leaving. He's divorcing you.* "I thought you went to see Della. Shouldn't have been much room for me in that head of yours."

"And yet there was," he said, shoving his hands into his front pockets and giving her the kind of smile that usually charmed pants off. Forget the scaring.

She bent and scooped up dead flowers. "How did it go? And why's your collar nearly torn off?"

"Better than I expected, and the collar was part of it."

Renny tossed the dead flowers into a wheelbarrow she'd parked by the back steps and brushed her hands on her old cutoff sweats. "Hmm. By that description you'd think it went badly. So why are you really here? I'm your ex. Thought we'd blown out the candles on the cake and gone our merry way."

"Have we?" he said, trailing behind her as she

wheeled the barrow around to the front of the house where a truck she'd not seen before sat in her circular drive. "I thought I'd be cool with how we left things early this morning, but the further I drove away from you, the more I doubted what we have between us is over."

She stopped and turned to him. "Look, I've been doing some thinking, too, and I'm good with friendship. I may be even good with another round or two of experiments, but I really believe I need to stay on the path I'm already on. This reintroduction project pretty much makes or breaks my career and I have to focus. Plus, I'm happy with who I am, even if everyone else in the world thinks I need a man, kids and a golden retriever."

"So you're not looking for love?"

"Nope. I'm looking for more money for our reintroduction project. I'm looking for some cream drapes that will hang nicely against my robin's-egg-blue guest room walls, and I'm looking for the new spade I spent eight dollars on two weeks ago, but I'm not looking for love." She scanned the crabgrass poking out of her flowerbeds. It was easier than looking at Darby. She didn't want to betray any of her words with eyes that said something else. One day she wanted love, and she might fantasize about having it with Darby. But she wasn't stupid enough to bet the farm on that happening.

"Sounds weird coming from a woman," he said.

"Well, we can be happy without a man. Go figure."

For a few minutes nothing was said. She stooped and tugged at the crabgrass and dandelions, waiting for him to process her words.

"Okay, cool, so I borrowed Nate's new truck. Thought I might take a ride, maybe go out to our old stomping grounds."

Renny looked at him but said nothing.

"Wanna go?"

"I shouldn't. Got things to do here." Even as she said it, she knew she wanted to go. It was like wanting peanut butter when dieting.

"Why not? We're talking about a ride. Two old friends, laughing, memories—"

"The more time we spend together, the more dangerous it feels," she said.

"You just said you're not interested in love. You said friends and sex, but not love, so how is that dangerous? Unless you're lying." He propped a tennis shoe on the bottom step and cocked his head. "I asked if you wanted to go for a ride. In my brother's truck. Not on me."

"I get that, but why me? Your family's here. Shouldn't you be riding around with one of your brothers? Or fixing stuff at Beau Soleil for your mother?"

She glanced at him but he wasn't looking at her. He stared off into the distance, looking as if he were trying to figure out the answer. For a moment nothing but the wind made sound.

"I don't know. Today Della said she felt like she straddled two worlds, and I feel that way, too. But when I'm with you, I feel like…" He paused. "Like I'm home."

His words rocked her, and she looked away from him. She couldn't look into his eyes, because those visceral words were the kind that made her fall in love with him, and she really didn't want the heartache of loving Darby and watching him leave her. Again.

"Ren, come with me. I *need* you to sit beside me. Give me clarity. Give me comfort."

Finally she lifted her eyes to his.

"I need to be with someone who knows the true me."

But did she know the true Darby? Not anymore. He

was different, yet the same. Like the Darby of old, the man had charm and sex appeal in spades, but this was no boy with dreamy eyes and tempting suggestions. Here stood a man, a military lawyer with straight bearing and an occasional hard smile, a man who had a career that would take him far from the bayou…far from his roots. A man she didn't know anymore even if she'd shared in a most intimate act with him the night before. "I don't think I should."

But when she looked at him again, she saw something glitter in his eyes. It wasn't lust or anything resembling what she'd seen so far. No, this was a need every human had, a sort of desperate desire for someone to listen, to share in his world for a brief moment.

He blinked the emotion away. "Okay, you're right. It's stupid that I came here."

"Wait." She rose from her stooped position and stuck her hands on her hips. "Just a ride?"

Relief showed on his face. "Just two old friends taking a ride through the autumn beauty of the Louisiana countryside."

"I can tell you're an attorney. You know how to spin things."

He wiggled his eyebrows in a very non-lawyerly way and it made her smile. "Okay, let me grab some shoes and put on something that doesn't have dirt all over it."

"You don't need shoes. I like the way you look. Very cute in a farm girl sort of way."

"Suave," she said, trotting up the steps. "Let me wash my hands and put Chauncey out."

Not giving him a chance to protest, she left Darby and her good intentions for staying away from him outside. Three minutes later, after a swipe of the hairbrush, a scrubbing of her hands and a rummaging through her closet for cute polka-dotted flip-flops, Renny re-emerged to find Chauncey rubbing up against the man sitting on her front steps.

Smart cat.

She liked the profile of his back—wide shoulders stretching a worn T-shirt, tapered waist, firm butt—all very nice. Darby's hair was short and didn't even reach his collar. She could remember a time when its shaggy length curled beneath her fingers like silk ribbon. He'd worn it longer than most guys because why would anyone want to lop off gold streaks painted by the sun? She wondered if he would grow it longer again…and if the sun in Seattle was strong enough to bring the light gold highlights back.

Why the heck did she care?

"I'm ready."

He glanced back over his shoulder. "Perfect, though I like you barefoot. Those are pretty toes."

She looked down and wriggled those ten digits. "Um, pretty? Nah. Feet are really ugly when you think about it."

His gaze slid down her body and landed on her feet. It felt like his hands on her body rather than a leisurely perusal and she felt the same energy of the night before stir within her.

Danger, Will Robinson.

Not going there.

"You're so weird, Darby." Easier to draw his interest away from her feet…or any part of her body.

"So you say," he said, walking toward the truck. Like the boy his mama had raised, he went to the passenger side first and opened the door. Renny obliged and walked toward him, but before she could climb inside, he set a hand on her shoulder. "Thanks for going with me, Renny."

She nodded, knowing this was likely as much a mistake as the "closure" she'd given him last night—three times. "Sure."

He loped around to the driver's side, turned the ignition and started around her curved driveway. Music blared from the radio, an old John Cougar Mellencamp song about small-town life and dreams of something bigger. She tried to keep her eyes trained on the road in front of her, but couldn't help glancing toward Darby as he turned out of her driveway and headed west.

A ghost of a smile haunted his mouth.

"Did you put this song in on purpose?"

He looked over at her and grinned. "What? This song?"

"You did." She wagged her finger. "You know what this song is."

Nodding, he pulled his gaze back onto the road. "The song that was on the radio the first time I kissed you. I swear this isn't a CD or synced to anything. It's on the radio. Must be fate."

Renny folded her arms over her seat-belted chest and refused to check his claim. Even if he was lying, the ball was in her court and she wasn't hitting it back. She had to let Darby go. Had to remember last night was a goodbye and not a hello.

Find your will, Renny.

Don't fall for him, Renny.

For God's sake, keep your legs crossed, Renny.

She crossed her legs and pointed out the old graveyard. "Remember when Grayson drove his grandmother's Caddy into the Forresters' crypt?"

Darby laughed. "We were drinking Cisco and you

were wearing that front-clasped bra we lost behind the first base dugout."

"That's what you remember? My bra?"

"I was seventeen. Sex was all I thought about. That, baseball and where the next party was."

"We were stupid," she said, watching the small community of Bayou Bridge parade by. Several people glanced their way as Darby drove through town at the pace of a tortoise. Another thing about him that had changed.

"But we were supposed to be young and dumb— it was good, clean fun," he said, speeding up to catch a green light, then turning off onto the highway that would take them out to the land his grandfather had willed him. It had been one of their favorite places to go because of the large pond and the open pasture surrounding the water. They'd fished, skinny-dipped and made out in the back of Darby's truck. They'd dreamed about the house they'd build there one day, complete with three kids and a dog named Barney, after their calculus teacher. "I don't have much fun these days. Growing up kind of sucks that way."

Renny remained silent because he was right. Growing up did suck. Sucked up all your dreams like a Hoover, pulling them into a bag full of lint, dust and pennies. Oh, it wasn't all sucky, but filling the mind with mortgage payments, dry cleaners and pension plans wasn't anything near as wonderful as prom, stolen kisses and flaming Dr Peppers.

The sun moved toward the horizon, throwing golden splendor on the trees finally cloaked in yellowing leaves and casting shadows on the buff-colored leather seats. She watched the patterns flicker on her bared thighs and tried to skirt around the memories pulling her back into the frame of mind she'd been in last night. The frame of mind that had her panties on the floor and Darby back in her bed.

"Why are you so resistant to being with me?"

His words might have been a gavel slamming against wood. "What do you mean?"

"You're all prickly and standoffish."

She jerked her head. "I'm in the truck with you. I had sex with you last night. What's standoffish about that?"

Two-mile markers whisked by before he spoke. "You may be *here,* but you're guarding yourself. I thought we'd put the past behind us, that all had been forgiven, and we'd moved on to being friends again."

"Is it all so black-and-white with you?" she asked, trying to stay calm as Darby waded into uncharted waters. "I wish I could be so dismissive of a broken heart. Of what we did last night even. But I can't toss everything I've felt these past few years away so easily. What happened to us hurt—probably my heart more than any other part of my body. Those feelings don't magically disappear because we found out our parents lied to us. They don't disappear because I drank too much wine, got ambushed by those love letters, and ended up with my ankles around your neck. I spent a long time resenting you and, for good reason, I don't want to open myself up to hurt again."

"You think I'm going to hurt you?" His voice mimicked that gavel again, and his hands definitely tightened on the steering wheel.

"I think you've always held that power over me, and I've worked really hard on controlling my own life."

He reached the turnoff and left the road that would take them beyond a patch of woods and open up into pasture holding a large pond stocked with Florida bass and memories that might better be left beneath the shimmering surface.

Darby followed the old path down to the water and parked beneath their tree—a large sprawling oak his great-uncle had thoughtfully left standing when he'd cleared the land for the herd of longhorn cattle he'd planned on raising. The oak had remained; the cattle had long since disappeared. Darby killed the engine and turned to her. "I'm not trying to hurt you, Renny."

"Then don't."

CHAPTER TEN

RENNY POPPED THE TRUCK'S lock, slid out of the vehicle, and hopped onto the crunchy grass below. The fading sun glowed, making the sky orangey and the pasture smudgy as daylight said farewell, but she didn't feel peaceful. No, inside she was a swirling mess of doubt, fear and hope…and she really didn't want to address it at the moment. Easier to avoid.

She walked around the front of the truck and toward the water lapping at the thick reeds. "This has always been one of the prettiest spots in the parish."

Darby didn't answer because he was lowering the tailgate and pulling something from the bed. Renny returned her gaze to the pond as he thumped around. A few mallard drakes with their hens bobbed along the far side of the pond, milling around a flock of Canadian geese that honked beneath a cluster of weeping willow. The pond looked in good condition considering the late dry summer they'd had.

"Hold this," Darby said, poking a fishing rod toward her.

"Fishing?" she asked, glad he'd moved on, bypassing the tension she'd felt in the cab of the truck.

He flashed a smile as he set a tackle box at his feet and unhooked a plastic worm from the eye on the rod he held. "I was stationed near lots of water but never took to fishing in the ocean. Many a night I lay thinking about this little patch of pasture with my pond sitting here, waiting on me."

She smiled, not with relief, but at the longing in his voice. He had professed he would leave his life in his home state behind, but she could hear the wistfulness in his voice. You could take the boy out of the bayou, but you couldn't take the bayou out of the boy...or the pond.

"Wonder if anyone comes out here anymore?"

He shrugged. "Maybe horny kids like us."

His words made her sad for some reason. "Speak for yourself."

He squatted down and opened the box before squinting up at her. "I am, but I wasn't the only one needing a good lay last night."

"Darby Dufrene." She put her hands on her hips. "I'm tired of talking about last night. I declare it 'French'."

When they first started dating, Renny's mom often stood a smidge too near the phone while they talked, stretching her ear so she could foil their nefarious plans of sneaking out. If there was something that couldn't be spoken of, they used the class they both shared as the secret word for keeping something hush-hush.

He chuckled. "Really? So it can't be spoken of?"

"Nope."

"Okay, then. French. You can pretend whatever you want, but it happened and it was gooooood."

"Shut up and let's fish." Renny bent and grabbed a lime-green speckled top water bait and expertly tied it on the line with a fisherman's knot. "How old is this line? Don't want it to break when I land a three-pounder."

He glanced at the surface of the pond. "You think we can land one that big?"

"I think *I* can," she said, heading for the place where

the old pier had sunk. Had to be a nice fat bass swimming around the half-sunken structure. She let the bait fly with a precision cast right that landed exactly where the rotting wood met the water. Not two seconds later, something hit.

"Ai-yah-yah! I got one," she hollered, setting the hook and fighting the pull of the line. A fish jumped, flashing silver above flying droplets before sinking beneath the surface again. She reeled fast, knowing from the weight it was a big fish.

"Don't stop reeling. You got him," Darby shouted, running toward her.

"Oh, my gosh, it's a big one," she shouted.

"That's what she said," Darby replied, halting beside her, propping fists on his hips and watching her.

Renny started laughing. Only Darby would throw out a double entendre while she stood in cast-off clothing fighting a bass on the end of her line. A girl could really fall in love with a guy like him.

"That's it. Keep it tight. Now give him slack. That's a girl," he said as she brought the fish to the edge of the pond.

"You act like I don't know how to catch a fish, Darby. You forget I won 'big bass' at that tournament we entered. Remember?" She reached down and jabbed her thumb into the fish's mouth, hooking it and bringing the bass up. He was a big one, fat and white on the bottom with a nice iridescent green striping along the darker sides.

She held the fish aloft and raised her eyebrows. "Told you I could reel one in."

For a moment Darby stood and stared at her, his blue eyes darker against the waning light. In them, she saw something deep and dangerous…something bordering on hope, teetering on desire, and skirting around love.

It made her swallow. Hard.

But then Darby pushed the kill switch on his emotions.

"Woo, nice one. Probably a little over two pounds." Darby took the fish from her and held it up, turning it so he could get a good look before handing it back. "I better get cooking if I'm going to prove my prowess with a rod."

"That's what he said," Renny quipped, slipping the fish back into the shallow water and watching it as it flipped its tail twice and swam away.

Darby shook his head, a silly smile fixed into place. "I forgot."

Then he turned and walked back to where he'd tossed down his rod and reel, leaving her to wonder what it was exactly that he'd forgotten.

But she kind of knew. They'd been good together in other ways besides the sheets…or in their case a lack of sheets. When you're seventeen all that's necessary is a little privacy and a little time. But they had been friends, too. Fishing together, hunting together, hanging out, discussing their goals, dreams and why the Atlanta Braves would win the World Series. Being together had been like plugging in the Christmas tree lights every night, giving a sort of energy, glow and rightness to the season. But that's what it had been—a short-lived season.

She put her thoughts back on the task at hand and, after checking her bait, she and Darby spent the next half hour bemoaning missed strikes, reeling in smaller bass and finally sinking down into the grass and sharing a beer from the cooler Darby had packed in the tool chest. Several minutes ticked by in companionable silence as the world around them settled into the inky night. Stars showed off, as a few fireflies arrived to give them competition. Cicadas chirruped and the breeze died, leaving the air hot and still.

Darby settled back on the trunk of the old oak, brushing against her shoulder. "Been a while since I've enjoyed myself like that," he said, his voice soft in the stillness.

"Mmm," Renny said, plucking a lanky piece of grass that brushed her shin. She supposed it had been a while for her, too. She worked all day then spent her remaining hours doing the same sort of things—laundry, restoring furniture, and avoiding any kind of activity that meant taking a risk. But the impromptu choices she'd made over the past forty-eight hours had jarred her awake to who she'd become. She liked who she was, but maybe she did need more than a cat and a steady diet of peanut butter sandwiches. At the very least, Darby's coming home had given her better insight into that department of her life. "Me, too."

"Hey, Renny, you know what you said earlier about hurting you?"

She nodded.

"Well, we were both victims of others' manipulations or whatever our parents want to call it."

"I know, but that doesn't change the nature of the beast. Doesn't change the way I felt. I never want to feel that way again."

"I understand, but I'm not trying to hurt you…just explore what this is between us. If it's friendship, fine, but if it can be something more, shouldn't we find out?"

She pulled her gaze from the glow of the new moon falling on the pond and looked at him. "I don't know. Maybe. But I can't help wanting to protect myself,

Darby, because in a week or so, you'll move on to Seattle or wherever you're running off to and I'll be left here with more memories…and bitterness."

"You think I'm running?"

"What?"

His forehead furrowed as he took his turn in studying the water before them. "Me. Running. You think that's what I'm doing?"

"I don't know," she said with a slight shrug. "Are you?"

"Moving to Seattle isn't running away from my past, it's starting a new life. Blank slate and all that."

"A blank slate always sounds nice."

He sat still as stone for a minute. "But maybe there's more here in Louisiana," he said, folding his arms across his bent knees. She felt his eyes on her and hope leaped in her chest like a small bird popping onto a spring branch. If she stripped herself bare, she'd admit she wanted him to want her, to want to stay in Louisiana and build the life they'd always wanted together. But thinking that way was crazy.

It had been only three days since she first laid eyes on him again.

They weren't in love.

Hell, they were getting a divorce.

It was ridiculous to hope for something so absolutely unlikely. She had to stop herself from turning down a dead-end street.

"There's always more here, Darby. It will always be your home, filled with people you loved past and present. You could live anywhere else in the world for years and years and that would still hold true. The main question is why have you always avoided coming home?"

He didn't say anything for a while, so she waited.

"Because hurt lives here. You, my dad, my reputation as a loser—all those things I didn't want to face. It was easier to stay away and build a new life, be a different man—one who didn't drink too much, didn't drag race or let people down. I grew up and became someone unexpected—a responsible, successful man."

"You projected people's judgments onto yourself. Darby, you were a kid, even tougher, you were a Dufrene. Sure everyone knew you but they didn't fault you for doing what you were supposed to do—act like every other teenaged boy. Let the past go. No one blames you for who you were. I don't blame you for the accident. We both made that decision."

His blue eyes reflected the stars, pools of light and mystery. Darby was way more complicated than anyone had ever given him credit for. Old wounds still ailed him, and he needed healing, but she wasn't there to be salve to his soul. She couldn't give him all of herself, leaving her heart vulnerable. "Are you coming around because you need healing?"

He shook his head. "No. Maybe. I don't know."

She hadn't meant to voice her doubts, but they'd tumbled out, stacking up more baggage for Darby to shoulder. But being truthful was better than sitting on her feelings.

"I'm not using you, Renny," he said, turning to her, dropping down a knee so he could move closer. "I can't seem to help myself. I want to be around you. You make me feel…like I— Shit." He struggled to his feet and walked to the edge of the lake. "I don't know. Forget everything. I'm screwing things up and taking you along with me because you're like a comfortable pair of pants."

She stiffened and alarm crept round again, clocking

her on the head, reminding her this wasn't about falling in love or starting over. It was about packing the past away, comfortable pants and all.

He spun around. "That's not what I meant. I mean I feel better when I'm with you."

She tried to pretend his words didn't hurt as much as they touched her. She was safety to him, whether that was a good thing or bad. "Maybe you shouldn't use me for a crutch. Maybe you should leave me alone."

He stalked back toward her and lifted her beneath her arms. Her bad leg buckled and she fell into him, but that didn't matter because he hauled her against his hard body.

"Darby." Her mouth fell open, which seemed to suit him fine. His lips covered hers, hard, punishing, almost desperate. His arms were steel, squeezing her tight, as his hand knotted in her hair, pulling, forcing her head back so she had no choice but to surrender to his kiss.

And it felt good. Hot flames licked up her body, volatile and wicked. After three seconds of his mouth on hers, his left hand moved to her ass, and she knew she didn't want him to leave her alone. In fact, she wanted him to lay her down on that half-dead grass and teach her a lesson about challenging a man who didn't know what the hell he wanted.

He ripped his mouth from hers. "I want you. I can't stand knowing you're sitting at your house away from me where I can't see you, touch you, taste you. I want you, Renny, when I shouldn't."

Her breath came in short, turned-on puffs, and she couldn't seem to find any words to combat his admission. So she rose on tiptoe and kissed him again.

"Oh, hell," he groaned against her lips before dipping his head so he could turn her awkward peck into a full-fledged hot, wet kiss.

She slid her hands up to his shoulder, brushing against his short-clipped hair and anchoring his head between her hands, and kissed him with all the pent-up frustration that had been knotting in her belly since the man had shown up.

Finally he lifted his head and looked down at her for a few seconds before leaning his forehead against hers.

"I want you, too, Darby, but I refuse to be hurt. Don't ask more of me than I'm willing to give."

"And what would that be?"

"You can have my body, you can have my friendship, but I won't give you my heart. Not again, even if it wasn't your fault. You're leaving Louisiana, and I'm not."

He closed his eyes. "I'm not asking for your heart, Renny. I'm not asking for anything but the possibility of what the next week or two could bring. Can we leave it at that? Can we just *be* for the next few weeks without trying to define things?"

"Sounds rather convenient for you."

"No. Not convenient, but necessary. At least from my vantage point."

"So you want me to *be* with you with no expectations?"

"Yeah. I mean, no."

Her laugh was dry. "You don't know what you want, and I understand. Ever since you came back and those old stirrings cropped up, things are cloudy, but you can't expect me to take all the risk."

He released her. "Don't say you won't see me. I like having you—"

"Be your comfy pants?"

He smiled. "That was a bad analogy."

"You think?" She picked up the rod she'd abandoned and started for the truck.

"I didn't mean it as an insult. I like comfy pants and I need you, Renny. More than you know."

She turned back and looked at him silhouetted against the pond. "I don't trust myself around you."

"The feeling's mutual, but it's like the top has been ripped off the past and I can't stop what's coming out…even if I want to. Maybe this is why I never came home—I didn't want to feel the way I felt when I left. All that resentment toward my father, that betrayal by my mother, and then there was you."

The anguish in his voice swayed her, made her doubt throwing up any walls, but she knew that, like the ocean, being with Darby would be treacherous—it could bring destruction and leave her broken on the rocks. Things had happened so fast she didn't want to pull on a bikini and plunge into the waves without thought. Better to stay on the beach and wade into the tide slowly. "But I didn't hurt you. I had nothing to do with what happened. And I can't heal you."

He turned his head to the pond, giving her his profile. "Guess I'll have to live with what I've created."

She turned and walked to the truck and whispered, "But can I?"

DARBY STARED AT THE CELL phone he'd tossed onto his bed. Not good.

He'd finally talked to Shelby, and it hadn't been fun. She hadn't been very sympathetic to his plight of being confused about their potential future. In fact, she'd been a little aggravated—not something he'd heard from her in all the time they'd spent together in Spain. But could he blame her?

Especially when he'd told her he needed to postpone the job interview, put everything on hold in regards to Seattle until he could figure out what he wanted. He'd also told her he couldn't commit to a future with her. Wasn't exactly fair, but it was honorable. He couldn't move forward until he figured out an answer to the two questions Renny had thrown at him earlier that evening—who he was and what he wanted in life.

At that moment, he was answer-free.

And feeling a little guilty he'd strung Shelby along, unintentionally or not.

Because he'd heard the hurt in her voice when he'd given her the news.

"Well, should I come down to Louisiana? Sounds like you need someone on your side. I'll be happy to be your shoulder, Darby." Her words were exactly what he wanted to hear, but Shelby's shoulder would be one more complication he didn't need. Yeah, the last thing he wanted was his now ex-girlfriend on the front porch with her engaging smile and warm nature.

God, why did life have to be so complex?

He'd thought divorcing Renny would be easy, that he'd feel next to nothing when he saw her. Instead, he'd been slammed by feelings he'd buried deep inside him—pressed down, folded like a forgotten love note tucked in a drawer of his heart. And he wanted her. Burned for her. Taste, touch, smell—all of the senses ignited around her. So he couldn't go to Seattle and start a new life with Shelby. Not until he emptied himself of the past.

"Don't worry," he'd told Shelby. "I'll figure things out. I'm just stuck between two worlds right now, you know? I don't want you or your father waiting on me. Not fair to either one of you."

"What are you saying? You aren't coming here at all?" Her voice had held panic.

"I'm not saying anything for sure, but I don't want to lead you on a wild-goose chase, Shelby. At this juncture, I'm still planning on Seattle, but that could change. Louisiana is a sticky situation." *Like I had sex with my secret wife. And I might be falling back in love with her. And I might have missed home more than I thought I did. And I might never see you again.*

Somehow he didn't think Shelby would appreciate that last unspoken bit so he didn't say it.

"I should come down there. I have a month before I start my new job."

"No, there's nothing you can do, Shelby." *Except muddle the water.*

"Darby." Her voice lowered, and he felt crappy at the little lost girlness of her tone. "What about us?"

"Shelby, this sounds really selfish, but there can be no us right now. I'm telling you this because I totally respect you. You're a wonderful friend, and I had hoped we might move in a more intimate direction, but I can't right now. I'm sorry."

Silence had sat on the line for a few seconds.

"If that's what you want, but I'm not giving up on seeing you climb off that airplane. I know we could be good together, but I won't force you to be with me." Her voice sounded determined, and an inkling of worry cropped up. Shelby was sweet, kind and obviously not as passive as one would think.

"You're no consolation prize, Shelby. I would never treat you as such. I care for you too much. I need to be sure before I come to Seattle. If I come to Seattle."

And the conversation had ended with a thud. Like the other shoe dropping. Or a dog crapping in the pristine white of newly fallen snow.

Nothing pretty about cutting a person loose.

But he couldn't have both worlds.

He'd have to choose.

But not tonight.

And not tomorrow.

And probably not the next day.

He'd thought on the way home from Renny's about her firm stance she wouldn't risk her heart. His rebuttal was they needed time, and hopefully, time would lead to clarity. If Shelby found someone else, then it validated what he felt. If Renny found someone else, he'd trip the guy, drag him into a dark alley and beat him down.

Something about that last thought told him about the direction he headed, but he didn't want to admit his initial plan of divorcing Renny, leaving Bayou Bridge and carving out a new life on the West Coast was wrong. Maybe because he'd sat down, listed pros and cons, talked ad nausem with Hal and Shelby, and made this commitment to himself—that he would not go home to Bayou Bridge. That he was done with his former home. Done with his former life. Done with his former love.

Not yet. His mind whispered.

Maybe not ever. His heart echoed.

CHAPTER ELEVEN

DARBY SAT READING THE Bayou Bridge newspaper and sipping chicory coffee in the kitchen of Beau Soleil. Not much was going on in town, though it seemed like the Bayou Bridge Rebels were facing a huge football show-down with St. Thomas Aquinas later that week, which meant that Abram would be busier than usual. Darby hadn't had much opportunity to visit with Abram who was occupied with his team and the new life he'd built in their hometown. During their lunch Abram hadn't even talked about football, only his girlfriend Lou's up-coming band gig at a country-and-western bar in Lees-ville in a few weeks.

So not like his brother who lived, ate and breathed football, but he guessed love did strange things to a fellow.

Love.

Scary word.

"Hey, I missed you at dinner last night," his mother said from the open doorway, interrupting his musings on love, football and the lack of news in Bayou Bridge. "Thought having you here would mean actually see-ing you."

Guilt flashed as he set the paper on the table. Funny, how he'd not felt much guilt until coming home. "Yeah, sorry about that. I took Renny fishing."

"Oh?"

"Yeah. Uh, just trying to burn old bridges."

"Is that what you call it?" Picou picked up a framed photo of him and his brothers sitting on the desk next to the window that overlooked the tree he'd used to sneak out many a night. "I would think spending lots of time with an old flame would burn something…just not bridges."

He tilted himself back in his chair, drawing a frown from his mother, so he thumped back onto all four legs. "We just went fishing."

"Fishing? Well, Renny always liked being outdoors, didn't she? Guess her job choice suits her."

"Why did you let Dad split us up?"

His mother sighed and joined him at the table. "You're really wading through stuff, aren't you?"

"I think I might need bigger galoshes—the crap's pretty deep. Maybe the truth will help."

"The truth is easy. Your father tired of you gallivanting all over the parish, tearing things up, drinking yourself into a stupor and acting like a boy who had a death wish. Truth."

Darby regarded her with little expression. How did that help clarify anything? "Couldn't we have talked about it instead of packing my bags for military school? Pretty radical to make me feel like I'd screwed up so badly you didn't want me anymore."

His mother smiled and laid a hand on his, giving a gentle tap. "Is that what you really thought? I didn't want you around? And how conveniently you forget the talking we'd done over the years."

Fine. He knew his mother loved him. And if he tried hard enough, he could remember lots of talking. His father strutting around the library, shaking a thick finger at a boy who'd rather eat glass than do as his parents suggested. "Guess I heard only what I wanted to hear. Felt what I wanted to feel."

"You were stubborn—and angry," Picou said, fiddling with the end of the braid that trailed down her shoulder. Her blue eyes were starting to fade and it struck Darby that she was close to sixty-five years of age. Mothers weren't supposed to get old. They were supposed to stay the same. Forever.

"But you could have stopped him."

She shrugged, dropping her braid. "Maybe, but I couldn't wholly disagree with him. You were intent on proving to everyone you could do as you wished. I didn't want to lose another child, and many of your shenanigans were death defying…like you wanted to die. So many brushes with death wear a parent down."

"I was just a kid."

"A kid with survivor's guilt. A kid trying to prove he was infallible."

Darby shook his head. "No, I wasn't guilty I had lived and Della hadn't, or at least we thought she hadn't. I just didn't like Dad trying to control me."

"Protect you," Picou murmured, sliding a hand to his hair, smoothing an imaginary cowlick with motherly intent. "You couldn't see what losing Della did to your father. He was a man who'd lost control of a world he'd always run with an iron fist. Having a child taken and presumed murdered rocks your world in a way that's unexplainable. Some may have channeled energy into pursuing and finding the culprit, but your father drew a shield around his family and tried to keep what he had left."

"But he smothered me."

Picou sighed. "Yes, he did. But that wasn't his intent, just an unfortunate result."

"You would think he wouldn't send me away if he wanted to protect me."

"You would think, but as you now see, being an adult is rather complex. Your father and I were having problems in our marriage—problems that started when Della disappeared. It's not easy to live with grief and it set a gulf between us."

Darby felt a weight in his gut. A child never knew what parents felt—until he got older and the rosy glasses of childhood were broken by the reality of a life that had sharp corners and deep potholes.

"By the time you hit high school, your father wasn't well. The doctors put him on medication, but his heart was weak. He'd already failed in controlling you, and he'd already looked at various military schools he thought could do what he could not. Even though it would take you away from us, it would take away the temptations you liked to court here in Bayou Bridge."

Renny. Yeah, she'd definitely been temptation with her wide smile and sexy laugh—she'd hooked him and reeled him in as easily as she had that bass last evening. But, she hadn't been a bad influence, quite the opposite. Renny had been smart and ambitious with high grades and scholarship offers on the horizon. She'd also been down-to-earth, easy to like and destined for good things. "But Renny wasn't holding me back."

"No, she wasn't. You were holding her back."

Ouch.

"So you sent me away because I was a bad influence on Renny? You lied and kept us from each other because—"

"No, because you both needed to grow up. That accident nearly killed her and her mother agreed not to press charges against you if we would keep you away from her daughter, and, honestly, honey, you needed to leave Bayou Bridge for a while. Gaining maturity wasn't going to happen where you were comfortable."

He stood and walked toward the antique chest his mother had bought him that had once sat in his bedroom, but now served as a coffee table in the new seating area his mother had created in lieu of the old banquette. He'd loved that trunk and hadn't wanted to take it with him, thinking he'd be back soon.

His mother had taken him to New Orleans for Mardi Gras when he was nine, and he'd seen the old steamer trunk in the window of an antique store and had become fascinated with the brass fittings and intricate silver-plate placard. Picou had taken him inside and bought it without blinking an eye. She'd later sat him on an iron bench as they waited for the streetcar and told him it was a portent. She'd known it meant he would go far and wide before he found his home.

He'd thought she was cuckoo—he'd wanted it because he loved pirate tales and wondered if there might be secret compartments with treasure maps.

But maybe she'd been right.

Maybe he'd spent over a decade living away so he could become the man he was—a man who was a bit confused about his direction, but outfitted with a compass and knowledge that he could find his way.

Darby turned and studied his mother as she perched on a bar stool, eyebrows lifted slightly, as if she expected his answer, so he gave it to her. "I guess I see your point."

"Do you?"

"Your hands were tied."

"Partly. We could have let the chips fall where they may, but your father, along with the judge and district attorney, thought giving you a new perspective would be best." She paused, a ghost of remembrance in her eyes. "It wasn't easy sending you away. Lord knows I begged your father to change his mind, but he saw what I could not. My only regret was hurting that girl. Renny never deserved to think you didn't care."

"And I didn't deserve to be kept from the girl I loved."

Rising, she came to him and gave him a pat. "And I'm trying like the devil to give you a second chance. It's the main reason I didn't pitch a fit about you missing dinner."

He shook his head. "Mom, what is or isn't between me and Renny isn't your concern. You can't fix the past. Renny and I are two different people on two different paths."

"Oh, pish. Like you can't merge two paths. Makes for easier traveling when you're walking the path with someone who fits you like an old comfortable—"

For a moment he thought she might say pair of pants.

"—shoe."

"I don't think Renny would like being compared to a shoe, Mom."

"I have a fondness for a good pair of shoes, so I don't find it insulting in the least. Feel free to call me an old shoe any day of the week." With one last pat she waltzed out the door. Like literally waltzed, keeping time with a one, two, three count.

Darby shook his head and glanced back at the trunk. Journeys were odd. A person could set out knowing where he was headed and then end up in a ditch or on the wrong road, or in an unexpected place of rightness. The question was did he want to backtrack and take the road to Bayou Bridge, the road back to the girl who still sparked something within him?

Or a new road promising a whole new life?

He wished the answer would appear, but the kitchen of his childhood held no answers. Maybe he needed to talk to someone who could give him perspective, so he walked up to his room, grabbed his cell and called the person he knew would shoot it to him straight.

"Yo, buddy! How's life on the bayou?" was the greeting he received from Hal Severson. After several minutes of chatting about the new JAG Corp officer, Della and the progress he'd made with her, he moved into murkier waters and told Hal about Renny and the fact they were married—and that he'd rediscovered feelings for her.

"Dude, that's the strangest thing I've ever heard," Hal said. "You're married? And you didn't know it?"

"Looks like it," Darby said, kicking off his shoes and lying back on the just-made bed. Hal might have some good insight, and Darby trusted him.

"Wow, that blows the mind."

For a few seconds, his friend was silent. "So you're saying there wasn't much closure between you and this girl, and now you're into her again? What about Shelby? Thought she looked like part of your future?"

"She did. I mean, she does. I'm not sure about anything anymore, Hal. That's why I called you. Thought you might give me a different perspective. Around here, I feel like everyone's pushing me toward Renny."

"Why?"

"Because of the way things were left between us. My mom thinks that if she fixes the past—it's part of this prophecy she got from a voodoo priestess—she can have everything the way it should be…with a cherry on top."

"A voodoo priestess?"

"Don't ask," Darby said, wishing he hadn't brought that up. "Thing is I still feel connected to Renny, and these feelings I have are really intense."

"As in romantic? Have you kissed her or made any overtures?"

Darby frowned. "What's that got to do with anything?"

"Oh, man. You slept with her. Dude, that's way complicating things. That's a total screwup, man."

"Aren't you from Oklahoma? You sound like you stepped off Venice Beach. And no judgment please."

"What do you want me to say? Lie to you?" Hal's voice was a mixture of amusement and concern. "And don't forget, Shelby's my friend, so I'm not unbiased here. She and I worked together on several programs for the base school, and she's a gem and not deserving of being hurt."

"I know. I'm not hurting her. We aren't together. Not really. We were an expectation, and come to think of it, you sort of made her an expectation."

Hal was silent for a moment. "Maybe I did. Sometimes friends think they know best and push for what suits them, but this is not about me or what I think is best for you. It's about you and what you want. As for Shelby, you need to shoot straight because I happen to know she thinks you are headed in her direction. You pretty much indicated that when you scheduled a job interview at her father's firm and packed up all your earthly belongings for Seattle."

"I know. I've already talked to her. She's not happy, but I was honest."

"Good. So about this thing you have with—what's her name?"

"Renny."

"Yeah, Renny. I'm not saying to not follow your heart, but you have to make sure your feelings aren't some leftover remnant of a time when things were easier for you. God puts things in front of us that need to be there. Renny could be a barrier or could be a gift. You'll have to figure that out."

"That's the kicker. When I'm around Renny, I feel like I came home because here is where I'm supposed to be."

"That might be the case," Hal said, with a sigh. "Nothing wrong with spending some time with her and seeing if what you feel for her is real."

"You think?"

"Yeah, but don't be afraid to use distance to give yourself some clarity."

"You think I should leave Bayou Bridge?" Darby sat up, not so comfortable with his rock-solid mentor's decree. Didn't sound like Hal to suggest he run away from a problem.

"Not yet. You have things to sort out obviously, plus I don't need Picou hunting me down and working me over. But, when the things get too intense and you feel like you just climbed off the Gravitron, pull away and give yourself some space. I understand there are others involved here, but you're also trying to decide your future, so it's okay if you need to pull back. It's also not a do-or-die situation. If you go to Seattle, it doesn't mean you pick Shelby. If you stay in Bayou Bridge it doesn't mean you're destined to be with this girl. You're trying on absolutes."

Darby supposed he had made it too black-and-white.

First, he needed to focus on himself without contemplating love, or the lack thereof. He had to decide where he belonged. He had to decide if coming to Bayou Bridge meant coming home.

"And remember, just because you figure out what you want doesn't mean happiness will fall into your lap with a smile and kiss, but at least you won't be trying to pull on a shoe that doesn't fit just so your feet are covered."

Darby flopped back onto the bed. "What is it with everyone and shoes? And what's a Gravitron?"

"You never rode one at a carnival? The things that suck you up against the wall?" Darby heard Hal's smile and could visualize his old friend with his socked feet propped up in the patched recliner he refused to throw out. "Look, I know you, son. For the past eleven years you've been told what to do. Heck, I guess you've been told all your life what to do. Even I set Shelby and the idea of Seattle in front of you. Now, you're faced with making a lot of decisions at once—where you live, where you work and if you even want a serious relationship. You're rudderless."

Darby had never thought about it in that light, but his friend was correct. This was the first time he'd ever had the freedom to decide anything for himself. No wonder he struggled with a direction. "You're a smart man."

"Darn right I am. Why do you think the Lord called me into His service? He doesn't pick dumb-dumbs."

"Yeah, He leaves them for the court system."

"That would be the devil's work, my friend."

Darby laughed. "I thought giving myself time would be all it took."

"Time's not a bad thing, but you can't just bob in the

current. At some point, you've got to take off for shore. Your job is to figure out where that shore is."

"I'll find my course," Darby said.

"I've no doubt you will, but don't forget to nourish your spiritual life. Remember, God has a plan for you, Darby Dufrene, whether it's in Louisiana, Seattle or Timbuktu."

Darby said goodbye and hung up, thinking about the chaplain's words. Darby had never been overly religious, though he'd gone to Catholic grammar school and had been forced to attend Mass by his mother and father. It wasn't until he met Hal that he'd even thought about God and what role He played in his life. So was Hal right? Did God have a plan, and had Renny been part of it all along?

Or was his marriage and ensuing strong feelings for the girl he'd once loved part of a roadblock he had to get past in order to move forward?

He wasn't certain.

But what he was certain about was the fact he needed to be proactive. To get off his keister, lick his finger and hold it up to test the wind. Only then could he figure out where to point the prow of his ship.

And all things pointed toward Renny. She may not be willing to risk her heart, but shouldn't he be willing to risk his? Perhaps it was time to stop flirting with fate and grab hold with both hands.

If Renny was his future, he wasn't going to be certain until he started swimming toward her.

CHAPTER TWELVE

RENNY WATCHED HER MOTHER as she thumbed through the sales rack at the discount store. Bev was a shopaholic and loved to paw through all kinds of junk at bargain stores specializing in the stuff no other decent shops wanted.

"Ooh, look at this sparkly shrug. I can wear this over my gown for the Krewe of Janus ball. Do you think it will match the beading on that blue gown I bought last summer?" Bev wiggled the hanger, making the sequins dance.

Renny had no idea what her mother was talking about, so she nodded. "Sure. It's kind of neutral."

Bev eyed the swatch of beaded net critically. "I don't know."

"Well, we can look over there." Renny pointed to another crowded rack. "It's your birthday present, so I don't mind your choosing something at regular price."

"But there's an extra thirty percent off this rack. Why spend money when you can save it?" her mother said, hanging the glittery gray shrug back on the rack and turning toward the rack with the new arrivals. "But then again, you did stand me up on my birthday lunch."

"But then again, you lied about my husband leaving me."

"Husband?" Bev snorted. "Not really. And how is that divorce progressing? Has he filed the petition?"

Renny shook her head. "Not yet, but he will as soon as Sid Platt drops off the papers for him to sign. Would have been done yesterday, but Darby said Sid got held up with something more important. I'll waive service and it will shave off a couple of weeks on the process, but the petition should be filed within the week."

Bev picked up a cashmere coat of puce with a gray faux fur collar and held it in front of her. "Good. Aaron has a nephew who has a friend who's a pharmacist. I always thought it would be nice to have a man who knew a little something about drugs. What do you think? Want to go to coffee with Bill?"

"You don't know how much that statement explains about you. And, no, I don't want to do coffee with Bill... or anything else with him. And just because I forgive you for ruining my one good relationship doesn't mean I'm up for you screwing another one up for me. I'll find my own bad dates, thank you very much. And, Mom, I don't need a man to be happy."

"I know. I don't need a man to be happy, either, but we women can have everything nowadays. I believe there was a perfume commercial that intonated as much back in the eighties. Always been my theme song... 'cause I'm a woman."

Her mother was cracked, that was the problem. "Okay, Gloria Steinem, calm down. It's just that all my life you've harped on me succeeding at all costs. You said yourself days ago that you sabotaged my relationship with Darby to insure I didn't throw my future away. I'm *in* my future—I'm a successful biologist who defied the odds doctors set before me. So why do I need Bill or Bob or whoever the pill guy is?"

Her mother's lips pressed into a thin line as she jerked hangers along the metal rack with ear-grating frustration. "Because I want grandchildren. Barbara Hassell has two already and she gets to buy them the cutest clothes, and besides it will take your mind off your soon-to-be ex-husband."

"You're trying to set me up with some guy in order to assure grandchildren you can buy cute outfits for and to keep me from seeing Darby?"

"Of course not. Ridiculous," Bev said, finally looking up at her. "I wanted you to be successful, not lonely."

"I'm not lonely. I have friends and purpose," Renny said, trying to figure out why her mother had suddenly grown so concerned with her social life. Was it Darby? "And I'm not losing my head over Darby Dufrene."

"So you're in control of that situation, are you?" Her mother peered at her from over a rack stuffed with coats.

Renny felt as if her mother had slapped her with that question. Maybe because she was afraid she wouldn't be able to keep her hands tight on the reins of her heart. "Yes, I am."

"Good."

"Good."

For a few minutes they each browsed the racks, pretending their thoughts were of clothes and not of the complexities of life.

On some level, Renny wished she had not picked up the phone when Bev called the previous night in tears because her daughter hadn't shown for her birthday luncheon on Sunday. Even the meek Aaron had sent Renny a strongly worded text about blood being thicker than water, and some proverb from the Bible about forgiveness.

Point made, Aaron the chiropractor, point made.

After having listened to her mother, Aaron and her

conscience, Renny invited Bev for a Tuesday evening of shopping and martinis at their favorite restaurant. After all, though Renny still ached from the betrayal, she loved her mother and could somewhat see the view from her shoes…even if what Bev had done had been deceitful.

Forgiving her mother hadn't been easy, but necessary. Renny loved her mother more than she hated what she'd done.

Besides, the outcome of her and Darby staying together likely would have been the same. Back then, she and Darby had come from two different worlds, and Renny would not have gone much longer agreeing with Darby on his version of their future together. He'd always been the one to plan—sometimes offering her little say-so in what would happen once they married and graduated from Bayou Bridge High. She'd been so in love with him, she'd never questioned his ideas. So what good did it do to nurse a grudge against the one person who wouldn't disappear from her life? Her mother hadn't kept the two of them apart out of spite, only out of her misconstrued idea of protection.

"So why do you think I can't resist Darby?" Renny finally asked.

"Because you are like me." Bev glanced at her, brown eyes probing the mirror reflection of her own.

"Really?"

"More than you know," her mother said softly, moving to another rack, dancing her fingers across the hangers, looking but not really seeing the garments before her.

"What's so bad about Darby?"

"He's not bad, but I always felt like he drowned you out. You didn't complement each other the way a man and woman should. His personality blanketed you, maybe because he was a Dufrene, different from me and you."

"You judged him because he came from a wealthy, influential family?"

Bev shook her head. "No, but I know you sensed it, too. You were never quite sure about him. That's why you believed he was done with you. He was always a one-foot-out-the-door kind of guy, always looking for a better situation."

Renny shook her head. "That's not true, because he didn't actually leave me. I just thought he did."

"Maybe so, but neither of you fought very hard to get back to one another…I always thought that telling of your relationship. It ended up best-case scenario for you both."

Had it been for the best? Renny wasn't sure. Something was off-kilter about Bev's conclusions, and at the same time there was truth in her observations. Renny had never been absolutely certain of Darby.

"Now this is nice," her mother said, wrapping the gauzy shawl around her shoulders and doing a pirouette, effectively ending the conversation on the note she wished.

And Renny let her. "Great, let's buy it and move on to Chelsea's. I'm starving."

Her mother spent another thirty minutes perusing the shoes section, which was a "quick" look according to Bev, before they got out of the store and back into the parking lot.

Renny's phone dinged with a text message just as Aaron pulled into the lot in his convertible Jaguar. He was pretty successful at cracking backs and liked to prove it.

"Hey, bunny," Aaron said, as he rolled down the window. "We've got reservations at Catahoula's for seven-thirty. Better get a move on."

Bev looked at Renny and fluffed her hair. "Well, darling, it sounds nice, but I'm planning on having dinner with my Renny. Just a little girls' night out thing."

Aaron's face fell. "But I sent Renny a text about tonight. You got it, right?"

Renny pulled the phone she'd been trying to hide in her purse out, noting a text from an unknown number. She scrolled down. Sure enough Aaron had texted his special plans for her mother, including a supersecret surprise. Uh-oh, did that mean what she thought it meant? "Uh, sure, I got it right here."

"Aaron, honey, I appreciate your wanting to take me out two times to celebrate my birthday, but I'm not prepared to go to Catahoula's tonight. Let's go some other time."

"Well, I have a little something planned and—"

"Oh, go ahead, Mama. We'll have drinks another night. I've got to get to work early tomorrow anyway." And she'd read the unknown text—Darby wanted to meet her at their favorite old stomping ground, McCavity's, a little bar and grill in the middle of downtown Lafayette where she and Darby and their friends used to wolf down chili fries and drink beer using the ID Robbie Tarver had swiped from his older brother.

After their words at the pond two days ago, she hadn't expected to hear from him…at least not so soon. She'd given him some things to chew on, and, honestly, she'd been certain she'd scared him off. She wasn't in the business of making Darby feel better about himself and she wasn't going to take all the risks if they wanted to move beyond what they currently had. Were they friends, lovers or something destined to end badly?

She wasn't sure. What she was adamant about was not putting her heart out there to be kicked around. She could handle a lot of things but having Darby walk away again would leave her bleeding and broken.

Control.

That was the key.

Her mother eyed her with a guilty expression. "Well, okay. I hate to leave you, sugar. Why don't you call a friend to join you for dinner? Maybe that nice Carrie? She's a sweet girl." Her mother tucked a piece of hair behind Renny's ear and straightened the tie of her short-sleeved sweater. Her mother's actions made Renny wish she'd gone in for a trim and maybe a manicure. Bev made beauty a priority in life.

Renny brushed Bev's hand away. "I'll be fine. Maybe poke around a few places I haven't been in a while. Y'all go on ahead."

Her mother tossed the bag with the shawl into her own sporty convertible and climbed into Aaron's car. The man looked pleased his plans had taken shape. No doubt a piece of expensive jewelry sat in the breast pocket of his jacket.

Her mother put down the window. "Oh, and, Renny, sometimes the past is better left in the past. Look ahead, my darling."

Then Aaron drove away.

"Well, there's a revelation," Renny said to herself.

"Huh?"

She turned and saw a woman in sweatpants with a kid in tow staring at her. "Oh, sorry. Just talking to myself."

The woman waved her off and tugged the kid toward

the store. Renny stood there in the middle of a parking lot in front of a strip mall in a run-down part of town trying to decide if she should meet her soon-to-be ex-husband for drinks and decadent cheese fries.

Did she have anything better to do?

And, really, was there anything better than doing Darby Dufrene?

Not in her experience.

DARBY SET DOWN HIS BEER as she walked into the crowded bar. "You came."

"That's what he said," she quipped, hooking her purse on the back of the chair and waving a waitress over. "I've been shopping with my mother and I need a Bud Light."

He wasn't sure if she was talking to him or Katy, their waitress, but it didn't seem to matter. Katy took off for the bar.

"Rough day?" he asked.

"Not really, though dealing with my mother is always challenging. Always feel like I've been put through a wringer and come out a little worse for wear." Renny pushed back her hair, giving him a glimpse of delicate ear and sweet, satin neck. He wondered if she smelled as good as she looked. Probably doubtful he'd find out with the scent of beer and fried foods smothering the place.

"Thought you were angry with her about keeping my letters."

"I was, but I'm good at forgiving. Remember? I was angry with you, too. But I got over it—three times over it, if I remember correctly." Her eyes blazed some sort of challenge, and this woman in front of him became something bold and outrageous, something far removed from a quiet biologist. It was as if the years peeled back, layer after layer, giving him the spicy, smart-mouthed bayou beauty he'd worshipped years before.

"You remember correctly, though if you want to make it four, I'll meet you in the ladies' room."

"I'd rather be tarred and feathered than have sex in the handicap stall of McCavity's." She picked up the menu he'd slid between the salt-and-pepper shakers.

"You could do both. Sounds kinky."

She leveled those golden brown eyes at him. "Not on the menu, big boy."

"Damn, thought I might get lucky."

Renny pulled her gaze from the menu and studied him. "You know what I am?"

"Gorgeous? Sexy? Smart?"

"No, I'm the kid that can't stop playing with fire. You know that kid, right? Been burned but still lighting the match and letting it burn till it singes her fingers? You're a sickness, you know."

He didn't know what to say to that.

"So, here we go again. Why did you invite me here?" she asked as she perused the menu.

He pushed the edge of the paper down, drawing her attention. "Why did you come?"

"I don't know," she said, her tone a little angry. At him or herself?

"Well, I actually have a reason. I've been thinking a lot since I dropped you off at your house a few nights ago, and I have something to ask you. But first, I want you to understand where I'm coming from."

She allowed the paper to drop and her eyebrows lifted. The waitress set an icy beer on the table as if she knew it was needed.

"I've spent the past few years living within parameters. The navy's been good to me, but I didn't want to stay in. As I considered what life would hold for me, I never thought about coming back here. I didn't want to deal with my past, and we've gone over how I'm good at avoiding anything that makes me uncomfortable, so no need to beat a dead horse."

"Okay, I won't." Renny took a draw on her beer and nodded as if to encourage him.

"But I came home, and all the plans I had for myself suddenly didn't seem so solid, especially when we found out the way we ended wasn't, well, the way we thought. So I've been questioning whether my initial plan to live anywhere other than Bayou Bridge was the right plan. And then there's you."

He stopped because he knew what he was about to ask of her could be met with crickets.

"You constantly ask me why I keep showing up, and it's not because of things left unsaid. What's going on between us is something new, something different. I don't think what I feel for you is based strictly on the past."

"You're saying your feelings aren't leftover."

He nodded. "Right. Not leftover."

The waitress appeared at his elbow, interrupting to collect their order, before melding back into the background.

"Okay," Renny breathed, tucking the menu back between the salt-and-pepper shakers. "You were saying…"

"…that I understand where you stand. I respect you enough not to ask you to risk your heart, but I *would* like to ask for a compromise."

"A compromise?"

"Are you willing to start over?"

Her brow furrowed. "Start over?"

"Hear me out. You said something that struck me

as important a few days ago. You said we're different people on different paths. That's true. We are different. There's a lot about you I don't know, and I want to know you, Renny. So I'd like you to consider dating me for the next few weeks."

"You want us to date? Isn't that a little backward? We already had sex."

He couldn't stop the smile at his lips. "Yeah, a little backward, but I don't want to walk away from you yet. I think we both owe ourselves the chance we didn't get all those years ago."

"So you want us to date, get to know one another, and then decide if it can be more than…"

"Dating."

"But that's taking a risk."

"No more so than you take with any other guy you date. I want to be any other guy. The past is behind us, and I'm calling for a mulligan. That is, if you agree."

Renny's eyes left his for a moment. Then she looked back. "Starting all over?"

"In theory. I want to know you better, and I want to explore this direction. Things between us may not work out, so it's a risk for both of us, but it's the same risk every person takes when pulling in close to the fire. Either one of us could get burned, but I think it's worth a shot. What I feel when I'm with you tells me so."

"I don't know. It sounds rational, almost too rational for you," she said, a slight smile hovering around her gorgeous lips. "But rational appeals to me, and you make a good point—we never got to choose each other."

"So?"

"So, as a scientist I like process, and oddly enough, I think you're right. There *is* something between us, something more than sex. The only way we'll find out if there could be a future is to experiment."

"I like your experiments."

Renny shot him a withering look. "Not that kind of experiment. I'm thinking more along the lines of cheese fries and ice cream. So, sure, let's get to know one another and see where we stand in a few weeks. That doesn't seem so precarious."

Relief pooled in his stomach. Until that moment, he hadn't realized how much he'd hoped she would agree to his plan. After talking to Hal, it had struck him as the easiest way to test the winds. He had to know what he was headed toward, and though he knew the places Renny liked to be kissed, he didn't know much else about the woman she'd become.

"So, I want to know about your job. Your life. What you dream about," he said, taking another sip of his beer as the rest of the world swirled by, chatting about football, tapping their feet to Sheryl Crow crooning over the speakers and munching on food that hardened the arteries.

"First tell me about why you chose Seattle. Seems random."

He settled in, ready to be date-like. "Well, I visited once a few years back for a friend's wedding and thought it was a cool city—there's a sort of naturalness layered with sophistication that appealed to me. Then a couple of months ago, I met someone whose father was looking for a partner, and she thought I'd be a good fit. Washington State is so different from Louisiana, and I guess that appealed to me."

"You said *she*."

"What?"

"This friend. She."

"Oh. Well, her name's Shelby. She used to teach at the base school and we struck up a friendship."

"Is she the reason you're considering Seattle?"

"I won't lie. She's a cool girl and I had thought I might go that direction."

"And now?"

He shifted his chair and tried to forget the guilt associated with Shelby. "Now, I don't feel the same way. I realize I tried to make Seattle and Shelby fit because they seemed a natural progression."

"Oh," she said, peeling the label on the beer sitting in front of her. She looked too thoughtful, and he wondered what she thought about Shelby. Jealous? More seeds of doubt tossed in her path?

"I'm not with Shelby. We're not an item. Actually, I called her as soon as these feelings for you started."

Her eyes met his and he could see the doubt in them. Already their "dating" felt rocky.

"So, your turn. Tell me about going to school at LSU, and then didn't you end up in Virginia for grad school?" he asked.

"University of Maryland. I eventually interned at the USGS Patuxent Wildlife Research Center while I worked on my PhD in research biology. After visiting the center, I fell in love with the work they were doing there with the whoopers and the rest is history."

"You're really passionate about that bird, huh?"

Renny smiled, and the tension melted away. He liked to see the enthusiasm she had for her work. Her whole face changed and he saw that young girl's enthusiasm, a sort of joy that a guy wouldn't expect over an awkward-looking bird. "Yeah, they're interesting birds and the USGS is doing incredible work in reestablishing many endangered species, including that of the whoopers. I love what I do because I'm helping to restore natural species to my state. It's like I'm giving back to Louisiana."

"A doctorate before thirty. Impressive," he said, as the waitress set a plate containing his sandwich in front of him. Renny had ordered an oyster po'boy and the chili fries went between them.

"So why did you become an attorney?" Renny asked, plucking a fry from beneath the oozing cheese and chili and taking a bite. Her face told him that the decadent side item hadn't changed in the past ten years. It also reminded him that he liked to see Renny react to all things pleasurable. His groin tightened and he had to remind himself they were "dating."

He shrugged. "Not sure. Guess I thought I would be good at it."

"So no passion for being an attorney?"

"A little. Once I committed to the navy, I had to think about my path. I settled on law school—NYU for international law—and that was that."

"NYU is hard to get into."

He lifted a brow. "I know what you're thinking. I never worried about studying, but that doesn't mean I was a moron."

"I know."

"I became obsessed with making the grade in college. Funny how I was in Maryland for four years while you were at LSU. Then you came to Maryland and I went to New York City. We chased each other."

"You regret it?"

"What? Being sent to military school? The navy? Law school?" He took a bite of spicy chicken and thought about all those things. "A little. I missed you… and home."

"But it was good for you." Her words held a question.

"It was good for both of us, I think. My mom said something yesterday that struck me as true. She said I would never have grown where I was comfortable."

Renny tilted her head and seemed to mull over those words. "Hmm, interesting. Maybe we both experienced the world in a way we never would have had we stayed here. Had we actually chose to be together."

"I still would have liked the chance to decide for myself."

"Then you'd not be who you are today."

He swiped a French fry and popped it into his mouth. "I could have been better."

"Or in Angola."

He took another swig of beer to wash down the heat. He'd gotten unaccustomed to Louisiana seasonings living overseas. Cayenne pepper burned like fire on the tongue. "True, though I'd like to think I'd had a damn good reason to keep my nose clean."

Renny's eyes flashed something tender. "Maybe, but who knows? *We* won't, that's for sure."

They fell silent because, like a bad penny, the past was inevitably going to turn up now and then, no matter how much he wanted to move forward.

"So tell me about Della," she said, digging into her food.

So he did, trying to stress to his libido he and Renny were nothing more than a man and a woman on a date—a first date if they were going to stick with his plan. He already knew how good they were together in bed, but if he wanted to figure out where his future lay, he needed to pay attention to the woman Renny had become. He also had to give them some time to get to know each other. Time to figure out if the feelings they shared were residual. Or something stronger, strong enough to move them forward to… Well, he wasn't sure exactly where they were going. Just trying to figure out if they wanted to strike out toward that evasive something together.

His libido didn't like it much.

But them are the rules, libido.

After boxing up leftovers, paying and walking Renny to her car, he momentarily forgot the rules.

If only she hadn't touched his arm. If only she hadn't smiled that smile. If only she hadn't pushed her hair behind that sweet ear as she searched for her car keys.

Darby grabbed her arm and spun her around until his lips covered hers. He'd surprised her because her mouth fell open, an unknowing invitation he'd never pass up. One of his hands found the small of her back while the other cupped the back of her head. She tasted wonderful, like yeasty beer tinged in Louisiana hot sauce. She tasted like his past and, dare he think it, his future. Whatever it was, it was right.

Finally, he broke the kiss.

"That's not a first-date kiss," she said, her lips glistening beneath the fluorescent lights of the parking lot.

"So sue me. I broke the rules." He smiled down at her.

"It still feels dangerous, Darby. I'd like to think I can control how I feel about you, but I'm scared I won't be able to stop my heart from taking the plunge over the precipice."

He looked away because he was afraid, too. "But it's better than not trying. Could we walk away, knowing we didn't even try to hold on to whatever vibrates in the air between us?"

She sighed and leaned against his chest. "I don't want to hate you again."

He wrapped his arms around her and held her. "I don't want to have regrets, Renny. I've already lived with those. If we decide to walk away from each other at least it will be our decision this time."

"You're trying to be rational again. I don't think you can be rational about love."

"But this isn't love. Yet."

She pulled back from him. "It's getting hard for me to distinguish what I feel anymore."

Her lips tempted in the lights thrown off the bar and grill, so he did the only thing he could—he kissed her again.

This time her arms curled around his shoulders and she kissed him back with matched fervor. And it felt so good, so damn right, to have her in his arms.

This time she pulled back. "You're making me crazy."

"Feeling's mutual. Everything I thought I wanted has flipped upside down, but I'm trying to roll with it."

Renny nodded. "So, you'll call me?"

"I'll call you."

He stood in the parking lot until he could no longer see her taillights in the distance. As they faded out of sight, the words his mother had spoken to him days ago echoed in his ears. A prophecy made by a mambo:

A dark stranger comes from a distant place, bringing shadows and light, twisted in fate. The sun will not set on Beau Soleil until old wrongs are set right and the great bird comes home before again taking flight.

Twisted in fate.

Old wrongs set right.

Taking flight.

Things felt twined about him, wrapping fingers of fate about him. He didn't want to believe in prophecies but something propelled him toward Renny and at the same time rooted him in the land of his birth.

No matter what his future held, there was no doubt he was meant to be here. On the road that led to Bayou Bridge. Even if it took him away again.

CHAPTER THIRTEEN

"WHERE ARE THOSE MORTALITY reports for the brown pelicans on Grassy Isle?" Carrie asked, dumping an armload of files onto the thing she called a desk. Renny wasn't sure she could call it a desk since it basically resembled a pile of paper. Her coworker wasn't exactly organized in her work space, though she usually knew exactly where to find what she needed.

Except those reports.

"I think Lynn took them home, and he's still on vacation."

"I may be blonde, but I drew that conclusion when he didn't show up for the past few days."

"Ouch," Renny said, clicking her screen shut on the computer. "You're a grouchy goose. What's wrong?"

Carrie sighed and sank into her swivel chair. "Nothing. Everything."

Renny didn't know what to make of that. Maybe her friend needed a hug? Or a fresh cup of coffee?

"I had dinner with Ernie last night and he told me he doesn't want to get married this spring. He wants to save more money so we can buy a house first."

"Oh," Renny said, thinking maybe Carrie needed more than a hug or coffee. More like some rope so she could hog-tie Ernie and drag him to the altar. The man had backed their wedding up two times before and

Carrie's patience wore thin. Renny didn't blame her friend. Nothing good about being in limbo.

"Yeah. I'm beginning to think this isn't about money. That it's about frigid feet. It scares me because I've invested all this time and energy into this man."

"What about love?"

Carrie wrinkled her nose. "Well, that, too."

"Marriage is a big undertaking and it's not a bad idea to be absolutely certain." *Says she who'd been married for eleven years without anyone knowing.*

Carrie looked close to tears. "You're not helping. I have the dress, the church reserved and a bridal tea planned at the Rotunda, but none of that matters if I don't have a groom. Do you think I should give him an ultimatum?"

Renny bit her lip, knowing she was absolutely not the right person to ask anything regarding men, weddings and ultimatums. "I'm not sure if—"

A knock on the office door interrupted her ineptness at playing relationship counselor. "I'll get it."

Renny struggled up from the cushioned depths of her chair, crossed the room and pulled the door open—and found Darby reading the plaque outside the office and holding a picnic basket.

"Darby?"

He ripped his gaze from the plaque and smiled at her. "Hey, thought I might take the old ball and chain to lunch…or rather bring it to her."

What was he doing here? Dating? Sure. Showing up at work? Um, not so much. She wasn't ready for the questions—and Carrie breathing down her neck.

Her friend peered over her shoulder. "Ball and chain?"

Renny spun around. "Oh, um, this is—"

Darby leaned around her and offered a hand. "Hey, I'm Darby, and I was teasing her about the ball-and-chain thing. I have an odd sense of humor."

Carrie took his hand, sweeping him from head to tip of boot with an ambiguous mixture of curiosity and befuddlement. "Hi, I'm Carrie, and she has *never* mentioned you."

Her friend's gaze found hers and she shot accusation with her brown eyes.

Darby gave Carrie his toe-curling grin. "She hasn't? Well, that's strange. We've been married for eleven years."

Renny stepped back onto Carrie's toes.

"Ouch!" Carrie pushed at her back before squealing, "Married?"

"He's joking. I haven't seen him in eleven years. All that sun in Spain cooked his brain." Renny smiled through gritted teeth. "And he does have an odd sense of humor."

Darby nodded, with a stupid smile. She gave him a daggered glance. "So do you want to die now or later?"

"Later, please," he said, holding the picnic basket off. "I want my last meal first."

Carrie hopped on one foot, looking back and forth from Darby to her. "You have a date?"

Darby laughed. "Exactly."

"Well, this *is* interesting." Carrie looked at Renny and lifted her eyebrows. She might as well have added *you dog* to her proclamation.

"Well then, old friend, should we go?" Renny asked.

Darby frowned. "You don't know where we're going. *I* don't know where we're going. I only got as far as asking Lucille to pack a picnic. Caused lots of speculation at Beau Soleil."

"Beau Soleil," Carrie repeated, narrowing her eyes. "Even more interesting."

"We should be off," Renny said, grabbing Darby's elbow hard and steering him toward the outer door to the facility. "See you in about an hour, Carrie."

"Nice to meet you," Darby called over his shoulder, allowing her to lead him like a lamb to slaughter. Which he was. Of course Darby was nothing similar to a lamb, but the bloodbath was about to go down.

"What made you think you could come to my office? I agreed to dating, but not to letting everyone *know* we're dating," she muttered as Carrie called back platitudes.

He tossed a final wave over his shoulder and looked down at her. "What? I thought we were learning about each other. Thought I'd check out the station and bring you some lunch."

"You told her we're married. Are you insane?"

"I was joking. No one's going to find out until we tell them…or until they read the filing in the newspaper. So what does it matter? Just trying to flirt and set the mood for a nice little picnic."

"You should have called and I could have met you. Now I have to go back and answer all her questions— she's going to be worse than being stuck in a room full of mosquitoes at sundown."

"That bad, eh?" Darby smiled, opening the car door and giving her a questioning look. "Is there a place nearby where we can picnic?"

"Guess we can drive down by the launch and eat in the car."

He nodded and set the basket in the backseat next to a folded quilt. "Fine, but I'm warning you, these seats are small and don't go back far. Going to be hard to make out in them."

Renny shot him an exasperated look. Darby was in an awfully good mood. He grinned at her and something about the sun shining, the promise of Lucille's cooking and lunch with a good-looking man lifted her spirits—even if she faced an inquisition once she returned to the office. "We can use the hood. No one will be around."

"Really?"

"No."

"Damn. I had hope for a minute there."

She clicked the belt into the slot, wondering if they might get in a little necking on the car hood. Then it struck her how different she felt from last week. Darby was the used car salesman of her heart. Hell, she'd probably end up with her panties floating in the lake and a stupid lovesick smile on her face before the afternoon was over.

And for once she didn't feel so guilty about it.

After all, they were dating…even if they were married.

Darby started the engine and she directed him with a finger out the parking lot and toward the boat launch.

"Are you really that upset I surprised you with a picnic? I thought girls liked romantic overtures?"

"Well, you make it hard to be mad when you show up and do nice things for me, and you brought Lucille's cooking. That's seduction in itself."

He gave her a sideways smile. "I know how to choose my weapons."

Did he ever.

They remained silent during the rest of the drive to the launch. When they pulled in, they found only a few trucks with trailers parked in the gravel lot, and no one else in sight.

"There's no good place to spread a picnic blanket. Too wet. Guess we'll have to sit on the hood or trunk of the car or in the car." She glanced over at him as he parked in an empty slot facing the water. He looked like the young devil-may-care Darby he'd always been. Seeing him this way made it easy to tuck her problems away.

Darby cleaned his sunglasses on his shirttail then opened the door. "I forgot how wet this area is."

"It's the wetlands," Renny said, climbing out and surveying the expanse of grassy marsh surrounding the brackish water of the lake. All looked remarkably calm though she could hear the whine of a boat somewhere off to her right.

Darby had just set the picnic basket on the trunk when she spotted the little pirogue Stevo kept tied to the wooden pier. He'd been testing water pH several times a day and because it was marked with Department of Wildlife and Fisheries and had no trolling motor or outboard attached, no one messed with it. A weathered pair of paddles leaned against the scratched aluminum hull. "What about the boat? We could row out to that little inlet over there and eat on the water."

Darby looked up from his rummaging within the basket. "Absolutely. I haven't had the chance to get on the water."

She wore her rugged waterproof Merrells but Darby had on expensive-looking running shoes. She nodded toward his shoes. "You sure?"

"I couldn't have dialed up a better day than you, Lucille's homemade bread and paddling along a Louisiana lake."

His words warmed her…or maybe it was the sun overhead. A cool front had slipped through the night before, giving them relief from the incessant Louisiana humidity, and gentle waves lapped at the grasses lining the shore. If Darby wanted romantic, it didn't get much more perfect for a gal like Renny, unless they'd had bait and fishing poles.

It only took four grunts, two curse words and nearly losing a paddle before they'd pushed off into the deeper water that would allow them to drift off the main channel. The boat was so small they had to tuck themselves out of the way of the fishermen's larger boats that kicked up waves big enough to make eating impossible.

Sweat rolled down Renny's back as she and Darby each took a paddle and made way toward a small copse of brush and scrubby swamp trees that would provide some shade, but she didn't mind the perspiration because there was something satisfying in the rhythm needed to propel the old boat forward. Dip, pull and rotate—they moved in natural harmony as they'd done in the past.

With the wind at her back, the sun warm on her neck and the man she'd always loved rowing in front of her, Renny could almost believe fate had given her a perfectly wrapped gift. What had Darby called it? A mulligan.

A do-over. Second chance. Whatever she wanted to call it. She had doubts, sure, but today things felt right and good, and she was glad she'd agreed to dating.

Darby reached out and took a low branch of a small tree and looped the rope of the boat around it in an expert knot. "Okay, let's see what Lucille packed us, who by the way, was thrilled to know I was having lunch with you. She said she sent you something special. Ah, here it is." He withdrew a small Baggie of Lucille's famous lemon cookies.

Renny took them from him, opened the bag and popped one in her mouth. "Mmm."

"Don't do things like that unless you want to find out what making out in a pirogue is like."

"I already know," she said, wiping the crumbs from her chin.

His eyes crinkled and she knew he remembered a few choice fishing trips they'd made. "Touché."

Renny took another cookie. "You know how to woo a gal, don't you?"

"And they say the way to a man's heart is with food. Guess they never met you. Who needs a bed and roses when you have lemon cookies and a pirogue?" He pulled huge turkey sandwiches with thick homemade-looking bread from the basket, along with a container of some sort of slaw and a bag of Zapp's potato chips and set them on the metal bench sitting between them. "Go ahead and get started. Didn't know how much time you had for lunch."

She grabbed a paper plate, set a half sandwich on it and glanced up at him. He watched her with a strange look on his face. "I have an hour if I need it. Usually I don't need it to slurp down soup or tear through a frozen entrée."

"Glad I brought you something more substantial than that crap. You could stand to gain a little weight."

"Are you kidding? Have you seen how big my butt has gotten? I need to start biking again if the old leg can stand it. I've been doing—" He leaned forward and silenced her with a kiss—a wonderful, sweet kiss that nearly caused her to drop the sandwich half in her hand.

After several seconds he lifted his head and tucked a piece of her hair behind her ear. "I like your ass fine."

Renny closed her mouth and looked down at her hand. She was hungry, but now she wasn't sure if it was for the sandwich or the man. Probably both.

She took a bite and glanced around them, at the way the breeze fluttered the leaves above them, at the way the wetland grasses swayed in a ballet of laziness. All around them, the land breathed. "I've come here hundreds of times, but I don't think I've seen the lake like this."

"I've missed it," he said, his voice tinged with longing, with pride.

"You know, I'd thought of staying in Maryland. Good opportunities presented themselves at the research center."

"But?"

"I kept thinking of the way the marsh looked at sundown, the way the herons coast over the basin early in the morning, the way my mama's jambalaya tastes… and I couldn't stay there. This is where I belong."

Darby took a bite of sandwich and chewed it slowly, his mind seemingly chewing just as intentionally. "Guess you have your own weapons in your arsenal."

"What?"

"Well, I've brought food for seduction, but you have the words."

"I'm not trying to sway you with words. That's how I feel, but that doesn't mean you're wrong for wanting to move away." Her stomach rolled a little at that thought because somehow in the course of a few days' time, she could hardly tolerate the thought she'd not see him again.

He didn't say anything further, and for the next few

minutes they ate lunch, a peaceful silence between them, interrupted only by the crunch of a chip. The lake lapped at the sides of the boat as the cool breeze, mixed with occasional sun on her skin, created that sort of sleepy deliciousness that usually ended in a nap.

"Thank you for lunch," she said, dusting crumbs from her lap.

"After that greeting I wasn't sure it was a good idea. You seemed embarrassed I showed up to take you to lunch."

"Not embarrassed, just still uncomfortable with everything that's happened over the past six days. Dear Lord, it's been less than a week."

"Seems like a lifetime, huh?"

"Yeah, but I don't want to sit here and talk about feelings. Not when there are more lemon cookies in this bag." She picked the plastic bag up and wagged the cookies in front of his nose.

He grabbed it, pulled out a cookie and popped it in his mouth. "A woman who bass fishes, eats multiple cookies and doesn't want to talk about her feelings? I'd marry you if I hadn't already married you."

"Real funny," Renny said, lifting a paddle. "We should get back."

Darby's phone rang, but he ignored it and stood, making the boat rock. "Just a bit longer."

"Darby, sit down. You're making the boat rock."

He ignored her and pulled her to him, wrapping his arms around her. "I'm not going back until I get a little kiss for all this effort."

"Oh, really?" She widened her stance because the boat rocked. "Even if you end up in the water?"

"Water Schmater."

His lips covered hers and she forgot about the boat,

the water and the world around them. In his kiss she tasted all she needed—hunger, sweetness, her past and, dare she hope, her future. It was good and didn't last nearly long enough for her.

After he broke the kiss, she looked up at him and he smiled, tilting his head down so his forehead rested against hers. The boat still rocked, but who really cared?

"Ah, Ren, you taste like coming home, girl." He sighed, and her heart fluttered, then doubled in size.

It felt so wonderful to stand in the middle of a pirogue, wrapped in Darby's arms with the hope blooming in her breast.

His phone sounded again. "Guess we can't hide from the world forever."

Renny sank to the bench, every bone in her body wanting to keep hiding from the world, from reality, from anything that might take him away from her. How had she gone from hating him to toes over the line in such a short amount of time? Because that's what it felt like—her toes were hanging over the line of love and now she wasn't even trying to stop herself from making that hop to the other side.

Exciting—and dangerous.

She'd sworn she could handle being with Darby and not make that leap, but had she really done a bang-up job at keeping boundaries? His lips moved as he read the text on his phone and she knew she'd not done the job at all. The lines were blurred and the waters even murkier.

Because she was falling in love with him.

"Mom says I have a visitor at the house."

She snapped out of her dangerous thoughts. "Definitely time to get back."

He gathered up the remnants of their lunch and shoved the napkins, empty bottles and bags into the basket. "It's probably just Sid. He said he'd bring the waiver today. Of course, he's being discreet, telling Mom he's stopping in to see me on his way to Baton Rouge. Have you read through the petition?"

"Yeah, it's a pretty standard-looking divorce." She lied. She hadn't read it. Something kept her from wanting to end the sham of a marriage even though there was nothing legitimate about it except the paper it was written on.

She glanced at Darby and he looked like he wanted to say more. Maybe he felt the same way—knowing that divorce was probably the best idea but still not able to put his signature on the line. Because...

What if?

That question had floated between them ever since they'd made love.

Darby untied the boat, sat down and grabbed a paddle. They simultaneously began paddling back toward the launch. After several minutes, Darby said, "Why don't you come with me? It will give you a chance to talk to Sid and you can sign the waiver."

Something masquerading as a lead ball sank into her stomach. Of course, this marriage had to end. The past was the past, and if there was a future, it needed to be played on an even and clear field. "I hadn't planned on it, but I need to photograph L9-10. Didn't have my camera Sunday morning and we need visuals for our records."

He smiled. "Perfect. Both Mom and Lucille will love having you for coffee."

"It's not a social visit, Darby."

They reached the launch, and Darby leaped out with the rope and turned to give her his best toe-curling smile. The same one he'd used on Carrie. The same one that usually got him what he wanted. "Lucille finally made me one of her famous bourbon pecan pies."

Damn. Those were really, really good. Almost as good as his smile. "Well, maybe just one little slice."

"That's my girl. I know I can always seduce you with sweets."

Or with your body, smile and honeyed words.

Damn, her mama had been right.

She couldn't keep her panties on when Darby Dufrene was around. Well, she could. But sometimes she just didn't want to.

CHAPTER FOURTEEN

DARBY FELT PRETTY PLEASED with himself. Renny had followed him back to Beau Soleil and he hadn't had to use anything other than his "please" smile.

Dating Renny had been the best idea he'd had in a while.

Oh, he wanted her beneath him again. He'd thought of nothing else but her cute belly button and the curve of her breast. The smooth, soft skin of her inner elbow, the way her hair smelled of some flower and her sweet lips driving him crazy.

He shifted in his seat as he pulled into the gates of Beau Soleil. Renny had always had that effect on him, ever since he'd first seen her in those cutoffs and bikini top on the side of a backcountry road. The triangles covering her breasts had been bright pink and he'd been able to see the outline of her nipples through the fabric. Sweat had sheened her chest and her brown hair had fallen out of her ponytail. He'd stared at those lips stained deep red with blackberry juice and had been sucked into desire so intense he couldn't breathe. All he could do for a good two minutes was stare at her.

So, yeah, wanting Renny had never been in question.

But getting to know her, laugh with her, admire her dedication to her work, seeing her as a grown woman had moved him in a distinct direction. Because it wasn't just about Renny, it was about being here in this place that was a part of him.

If someone would have told him a month ago that he'd be entertaining the thought of staying in Louisiana and making a new start with an old flame, he would have dragged that person to a mental hospital for automatic committal. He'd spent weeks agonizing over moving to Seattle, taking a chance on Shelby and working for a man he didn't know. He thought he'd made the best choice—until he'd come home.

The roller coaster of life had hairpinned and dropped him for a loop, but he was hanging on and going with it. There was nothing else left to do. If he'd learned anything over the past few days, he'd learned he couldn't control his heart, no matter how much reason wanted to trump.

He glanced back into his rearview mirror as they rounded the corner and the huge yellow ancestral pile appeared before them. This was the road that had brought him home, and behind him followed his Louisiana girl—the past he was prepared to pull into his future.

His heart swelled as he looked at the house that seemed older than even the trees. This weekend they would all be together. Della was coming tomorrow, Abram and Lou would be there Saturday morning and, of course, Nate's family would take the walk over. They'd sit down as a family, eating, laughing and healing, trying to recapture what they'd once had many, many years ago. And Darby knew he wanted Renny with him.

She belonged with him.

He swung into the gravel parking area, halting beside a car that didn't look like it could be Sid's. The man had always been a Cadillac man.

"Sid drives a Civic?" Renny asked when he climbed out. She'd already emerged, carrying the bag she likely kept her camera in.

"Nah, he showed me his new Escalade when I saw him last week. Must be Della or Abram's girlfriend."

Renny shrugged. "Well, I don't care who it is. I came for the pie."

"Oh, sure you did. I know you want to maneuver me into that cloakroom under the stairs and demonstrate your talents with your—"

"Don't go there, Dufrene," Renny growled slamming the door. "We're *dating*."

"Whatever you say, baby."

"Stop calling me *baby*."

"Whatever you say, blackberry girl."

Renny shot him a look that should have chastised as they climbed the steps of the wide veranda that stretched the length of the main house but didn't. He could see the pleasure in her gaze, the softness surrounding her mouth. She loved the flirting.

Lucille met them at the door. "Well, I do declare! My sweet Renny girl!"

Renny smiled. "Hey, Lucille, you look good. Haven't aged a bit."

"Girl, you do lie, but I'll pretend you don't." The woman who'd been the Beau Soleil housekeeper for too many years to count enveloped Renny in a hug. "Ooh, you just about gone to bone, girl. Let me get you something to eat. I done made Darby his favorite pie, but I got some chocolate-cherry cake if you want that. Picou's in her sitting room having some tea. I'll bring coffee and dessert to you. Sound good?"

"Whose car?" Darby asked.

Lucille peered around at him. "That's something you got to learn for yourself. Oh, but first, Mr. Platt dropped off an envelope for you. Said it was papers you was expectin'."

She handed him the envelope that had been sitting on the antique buffet in the hallway. "Now, you got company, so go on in."

Her words created unease in his gut. Had Sid said something about the divorce? Or was there a whole new reason for Lucille to eyeball him?

He set the envelope back on the antique buffet and nudged Renny toward the back room. She placed her camera bag beside the envelope. "Come on."

"Stop rushing me," she said, lagging behind him.

Darby smiled back at her. "Lamb in the lion's den."

"Oh, please, your mother's not a lamb," she teased.

He entered the room with a grin...that quickly died.

"Well, finally. I texted you over an hour ago with no response," his mother said as the woman opposite her rose with a brilliant smile on her face.

"Darby!" Shelby said, setting her teacup on the side table and hurrying to him. She threw herself into his arms—or rather against him—in a hug.

"Shelby?" He grabbed her elbows in an awkward hug right before her lips found his. The air sucked out of his lungs and he grappled for a grip on reality.

She dropped her arms and stepped back. "Surprise."

"What're you doing here?"

"Well, after you canceled the interview at Daddy's firm, I thought I better come down here. You didn't sound like the Darby I knew. Plus, I wanted to meet your family. You've told me so much about them."

A baseball bat to the head wouldn't have surprised

him more than Shelby standing in his mother's sitting room. He blinked as the baseball bat to the head beamed up at him for another full second before lifting herself on her toes and giving him another kiss.

Renny's shock slammed against his back.

Then he felt the crackle of her anger, monstrous and cold as a January wind.

Oh, shit.

"You have a friend with you," Shelby said, stepping out of his arms and leaning so she could see Renny. "Hey. Didn't mean to be rude."

Renny didn't say anything for a moment. Finally, after what felt like hours, she said, "Hi, I'm Renny Latioles."

"Nice to meet you. I'm Shelby Mackey, Darby's girlfriend."

For one brief moment, he actually thought about running out of the room like a pusillanimous dog, tail between legs, but he wasn't sure his feet could unstick themselves from the polished floor. Didn't matter that he'd broken things off with Shelby and had no fault in what played out. It was sheer instinct. "Well, not technically my girlfriend."

Something flickered in Shelby's eyes, something that scared him a little. She'd sized up the situation and perceived Renny as a threat. "Well, what do you call me then? We've been dating for over two months."

What part of "cutting her loose" didn't Shelby understand? He glanced toward his mother who looked sort of bemused, and he knew she understood what was going down on her expensive antique carpet. He also understood there were certain expectations for behavior, and he wasn't going to embarrass Shelby. Even if he knew Renny was mad as a wet cat. Surely, Renny could see he had nothing to do with the blonde stand-ing in the heart of Beau Soleil. "Mom, any more cof-fee over there?"

His mother shook her head and acted as if she hosted afternoon tea with Darby's girlfriends, past and present, every afternoon. "Sorry, but Lucille's making a fresh pot and bringing out some dessert."

Shelby stepped away from him and he could see the thoughts flitting through eyes the color of a Louisiana sky. "Am I interrupting something here?"

"Of course not," Renny said, moving forward and extending her hand. "I'm just an old friend of the Du-frene family, a biologist overseeing one of the birds inhabiting Beau Soleil property. I'm here to get some photographic evidence to support my research. Abso-lutely nothing interrupted."

"Oh," Shelby said, looking about as comfortable as someone with her dress caught in her panty hose. "Just looked like..."

"Nothing." Renny wiggled her fingers on the ex-tended hand. Shelby finally took her hand and gave it a shake before latching her hands behind her.

"Oh, good. For a minute there I thought—" Her words trailed off and there seemed to be little doubt about what she thought.

Darby opened his mouth to clarify the situation.

But Renny beat him to it. "You thought there was something between me and Darby?"

He closed his mouth as Shelby darted a glance his way and nodded.

"Oh, that's ridiculous," Renny said, moving toward the door. "And I should be leaving you to your com-pany."

"Must you go?" Picou asked, patting the couch next

to her, making Darby wonder if she enjoyed the evident discomfort displayed before her. Only someone as perverse as his mother would enjoy tension thicker than fog on the bayou. "Lucille's been looking forward to visiting with you since you and Darby first reconnected."

"No, I really—"

"Oh, no you don't," Lucille said, bustling into the room, carrying a tray with a carafe of coffee and several plates holding pie and cake. "I got your pie right here, missy."

"Lucille, I have to go."

"Oh, you can," the housekeeper said, nodding her head emphatically. Darby noticed that the black curly wig tilted a bit as she carefully set cream and sugar on the tray sitting atop the large ottoman between the couch and extra-large stuffed chairs. "Just as soon as you eat your pie and drink your poison."

Renny shot him an undecipherable look. "Sounds lovely."

But her words sounded anything but pleased. Nothing like being trapped by the niceties of life—and Lucille's ironclad rule that once she set out pie, it got eaten.

Renny sank down next to Picou as Lucille settled her girth in the chair next to the one in which Shelby sat. The housekeeper turned and looked at Darby expectantly.

"I'll stand," he said, turning to pour a finger of Kentucky bourbon sitting on a silver service on the built-in cabinet. Screw coffee.

"Gonna be hard eating this here pie standing," Lucille said, holding out a plate. If her infamous pecan pie hadn't been so damn delicious, he might have waved it off. But it was beyond good. And Lucille had gone to extra trouble for him.

So he crossed the room and took the plate and fork. The liquor burned in his stomach, giving him a droplet of courage. Not much. But enough to attempt conversation. "So when did you arrive and why didn't you call?"

"No need to get a hotel room," Picou said, scooping up a slice of cherry-chocolate cake, putting it on a plate and holding it out to Shelby, who scooted over in the big stuffed chair and patted the seat next to her, inviting him to sit. He shook his head.

Picou continued. "How long do you think you'll stay, dear?"

"I have a room at a bed-and-breakfast in town." Shelby gave Picou a plaintive smile before turning to Darby. "I just arrived today. I did call yesterday, but you must not have gotten the message."

Or not even checked his voice mails, something he always did religiously, but his mind had been preoccupied with Renny, dating and sending out résumés to firms in Baton Rouge and Lafayette.

"So I said to myself, 'You're missing your man and you've always wanted to go to Louisiana, so do it.' So here I am." The smile Shelby gave him looked practiced. She knew he wasn't happy about her being here, but she wasn't going to let on. Shelby was more of a fighter than he'd given her credit for.

He glanced to where Picou sat observing the conversation like a hawk atop a line. Next to her, Renny sat stony and grave, trying for nonchalance and failing epically.

"I've heard so many stories about Bayou Bridge, and I'm dying to see your old stomping grounds. You told me if I ever came down you'd take me to eat crawfish, see some plantations and go fishing out on your pond. I've never been fishing before but I'm game for anything," Shelby said, taking a bite of cake and nodding at Lucille. "This is wonderful."

Darby wanted to sink through the floor. Guilt burned a hole in his stomach, and he looked around for the closest way to escape. He was certain he could break the nearby window if he threw his full weight into it.

"It's full of bass," Renny said, her voice very calm and intentional. "In fact, you can usually nab one on the first cast, but be careful—there are snakes out there."

Her eyes found their target. Him. "Big, fat snakes in the grass."

Something socked him in the chest. It wasn't just Renny's anger but what sat beneath the surface—the hurt. He wanted to hit his knees and crawl to her, to explain to her Shelby had made assumptions, that he wasn't a snake...but he knew his pleas would fall to the wayside. She was mad.

"Really? Snakes? Sounds a bit much for me." Shelby gave a dainty shiver. "I've never seen a snake in the wild—only behind glass at the Woodland Park zoo where I volunteered in high school. I once helped out with a boa constrictor named Tina."

"Interesting," Picou murmured, lifting what he was sure was an empty cup to her lips. "Boas eat their prey whole."

For a moment the only sound in the room was the clink of the fork against the china.

"So, how did you two meet?" Renny said, accepting a piece of pie from Lucille.

Darby swallowed hard, and it had nothing to do with the pie turning to ash on his tongue.

His mother grabbed a piece of cake, took a huge bite

and chewed, watching a real life soap opera play out. "Yes, do tell."

Shelby's cheeks pinked a little as she spread a cloth napkin in her lap. "We met at an event at the officer's club. I taught at the base school—Algebra II and trigonometry—and his roommate Hal invited me to the event. Darby and I started talking and we just talked all night. After that, we started hanging out, having coffee, dinner, a couple of rides through the countryside on his motorcycle."

"You have a motorcycle?" Renny asked, looking as if she choked on the pie.

"A Ducati," Shelby said with a wry laugh. "I want to see him make that work in Seattle. It rains way too often to consider a motorcycle a reliable mode of transportation."

Picou raised her eyebrows. "Darby always loved going fast. Anything dangerous and he'd sign up for it. Gave me all this silver hair."

"Really? Doesn't sound like the Darby I know. He's always been so reliable and sensible. The navy must have made him more discerning." With that statement, Shelby's gaze slid to Renny.

Again, the room fell silent, so silent Darby could hear the ticks on the grandfather clock just outside the room in the hallway.

"I think we got a ghost out there in them woods," Lucille said, pointing toward the back of the house.

"What?" Picou said, her gaze following the direction in which Lucille pointed.

"A ghost. I've been seeing something white fluttering out in the woods. Saw it once a week ago Tuesday, and then I saw it again yesterday morning. Early."

"That's silly," Darby said, wondering if he should

kiss the housekeeper now or later for changing the subject to something more benign than dating Shelby and how much he'd changed over the years.

"Maybe something blowing around? Plastic bags sometimes catch in the wind. They've scared me before." Renny set the half-eaten pie on the tray and folded her napkin.

"There are spirits all in these woods," his mother said, sipping her tea, a thoughtful wrinkle marring the smoothness of her forehead. "Lucille knows what I'm talking about."

"I sure do," Lucille said, nodding her head, "but this one don't seem like no regular spirit. It's got business, it does."

"There are regular spirits?" Shelby looked a bit frightened, or put out. He didn't know her well enough to make that judgment. Three weeks of the two months they'd been "dating" had been spent with her in Seattle and him in Spain.

"Of course," Picou said as if she were discussing everyday subjects like gardening or doing the crossword puzzle. "But they don't manifest themselves so obviously. I agree with Renny. You're probably seeing things."

"Mmm," Lucille said, not looking the least convinced. "Strange goings-ons around here is all I'm saying. Keep having things go missing from the fridge, lots of knocking around at all hours of the morning, and specters out roaming."

Shelby's eyes were the size of a half-dollar and Darby could see her mind turning around the superstitious claims of the housekeeper. He looked at Renny. Her gaze bored into his, sparking with anger and maybe the desire to shoot him. "Uh, well, I'll keep an eye out, Lucille. Maybe we'll get to the bottom of these mysteries."

"Or maybe she's dreaming all this," his mother said, waving a dismissive hand. "Who would like more coffee? Just picked up this chicory blend from a specialty shop in New Orleans a few weeks ago. Isn't it good?"

"Why aren't you drinking it?" Renny asked, standing and smoothing her pants against her thighs.

"I don't drink coffee. Keeps me awake all night."

"Then you should go look for that ghost," Lucille said, wagging a finger. "'Cause I ain't dreamed up nothing."

"I'm going now," Renny said, moving around the back of her chair. "Thanks for the pie and coffee."

Lucille looked down at the plate. "You didn't finish it."

"Trying to watch my figure."

"Leave that to the boys, my dear," Picou said.

Renny tried out a smile but didn't quite succeed.

Shelby set her cup down. "Well, it was nice meeting you, Renna. A friend of Darby's is always a friend of mine. Hope I get to see you again before we leave."

"We?" Picou repeated, cocking her head.

Shelby's face pinked again as she stood. "Just slipped out."

Everyone seemed to process that info. Darby felt something hot and hard sink in his belly. This wasn't supposed to happen. Past and future on opposite sides with him straddling the center. Wasn't a good place to be.

Renny smiled and walked toward Shelby, putting out both hands to pull her into a hug. "I'm glad I got to meet you, Shelby. We're practically *family*."

Her gaze met his again and he got the message. He was toast.

"Oh," Shelby said, awkwardly returning the hug. "That's a wonderful way of putting it."

"Yes, it is, and so true considering you're dating my husband." Renny released her, turned around and walked out of the room.

His mother gasped, Lucille groaned and Shelby's hands dropped almost in sync with her jaw.

"Wha—what?" Shelby stammered.

"Shit." Darby set the empty plate on the end table with a clatter.

His mother looked confused for only a moment before dawning registered. Then her mouth curved into a smile. "You mean that marriage was legal? Is that why you've been so secretive?"

He shoved his hands through his hair. "I haven't been…well, I have, but it's complicated."

"You're married?" Shelby walked over and jerked his arm, her blue eyes pooling with hurt even though her words sounded incredulous—and maybe angry.

"That's complicated, too, Shelby, but right now I really need to talk to Renny."

He didn't wait for a reply because the slamming of the front door had rattled the crystal in the chandelier. As he walked from the room, he said a prayer.

The prayer was short mostly because Renny turned on him as he stepped onto the porch. Her camera bag sat on the top step and she held the envelope in her hand. She pointed a corner of it at him.

"You asshole," she hissed. "You have a girlfriend?"

"No," he said, sidestepping her because she looked as if she might actually punch him.

She turned and placed a steadying hand on the porch rail. "How could you?"

"What?"

"Hedge your bets like that. What kind of man does that?"

"Now wait a minute. I haven't been—"

"No." Renny whirled, eyes crackling, fists curled. "You said there wasn't anyone, but it's very obvious there is."

"I should have—"

"Yeah, you should have, you two-timing snake."

He grabbed her elbow. "I'm not two-timing. Shelby and I weren't exclusive."

She wrenched her elbow away from him and pushed him back. "Not exclusive? Not exclusive! Who are you?"

He damn sure didn't have an answer for that one. He'd been trying to figure that out ever since he'd seen Renny again. But he'd not been dishonest with her. In true Renny fashion, she overreacted.

She advanced on him. "Don't you dare tell me she doesn't think you're exclusive. No woman flies thousands of miles just to *be a friend* to a man."

"You're not listening."

"Because I don't want to hear your dumbass excuses."

"I think you need to calm down, Renny. This is not what it looks like. I never asked Shelby to come here, and I never lied to you."

Renny took a deep breath that bordered on a sob, before pressing a fist to her stomach. "You made me believe you were considering staying in Louisiana—for me."

"I was. I am."

"Yeah, I can see that. If that were true, Shelby wouldn't

be sitting in your mother's house eating Lucille's choc-olate cake talking about how much you connected and about how funny it will be when you drive your motor-cycle in the Seattle rain."

"Why won't you let me say anything in my defense?"

Renny shook her head, her eyes filling with tears. "Because I'm not stupid. You hedged your bets like my feelings didn't matter—like her feelings don't matter." She whirled, scooped up the bag and started down the steps, her limp somehow more pronounced, or perhaps it seemed so because he knew he'd hurt her once again. "I don't know you anymore, and that's the problem. I relied on a memory of a boy. And you've grown into a man—a man who thinks it's okay to play with wom-en's emotions."

"Wait, Renny." He followed her. "That's not fair. This whole last week has turned me upside down. I never expected to feel the way I do. You're acting like I planned this, and that's about as far from the truth as you can get."

She held up a hand. "I don't have time for this. Never should have let you talk me into…into…anything I did with you."

"Talk you into it? I'm fairly sure you participated fully in everything we did together. I didn't force you, Renny."

"No, but you pushed and pushed until I rolled over. Every time I opened the door, you were there, smiling at me, charming my socks and other unmentionables off. You're just like your mother, you lean on people until you get what you want—or maybe manipulate is the better word."

He dropped the hands he'd been holding up to her. That's what she thought? He'd forced his way back into her life? "I never tried to manipulate you, and I was always honest about my feelings."

"Sure. You're confused, so you use me as your crutch, as an excuse to forget about life for a while. Picnics, fishing and takeout. I'm nothing but a holiday to you. A little mini high school reunion. A—"

He grabbed her arm and jerked her. "Shut up and listen."

"Don't—"

"I said shut up," he growled, anger crashing onto him. His life had been bordering on chaos for the past week and now it was full-fledged out of control. He wanted to punch something. Run until he fell over in exhaustion. Scream his frustration into the wind.

She closed her mouth and stared at him. For a moment, neither one of them spoke.

"Take a deep breath. You know me and you know what happened in there is not what you're making it out to be."

"I don't know anything anymore." Renny pulled from his grasp, opened the folder and pulled the papers from the depths. Then she rifled through the bag holding her camera and withdrew a pen, clicking it and flipping up the pages until she found the signature line.

He sank against the back door, trying to still the frustration churning within. "Don't do anything you'll regret, Renny. All I have to do is have a little talk with Shelby and all will be taken care of."

She scrawled her signature onto the papers and slapped them on his chest. "Find a witness and file the papers."

"Ren—"

"No. I shouldn't have allowed all those old feelings

to spill back into my life. I knew things wouldn't work between us."

"Ren."

"We were never meant to be, Darby. That's the truth here. Never meant to be."

He clasped the papers to his chest, feeling like she'd punched him in the solar plexus. "We'll talk after you calm down. You'll see this was a big mistake."

"No, I don't want to talk anymore." She looked around and grimaced. "Damn it. I still have to get those freakin' pictures."

He opened his mouth to tell her they had something between them worth exploring, worth fighting for, something very real, but he knew it would be a waste of air. Renny was too hurt to listen. She needed to calm down. Besides he had cleanup to do inside with Shelby and his mother.

Shit. Things were a mess.

And he didn't know if all the king's horsemen and all the king's men could put together what had just fallen apart. Hell, he didn't even know a king to call. Or horsemen. Or why he thought in nursery rhymes when his world crumbled around him.

"Go back to Shelby. Go to Seattle. And forget about me." Renny turned and started walking toward the woods that led to the abandoned rice field.

"You don't mean that," he called after her.

Her answer wasn't verbal, but he got the message. The middle finger was universal.

He shoved a hand through his hair, giving it a hard tug before exhaling the weight of his problems into the Louisiana humidity. Renny disappeared into the foliage just as Shelby appeared on the porch.

Right.

No rest for the dumbassed.

He had another woman to deal with, and then after that, his mother would peck at him like a mockingbird after a tomcat. Then Della would come. And maybe more women wanting to rip the flesh from his bones.

He climbed the steps, divorce papers in hand, and faced Shelby.

Her blue eyes were a tangle of emotion. "Why didn't you tell me you were married? That message would have been loud and clear, Darby, and I wouldn't have come."

He climbed the steps and shook his head. "I really don't have an answer to that, Shelby."

Crossing her arms, she eyed him with an expression he couldn't read. "I feel like a fool."

"Join the crowd."

"That's comfort," she said, her words no longer soft, no longer Shelby-like.

"Well, it's all I got at the moment."

CHAPTER FIFTEEN

RENNY STALKED THROUGH the woods with reckless disregard for her footfalls and ended up with a bone-jarring slip that left her leg in torturous pain and the top of her head feeling as if it could explode.

"Shit." She dragged herself a few yards and sank down on a stump covered with lichen and bright green moss, clasping her leg and trying not to cry out, but it hurt like a mother.

"Ow, ow, ow," she said, leaning forward, begging the pain to abate. Tears already swimming in her eyes threatened to spill over, but she brushed them angrily away.

She wouldn't cry. About her leg. About Darby. About what a fool she'd been to hope for something that couldn't be.

He had a girlfriend?

Talk about not seeing that sucker punch coming. One minute possibility skipped around her and Darby, the next she'd taken a header down concrete stairs.

She closed her eyes as something worse than the pain in her leg slammed her.

Sheer utter desolation.

And the tears fell as her heart tore in two. God damn, Darby Dufrene. He had made her believe in love again even though she'd tried to shut the door against him. She hadn't been strong enough to resist the delicious assault the man had waged on her senses. The love for him she'd buried so long ago had burst through the scars, bubbling over with sweet temptation, sweet pleasure, bitter hope.

And he'd made her love him again.

She opened her eyes and focused on a scarred tree lying twisted against another. Like her—damaged and twisted. All because Darby was a liar.

Okay, he'd told her about Shelby, but he'd said they were over. If he'd been serious about staying in Bayou Bridge, serious about wanting her, that woman wouldn't have been standing in Beau Soleil acting like she'd already picked out their wedding china. Renny hadn't meant to spill the beans about being married to Darby, but something inside her, some devil, fought past common sense.

The only comfort Renny could take was the utter shock on Shelby's face.

A sob rose in her throat but she choked it down.

Darby wasn't worth it.

At that moment she hated him as much as she loved him.

Which was intensely.

Finally, after she'd sat through her pity party long enough, she wiped her face with the hem of her shirt and stood. Her leg hurt like a son of a bitch, but she managed to walk toward the area where the bird who'd started all this in the first place foraged through Beau Soleil land.

If it hadn't been for L9-10, she wouldn't have seen Darby.

But that wasn't true.

He would have found her if only because he needed a divorce. Well, that was done. She'd waived her right to be served and the petition would be filed. She wouldn't have to see Darby again. She could move on.

She crashed through the foliage and emerged in the clearing before remembering she hadn't brought her costume.

Great.

That's exactly why she didn't want drama in her life. Not now. Not when countless government agencies were depending on her to keep a clear mind and elevate the survival of the whooping crane above silly things like bass fishing, eating bourbon pecan pie or having amazing sex. More important things hung over her, so there was no time to be distracted or wallow in pity for her poor choices over the past couple of days.

Still, she couldn't do her work without the costume, not unless she wanted to spook the crane. But then again, maybe it was time for the bird to move on and seek another habitat—so Renny didn't have to come back to Beau Soleil. Maybe it was a godsend she didn't have the white draping and hat.

Renny stepped out, pulled the camera from the bag hanging at her side and scanned the area. The crane wasn't in sight. But that was fine. She didn't need to see the bird to get what she needed. A few clicks later, she had covered the habitat, documenting the area visually so she could add the photos to the reports citing the water levels, vegetation and pH levels.

She dumped the camera into the bag and started back, not even setting an eye on the bird who stalked Dufrene land, crunching through the underbrush of the woods, seeking the trail that would take her back to Beau Soleil, back toward the man who she could cheerfully strangle, his overbearing mother and the girl who'd flown across the country to claim him.

As she pushed through a tangled knot of withering vines, a flash of color caught her eye. Renny pulled back camouflaged netting and spied the plastic storage container Picou had had with her in the cart a few days ago. It had been hidden well, but the vine Renny had yanked had jerked off part of the netting.

Her heart was broken, but her mind still worked.

So why was Picou hiding something out in the woods?

Renny knew she wasn't to interfere in a property owner's affairs not relating to the species being observed, but something niggled in Renny's mind and before she could think any better of it, she stomped over to the container and popped the lid off.

Inside lay a white sheet and a puppet—the kind used by wildlife biologists to feed the cranes when they were young. Beside the puppet lay a homemade version of her own headgear and an empty bag of grapes, the withered brown stems stark evidence of an old woman's meddling.

Insult to injury. Anger flooded her.

How dare Picou Dufrene screw with Renny's mission.

Darby's mother was the reason L9-10 wouldn't leave Beau Soleil. The old bat was feeding the bird a most favored treat—grapes—in effort to keep it on the land. Picou jeopardized an entire project because she believed in some hocus-pocus hoo-ha about a "great bird." And she'd gone to a lot of trouble, obviously learning about the cranes, how they were raised, fed and approached by biologists.

Renny should go to Beau Soleil and demand answers. After all, Picou had virtually sabotaged Renny's work. But the thought of charging up the steps on her aching leg and facing Darby with his sophisticated blonde girl-friend made vomit rise in her throat. She'd deal with Picou later. Maybe she'd send agents to her door and arrest her for…something.

Renny closed the box, not bothering to disturb the contents any more than needed. It was evidence to be used against the woman—if Renny wanted to pros-ecute her.

If she could.

Jeez, wasn't life grand? Peachy keen? A bowl of cherries and every other stupid cheerful euphemism for happiness?

She wanted out of there.

It took longer than normal to get back to the plan-tation house, mostly because her leg throbbed. She emerged off the path into the gravel driveway and was nearly mowed down by a late-model navy Lincoln Con-tinental.

"Hey." Lucille's voice penetrated the fog of self-loathing that swirled around her. "What you still doing out here?"

She lifted the camera bag. "My job."

Lucille studied her for a full minute. Renny really wanted to be alone, but it felt rude to tell the woman who'd baked her lemon cookies to get lost.

"You ought not get too far down the road, baby. Outta sight is outta mind," Lucille said, jabbing her finger at her.

"I gather you're talking about more than walking over to my car?"

"You gather right."

"No offense, Ms. Lucille, but what you're talking about can't happen because Darby and I are water under the bridge. Darby doesn't know what he wants in life, and I don't feel like being a casualty of his confusion. I've been there and done that ten years ago."

"Mmm-mmm-mmm." Lucille tsked, shaking her head. "I guess I never saw you as someone who'd just give up."

"Give up what? There's nothing to give up. Darby has a plan and it doesn't include Louisiana or me. The sooner everyone accepts that, the easier it will be."

"You've changed, but I'm still betting on the girl who used to climb that tree outside that window just so she could spend an extra hour with her boyfriend. You was a determined child, and you loved that boy."

"That was a long time ago."

Lucille smiled and lifted her eyebrows. "Well, as they say the heart don't lie."

"I thought it was the hips," Renny quipped, starting toward her car.

Lucille's car crept right beside her. "They don't lie either, and my old eyes might be failing me in reading the good book, but they ain't missed what I seen when you two first come in the house today. Like peas and carrots again. That's what I do know."

"I hate peas and carrots," Renny responded, kicking a stone into the brush.

Lucille's cackle was the last thing she heard as the Dufrene housekeeper drove away with a wave.

"Nosy old woman."

Renny climbed into her car, stashed her camera and made like a cockroach when the lights came on. She ran for her hidey-hole, speeding down the road festooned with golden patterns of soft sunlight.

On the surface, it was a calm fall day.

But inside, Renny's heart ached, her stomach knotted and her brain juggled all the happenings of the day.

"Things really can't get any worse," she said out loud as she turned onto the highway and headed toward her house. And that's when her car died.

"What the hell?" She steered to the shoulder of highway. The car came to a halt in a lonely stretch on the highway as her gaze landed on the gas gauge.

"You've got to be kidding me," she screamed at the big E her needle had dipped past. The irony didn't escape her. After watching Shelby slobber all over Darby, eating pie that should have been golden but tasted like cardboard and signing the waiver for her divorce, she'd flippin' run out of gas.

Yeah, she knew what rock bottom felt like.

Renny leaned her head against the steering wheel and refused to lose it again.

Instead she picked up her phone and dialed the one person she knew she could count on—even if it meant hearing *I told you so.*

Yep. Rock frickin' bottom.

"So I CALLED THE AIRPORT and can't get a flight out until Friday evening," Shelby said as she passed the hot water corn bread to his mother without taking any. Darby knew Shelby was very particular about her food, electing to eat mostly organic with very little red meat. When Lucille had gotten back from town with groceries, she'd fried deer steak, pairing it with rice and gravy and purple hull peas cooked in salted pork. It was very Southern and a gift from the housekeeper who'd known his favorite foods since he'd first gnawed on a teething biscuit.

"You're welcome to stay with us until then. No need to keep your room at the bed-and-breakfast," Picou said, setting the platter in the center of the table.

"Actually, I'd be more comfortable staying in town,

though I do appreciate the invitation to dinner." Shelby set her fork down and straightened the napkin in her lap.

He knew she was uncomfortable, but didn't know how to make her feel any better about the situation. Even after their earlier conversation, things felt strained and he doubted it would ever be any better.

He'd wanted nothing more than to run away, sans Shelby, but he knew he owed the woman he'd been dating an explanation. And maybe rehashing the details would help him figure out exactly what he was explaining. Everything had gone to hell in a handbasket—which was an odd saying—but that's where he was. Watching his life go to hell.

So after Renny had driven away with a squeal of tires, he'd asked Shelby to take a ride with him, for no other reason than he didn't want to have the conversation anywhere near his mother.

For the first ten minutes or so, Shelby had been silent, but after he'd taken her into Bayou Bridge, she'd perked up and asked a few questions about the two bridges spanning the bayou and the charming storefronts lining the streets. He'd pulled in and parked in front of Scoops and Lattes, thankfully avoiding the after-school crowd, and treated Shelby to the one good thing he could give her at the moment—an ice-cream cone.

He started at the beginning with his finding the marriage certificate, while Shelby licked her ice-cream cone like a woman who really liked mint chocolate chip. Or a woman drowning her sorrows in high-calorie therapy.

Shelby wrinkled her nose. "So you're saying this boat captain was an ordained minister? That's incredible bad luck."

Or not.

After all, if "Rev" hadn't been a legit minister, Darby

wouldn't have had reason to seek Renny out again. That wasn't bad luck. It was karma, or something like that. "Yeah, so we're legally married."

Shelby put both elbows on the table and contemplated her cone. "So, this is why you're confused? Why you canceled the interview at my father's firm?"

"How could I move on to a new life when I still had an old one to deal with?"

She shrugged. "Why didn't you tell me in the first place? Wouldn't that have been easier?"

She had a point, but how does a guy tell the girl he's been seeing that he has a wife, and what's more, he was falling back in love with her? "I don't know."

"So you're getting a divorce. That's not that complicated, and you've had success with your sister, right? I'd say things are looking good for you, so why are you putting me off?" Shelby laid her cone in the empty dish he'd set aside. Her blue eyes seemed to peer into his, probing for the answer she wanted.

"Ever since I came home to Bayou Bridge, things haven't gone the way I planned. For one thing I didn't expect to feel anything for Renny."

"But you do?"

Moment of truth. "Yeah, I do."

"Well, our minds are tricky. They make us believe all kinds of things are possible when they're not."

"They do, but our hearts are ten times harder to decipher."

"Your heart?" Her mouth twisted. "I think I see where this is going."

He shook his head and glanced away. He was fairly certain if he led with *It's me, not you,* she'd upend her unfinished ice cream on his head. Even if it were the truth.

"I could give you platitudes, but what it boils down to is I left my heart here in Bayou Bridge," he said.

Shelby swallowed and he saw the raw pain in her eyes before she shifted her gaze to the front of the shop. "Well, at least you're speaking honestly to me."

"Well, I got nothing left but honesty sitting right alongside uncertainty."

"About me?"

He shook his head. "No, not about you. I wanted to make things with you work because you're beautiful, accomplished, and fun to be with. My head chose you and Seattle with this whole idea of a clean slate. But what my head didn't realize is my heart had chosen a road long ago. A road that led me here. To home. I just never realized it."

"But you were a kid," she said, spreading her hands apart. "How can you trust what you felt when you were eighteen? When I was eighteen, I tried out for *American Idol* wearing a Carmen Miranda costume. We're nuts when we're eighteen." Something in her expression shifted and he'd have sworn recalling when she was eighteen meant more than a silly costume.

"Carmen Miranda, huh?"

"Seriously. I thought I could sing. Randy Jackson destroyed the dream quickly, though Paula liked my fruit bowl."

He actually laughed. He was in the middle of purgatory and Shelby was making him laugh. This woman would make some man truly happy one day—he just wasn't that man.

"So you want me to go?" she asked quietly.

"You just got here."

"I already feel like an idiot. I don't need salt in the wound."

He nodded. "You do what you wish. I hope you'll always consider me a friend, and there is no one at Beau Soleil who would make you feel like an idiot. That's not the way we're wired."

"That's what I always liked about you. You have this sincerity that radiates off you. Too bad you're not in love with me."

"Things would be so much easier if I were. You're an awesome girl—everything a man could want. But—"

"You're in love with your wife."

Darby averted his gaze because admitting it felt too naked. "Maybe. I don't know. Everything's been so confusing, and not just for me. Renny's world got tipped upside down when I walked back into it last week and she's trying to figure all this out herself."

"She's a lucky girl even if she doesn't know it. Now, I think it's time for my exit." Shelby shoved her chair back and scooped up her purse, one of those expensive ones he'd seen in boutique windows with huge price tags dangling, and glanced down at him. "Unless there's anything else?"

The silence sat between them like a pregnant sow.

"I'm sorry."

Tossing her blond hair over her shoulder, she gave him a mysterious smile. "So am I. I had thought… Well, you were good on paper. I tried."

Shelby seemed to be talking more to herself than to him, and some prickling awareness penetrated the fog in his head. "Wait a sec, you're not really all that upset about this. Were you trying to make me fit?"

"I've been trying to find my way, too. That's what the teaching assignment and Spain were all about. Avoidance of things better left behind. Somehow, when you were so interested in me and Seattle, it felt like this was meant to be, like you might help me get over some of my past mistakes. I thought if I took you home, you might fix… Uh, you know what? I don't really want to talk about it."

He had no idea what Shelby was talking about, but it sounded as if she had her own motivations behind pursuing him. And somehow knowing she'd also tried to force a relationship made him feel better about dumping her.

Dumping her. Hmm. Not a nice euphemism for choosing another path. But either way it was what it was.

"We're good?" he inquired, scared of the answer.

She nodded. "As good as it gets right now."

And so they'd climbed back in his car, come back to Beau Soleil with a tentative peace between them. He knew Shelby felt raw from their conversation, but was glad she'd accepted his mother's invitation to a home-cooked meal.

Dinner that night was just him, Shelby and Picou. His brother and sister-in-law had gone to a friend's house for a cookout. Would have been easier if Nate, Annie and little Pax had dined with them. More boisterous, less awkward. But they were doing okay.

"I've heard so much about Louisiana that I've decided to spend tomorrow and Friday driving around the area and experiencing the culture. I saw they have a place nearby where you can dance to Cajun music, and I've never been to New Orleans or even Baton Rouge." Shelby said, taking a bite of the peas. "Mmm, these are good."

"Salt pork flavors them up," Picou said. Shelby set her fork down and studied the peas.

"You know, Darby's sister, Della, is coming and it

would be fun to go to Mulates. Why don't we plan to meet there when she gets in?" Picou asked, offering Shelby another piece of hot water corn bread.

Shelby waved the plate off. "Tomorrow I'm touring some nearby plantations. Oak Alley doesn't seem too far, and then there are many more along the river, but I can make it back this way by dinnertime."

His mother clapped her hands. "You'll love Oak Alley, and touring plantations is so interesting."

"But isn't your house a plantation?" Shelby asked.

"Technically, yes and no," Picou said, taking a sip of wine. "It's the right size and architecture, but was never used as a plantation. My ancestors were in shipping, not agriculture, though there was some sharecropping, I'm sure. Oh, and my great-grandfather tried to grow rice, but the land wasn't as fit as it is west of Lafayette and it never did well."

"Oh." Shelby said, refilling her wineglass. A nice flush had settled on her cheeks and she seemed to be warming up to his mother. At least something would come of her trip to Louisiana.

"Now, dear, tell me about your hometown."

Darby ate mindlessly as his mother and Shelby discussed the West Coast and the coastline. Seemed his mother knew an awful lot about Washington State.

All afternoon, when he'd had time to think, his mind turned round and round the conversation he'd had with Renny. Her words had sliced him. *We're not meant to be.*

The hell they weren't.

Wasn't that what he'd found out over the past few days? That was the main reason he'd suggested dating—to give them both time to adjust to what was absolutely true. So why didn't Renny already know they were meant to be?

No good answer. And what if she were right?

What if they loved each other, but it wasn't enough?

The doorbell rang just as Picou cut into the apple-walnut cobbler, ripping Darby from his thoughts.

"Oh, goodness," Picou said, setting the silver thing she used to scoop cobbler on her plate. "I wonder who that could be?"

"I'll get it," Darby said, fully expecting Renny to be standing on the porch, ready to fight for her man.

But it wasn't Renny.

It was Della, holding a bag and carrying a bakery box.

"Darby," she said, giving him a nervous smile. "I know I said I'd be here tomorrow, but something told me today would be better."

He took her bag, amazed he felt relief just by seeing the sister he hadn't known in over twenty-six years standing on the welcome mat. "I think there could be something to this twin thing. It's been a rough day."

"Really?" she said, stepping into the foyer and looking around. Like she was afraid their mother might jump out and chain her to the banister.

"Glad to see you," he said, dropping her bag at the foot of the stairs.

"Glad to see you, too," she smiled, rising on tiptoe to give him a brief hug

He jerked his head toward the dining room. "I'm living in a soap opera—a Southern-fried soap opera—with a secret—"

"Darby, who's at the door?" Picou was heading for the foyer and Darby felt his sister brace herself. "Oh!"

His mother stopped in the middle of the foyer, lifting

her hands before dropping them to her side. She looked shell-shocked, hungry and hopeful all at the same time. Her eyes ate Della up, but she didn't make a move toward her daughter.

"Hi," Della said, walking toward their mother, holding the bakery box like a shield. He knew they hadn't spoken at all since Enola Cheramie's funeral, which had been almost a year ago. Della had refused all contact, ignoring the family that she'd tumbled into like a hatchling felled from the safety of her nest. "I brought some bread from Boudreaux's Bakery. I know you liked it last time."

His mother took the box, but didn't make a move toward his sister. "Thank you, dear. I think it's the best French loaf in the state."

For a moment, no one said anything.

Finally, Picou smiled. "I'm glad you came for a visit, Sally. It's good to see you, darling."

Della opened her mouth, but closed it as Shelby appeared in the doorway of the dining room. He stepped toward the woman who'd fallen into his world, not like a fledgling, but like a…a…salmon? He didn't really know what Shelby had come like, but it had set him sideways. "Shelby, this is my sister. My twin sister."

Della held out her hand. "Hi, I'm Della Dufrene."

He didn't miss his mother's intake of breath. Something about the way her mouth fell slightly open and her eyes widened at his sister using a name she'd never used before made his throat feel raw and achy—a feeling he hadn't felt since he'd laid that carnation boutonniere on his father's casket.

"I'm Shelby Mackey, a friend of Darby's from Spain."

"Wow, you came all the way here from Spain?" Della

asked, a smile on her lips but questions dancing in her blue eyes.

"No, Seattle." Shelby dropped Della's hand and looked at him like she wanted him to give further explanation.

Instead he gestured toward the dining room. "Why don't we have cobbler and coffee? Del, did you have dinner?"

Della shook her head. "I'd love a little something. If it's not too late?"

His sister followed Shelby back into the dining room, but his mother didn't move. She stood there, holding the bakery box, looking as if she'd won the lottery.

"Mom?"

"How did you do it?" she asked, wiping the moisture from her eyes before tears spilled down her cheeks. "She called herself 'Della.'"

He moved toward his mother and curled an arm around her. "I didn't do anything but show up. God's been working on her, and she's finally found her way."

Picou shook her head. "No, this wouldn't have happened if you hadn't gone to her. You did this."

"If you want to think that, but whether I'd gone to talk to her or not, she would have come back to you, Mama."

Picou looked at him. "Maybe it's that whooping crane."

"Whooping crane?"

"The prophecy," his mother whispered, with a reverence in her tone.

"Mom, you've got to stop with that whole mambo thing. Even if there's a 'big bird' on the property. Come on. You're realistic enough to realize that the bird is a fluke. Now, let's go have that cobbler."

Picou smiled. "Let's do that."

He watched his mother walk back into the dining room with lightness to her step, and his heart warmed at the thought of his mother's happiness. Sure, they had some gaps to bridge with his sister, but they were on the right road—the road that led back to Bayou Bridge and the yellow house where his family had lived, loved and laughed for over a hundred and fifty years.

Yes, on the right road with Della.

But what about him?

He'd thought when Renny calmed down she'd come to him.

Maybe she would.

He'd give her some time, but if his blackberry girl had gotten turned around, she might need a nudge in the right direction.

CHAPTER SIXTEEN

RENNY KEPT HER EYES STRAIGHT ahead as her mother pulled onto the highway and headed toward the nearest gas station. Why had she called her mother and not AAA? Maybe she needed something concrete to grab hold of or maybe she wanted to bash Darby or maybe she wanted to continue the fight. She wasn't sure. All she knew at the moment was she felt like a wayward teenager who'd been busted for doing something absolutely boneheaded.

And that's because she *had* done something absolutely boneheaded. Like fall in love with her soon-to-be ex-husband who had a girlfriend and a new life thousands of miles away.

But she was no longer going to think about the man she'd left behind at Beau Soleil.

The man she left behind. Period.

"I suppose I shouldn't ask, but since I'm your mother—"

"Then don't," Renny said, setting the bag with the camera between her feet and fastening her seat belt. Her mother's car smelled like leather and perfume. She rolled down the window.

Bev delivered a wry laugh. "Oh, Ren, this is about more than gasoline. I can read your face like a novel. You went and did it again, didn't you?"

"What are you talking about? I came out to sign the

papers and take the stupid pictures of that stupid bird." Her throat ached with tears that threatened to make another appearance. Something about having Bev close made her want to both curl up in her mother's lap and pour forth all her disappointment and open the door of the moving car ready to tuck and roll.

"Mmm," her mother said, winding through the dense woodlands that covered the ten miles into Bayou Bridge. Bev looked over at her. "I *am* your mother."

What did she want Renny to say. "So?"

"So I know you. I know your body language. Your facial expressions. I see through those pretty brown eyes into your mind and heart. So you can't really hide from me, darling."

"You sound just like that crazy hack Picou Dufrene with her prophecies and ghosts, which by the way aren't ghosts. Giving birth doesn't give you insight."

"And you would know this how?" Bev smirked with that know-it-all-mom lift of the brows.

Renny snapped her mouth shut because she didn't know, and at the rate she "didn't" progress through relationships, her ovaries would be prunes by the time she found a man to procreate with. Not that she even wanted children. Or a man. Much.

Her mother turned the knob on the dashboard, and the sound of the Supremes and their declarations about hearing symphonies died. Then Bev pushed gem-studded sunglasses on her nose that blocked the blinding sunset. "If I had a small fortune, and I do, I would bet it all on the notion you've jumped back into bed with Darby, and not only that, but you've opened yourself up for heartbreak. Again."

"Oh, yeah?" Like Renny was going to admit history had repeated itself. No flippin' way.

"I know this because you're a lot like me," her mother said, sliding a glance at Renny she couldn't read because the glasses covered half her mother's face. She only knew Bev looked at her from the way her head tilted like a dog.

"So you've already said."

"But not in the way you dress, obviously."

Well, that sounded disapproving.

Renny glanced at what her mother wore. The silk pants alone would cost a week's salary and the bright magenta sweater had gold grommets around the neck. She looked like Marilyn Monroe mated with a Greek bazillionaire and had a baby Bev. No, not alike in their fashion choices. At all.

She'd never thought them alike in any other way. Yet, they both seemed to have made poor choices in the romance department. And they both had overcome adversity, molding misery into success. Both of them had vested much of themselves into a career, holding their hearts back for fear of being trampled.

So, maybe her mother was right.

They were alike.

Bev picked up the conversation. "Your father always held that same power over me. He smiled and I melted like chocolate on a summer's day. Whatever he suggested we do sounded like the best plan ever. I had no will when it came to him, and it left me in a bad place. Now I'm not saying Darby is—"

"He's not like my father. Darby may have a smile that melts Popsicles in an Arctic storm, but that doesn't mean he isn't a good man. He's changed." In some ways. In others he was still the same. Darby got what he wanted. He'd wanted her and she'd rolled over like a dog in heat.

"Says the girl still in love with him."

The hurt of the afternoon faded and was replaced by anger. "All of this is your fault, Mother."

"How? I told you to stay away from him."

Renny shook her head. "No, years ago. If you wouldn't have tried to control me, control the world around you—"

"You what? Would have become a successful biologist? Become an independent woman of means? Liked yourself?"

Renny glared at her mother. "You assume I would have been worse off than I am now. What if I were better because of him?"

"I won't apologize for what I did years ago. I saved you."

"Saved me? Really?" Renny shook her head. "No, you taught me not to trust a man. A whole life of 'a man will do you wrong' played on your stereo until I believed it. You are the reason I didn't fight for Darby all those years ago. You made me believe he was just like Dad—that he had left me, too."

Her mother's lips pressed into a thin Palace Pink line. "You're placing all the blame on my shoulders just because he didn't fight for you. Because you didn't fight for him."

"We may have worked. We might be two kids into a happy marriage right now."

"Or hating each other," Bev said. "Which one is more likely? Sometimes you have to step in to protect people from themselves. I wish I would have had someone to stop me when it came to your father."

"Aaron proposed, didn't he?" Renny slammed back against the seat, changing the subject because she knew what her mother had to say about her father. Second verse same as the first. "Did you say yes?"

"I don't wish to be married."

"Why? You say you love Aaron. You're happy when you're with him. He makes you laugh, he makes you—"

"Because I don't want to, that's why," her mother said, gripping the steering wheel hard, pushing her French-tipped nails into the leather. "And we're not talking about me. We're talking about you."

"One and the same according to you. You don't trust, and you've taught me the same. You expect to get shit on, and therefore, I've spent my whole life looking up and ducking under eaves."

"Why are you making this about me?" Bev said, passing a slower car, whipping around with little regard for safety.

"Slow down."

Her mother shook her head. "This is what you do to me. Make me so mad I can't function."

"I'm not trying to make you mad, but you picked me up expecting to rub salt into my wounds, wanting to wag your finger and say *I told you so*. It's not what I wanted or needed to hear, but you did it anyway."

"That was not my intent. I had no intention of berating your actions, so you can just stop painting me as the worst mother to ever breathe the air around her daughter."

Renny took a deep breath and tried to gather her thoughts. Pain echoed in Bev's last statement, and the woman was right—this wasn't about her. Much. It was more about Renny reacting to the hurt she'd been struck with back in Picou's sitting room. She looked to strike out at someone and her mother was a safe option. Probably why she'd called Bev in the first place. "Fine. It wasn't your intent, but it didn't stop you from doing it."

"It's just I love you and I can't stand for you to be hurt."

"I know."

"Maybe some of your hang-ups are my fault. I didn't do very well after your father left, didn't trust anyone other than myself. That led to success, but I think you're right—it's unhealthy to distrust people, to jump to conclusions about every man's intentions. Look at Aaron. His have always been good."

Renny nearly leaned over and pinched her mother to make sure the woman was real and not some alien cloaked in Bev Latioles's clothes. Her mother admitting to being wrong? To being judgmental and untrusting? Was this possible?

"Aaron's a good man, and he loves you."

"And he proposed to me."

"So you said?"

Her mother took a deep breath. "That I'd think about it."

"That's actually progress," Renny said, staring out at the passing scenery.

"And Darby?"

Her mother's question sat for a full minute like a big, fat elephant in the luxury sedan.

"I'm done with Darby," Renny said finally.

"Are you?"

"I've never had the best judgment when he was around. He's like the magic man in that Heart song. I don't seem to have much control when he plies his charm. I had thought things could be different. We're adults now. But Darby's not in the place he needs to be…and I'm not sure I want to wait on him to get there. Sometimes love isn't meant to be."

Bev nodded. "Sometimes it's not enough. Wasn't for me and your father. I loved that man. Hell, if he came back crawling on his knees, I don't trust myself not to drop to mine and meet him halfway. Some relationships, no matter what the heart wants, aren't healthy for either person."

Her mother's words felt like frigid ice water down Renny's back. She wanted to disagree. Love was supposed to conquer all. Not suffer under selfish want and need. Not smother under misdirection and misplaced intent.

Renny chewed on those thoughts as the car ate the miles of road winding through the flat wetlands. Finally, her mother pulled into a gas station.

"Will you be okay?" Bev asked as Renny grabbed her bag and opened the car door.

"Guess I'll have to be, won't I? Life never has stopped because a gal got her heart broke."

Bev shook her head. "Baby, if I could stop it—"

"You would. I know. I can always count on you to shoot me straight and pick me up when I take a face plant. That's what moms are for, right?"

"Something like that," her mom said, shifting into Park and giving her a slight smile. "Never easy watching your child fall down."

"I should have looked where I was headed." Renny sighed and closed the door.

DARBY WATCHED AS A MAN with a mustache wearing too-tight jeans whirled a laughing Shelby around the dance floor at Mulates, the quintessential standby in Cajun food and fun. His mother and sister sat at the table with him, watching the blonde act like she'd been born to two-step to a Cajun zydeco band. He hadn't realized Shelby was such a good dancer.

"She's actually pretty nice," Picou muttered, raising a pint of dark beer to her lips.

"You sound surprised," Della said, eyeing Shelby.

"She is. She expected to hate Shelby," Darby said. They'd already eaten, and after moaning in delight over the red beans and rice, Shelby had declared she wanted to dance. When Darby hadn't jumped right up and offered, she'd turned to the man at the next table and crooked a finger. That was all it took.

"I did not," Picou said, shaking her head. "I admit to having reservations about her, but I can be wrong."

Darby faked a heart attack, giving such a dramatic performance it caused Della to laugh until she snorted tea up her nose.

"See what you did?" His mother gave him the stink eye before thumping Della on the back.

"I'm good," Della coughed, waving her hands.

"Actually, Shelby reminded me of you," Darby said, hoisting his own half-filled glass and making a mocking toast. "Charming and bullheaded. Hard to admit being drawn to a woman because she's like your mother."

Della snorted again but, thankfully, not her iced tea. Della's responses must have pleased Picou because she finally smiled. "Nothing wrong with wanting a woman who's like your mother."

"Says my mother," Darby drawled. "Besides, Shelby and I are friends and that's where we'll stay. She's not my choice."

"Who says you get to choose?" Della asked, scooping a half-eaten hush puppy off the plate in front of her and popping it into her mouth. "Men always think they make the decision. Shelby looks capable of having who she wants. You make her sound like a booby prize."

Darby eyed his sister. "I'd never treat her that way."

One of the men at the next table tapped Della on the shoulder, arching a brow and jerking his head toward the dance floor. He wore a Univeristy of Louisiana–Baton Rouge Panthers shirt and Darby inferred the men were traveling to take in a Panthers game in Baton Rouge the next day.

"Sure," she breathed, looking as if she'd rather not dance, but she rose, leaving Darby with his mother and a table full of half-empty plates.

"I can't believe how relaxed she is," his mother said.

"Who? Della or Shelby?"

Picou looped her long hair behind her ears. For once, his mother dressed normally. Well, normal for her— jeans and a simple blouse. "Your sister. I think she's finally at peace with who she is."

He watched as Della moved gracefully and competently around the dance floor, giving instruction to the man who obviously hadn't much experience in dancing. "You may be right."

"Now, if we could only get you in that same spot," his mother said. "You belong here. Not in Seattle. But I want you to be happy, Darby."

"Guess I fell right into your trap, didn't I?"

"I never set a trap. Didn't have to. You had things waiting here for you, and now you're trying to use your head to make a decision that should be made by your heart."

"I'm trying, Mom, but I wonder if I'm screwing things up. I had a plan, a good plan, to go to Seattle and start a new life. And look at Shelby." He jabbed a finger at the woman who'd thrown herself into the dancing with a reckless abandon he'd never seen before. "She's a great woman. I could be tossing the baby out with the bathwater all because I've got the hots for a woman who's now so pissed at me she won't speak to me."

"Renny's got Cajun blood in those veins. Blowing things out of proportion is in her nature, even if she's a scientist with charts, graphs and logic. She'll settle down. Give her time." His mother motioned a waiter over and ordered another pint, then looked at him. "You'll have to drive tonight."

"I drove us here, didn't I?"

"Well, I like to be a responsible citizen…when I can."

He almost laughed, but the effort seemed too much. Again, he'd been flipped upside down when Shelby had shown up and Renny had blown up. All the steps he'd made toward Renny felt shaky, and since she'd not darkened his doorstep, ready to fight for him, he'd taken to doubting everything he felt.

"I want to tell you something I've not told a soul before," his mother said, accepting the beer from the waiter and moving her chair closer to him.

Darby quirked a brow. "Is it another ghost story?"

"In a way."

The song ended, but neither Della nor Shelby came back to the table. Perhaps they'd sensed his mother's wishes. Or maybe his frown kept them on the floor for another riotous stomping of the boards.

His mother didn't speak for a moment. Instead she seemed to be gathering her thoughts, preparing herself. "When I was a girl, at the end of my freshman year of college, I fell in love."

"I know the story."

"It wasn't with your father."

He leaned forward and placed his elbows on the scarred table. "Not Dad?"

"No. I went home on semester break with my roommate, Patty Greer, to her family home in Monroe. She was such a fun girl with the prettiest teeth. Of course, her daddy was a dentist so that explained her beautiful smile. So, anyway, she had an older brother, Gerald, who went to school on the East Coast. He was home on break, too, and the moment I saw him, I fell for him. He was not classically handsome like your father, but more of a rough-around-the-edges Humphrey Bogart sort, and for a whole week, we acted like lovesick fools. In fact, poor Patty got put out with me because I spent every waking second with her brother instead of her. She'd planned several outings, but I skipped them all. Ran wild with that boy all over Ouachita Parish. We went skinny-dipping, visited juke joints and drove all the way to Jackson, Mississippi, to see some drag races."

"This explains a lot, Mom."

His mother laughed, and in that instant he saw the heart of that eighteen-year-old girl. "Okay, you got your wild streak from me. Your father wouldn't have been caught dead naked in a fishing hole."

She took another sip of the beer. "And I loved Gerald. Thought I'd found everything love was supposed to be right in those green eyes. At the end of the week, it came time for me to come back to Beau Soleil for Christmas, and for the first time in my life, I didn't want to come home. But my daddy drove up in his new big-fin Caddy and loaded my suitcase in his trunk. I made up a story about leaving something behind and ran around the back of the house to where Gerald sat in his convertible waiting for me to elope with him."

She paused dramatically.

"But I couldn't do it."

For a moment, Picou closed her eyes as if the light in the restaurant was too much for her. But he knew it wasn't the light, it was the memories that overwhelmed her. Finally, she opened them, and inside he could see the regret and the sheen of tears.

"I wasn't strong enough to go against my daddy, to leave all I knew behind for Gerald. Just like I wasn't strong enough to go against your daddy. Not fighting for myself, my wants and needs, is something I've hated in myself for a long time. It's why I have claimed myself these past years since your father died. I'm never going back to being someone who lives to please others and not herself."

He'd never thought about his mother and the choices she'd faced in life. For some reason, children rarely saw their parents as anything other than the role they'd forced them into the day they drew their first breath.

"Well, it doesn't really matter now," his mother said, staring at the bottom of her empty glass. "My life has been very, very good, but I always had this piece of me that regretted not jumping in Gerald's car and following my heart."

"Why are you telling me this?" he asked.

"Because I got a little taste of what you're feeling that day as I stood on a concrete paver on the side of that farmhouse staring at Gerald waiting for me. It was a moment I will never forget. I chose to follow my head, and do what I thought everyone expected of me. To do what was reasonable."

She moved even closer, taking his hand. "Darby, everyone says you're most like me, and I guess you are. Whatever direction you go, sweetheart, I'll stand by you. But I want you to know it's okay to follow your heart. There are no guarantees in life, but it's not much fun living with regret."

He curled his fingers around hers. "So you wish you would have gone with Gerald?"

"If I had gone with him, there would be no Nate, Abram, Della and Darby, so, no. I can't regret the life I've made, but that doesn't mean I don't wish sometimes I would've chosen love over duty. Passion over principle."

She released his hand, shoved her chair back and tugged him by his elbow. "Enough talk of choices. I want to dance. The good Lord knows I don't have many more years left to cut a rug, so indulge me."

"I'm not great at dancing, so—"

"Oh, for heaven's sake, Darby, you don't learn how to live by watching. You learn how to live by doing. Let's go."

So he did, wondering how his mother always knew how to unstick him. Her words were like aloe vera on a burn—soothing and certain to bring relief. He needed to spend time analyzing his mother's words, but not now. Sometimes life called for doing—even if a guy may end up looking a fool.

Which he most certainly would on the dance floor of Mulates.

CHAPTER SEVENTEEN

RENNY STARED AT THE TRACKING band in her hand.

Damn it all to hell.

L9-10 was off the radar. Carrie had called her that morning and insisted she head out to Beau Soleil and check on the whooper. L9-10 had been stationary for over twenty-four hours—which wasn't good. Renny had planned on calling in sick because sappy movies and macaroni and cheese sounded like balm for her heart, but as the project manager she had no choice but to hitch up her pants, slide into her rubber galoshes and head to the battlefield.

She pocketed the expensive tracking device and looked for evidence of a struggle. She didn't see any scattered feathers lying snowy against the dank grass, so she started around the perimeter of the area, resigned to taking the time necessary to find the bird.

Was Picou still feeding the crane?

If so, the older woman could give her the particulars on when she'd last seen the bird, but Renny could think of nothing worse than going to Beau Soleil and seeking out Picou.

"Renny?"

Darby's voice jarred her from her deep thoughts and brought her back to full-fledged heartbreak.

She spun and crossed her arms. "What are you doing here?"

"I live here."

"No, you don't. Your mother does."

He looked big, gorgeous and determined. Her heart stutter-stepped, but she pulled her anger back into place. No longer would she take any chances on this man. Her mother had been right. Sometimes even love wasn't enough. And deep in her bones, Renny knew Darby didn't love her enough to make it work between them. Somehow, that had sunk into her consciousness and settled in, ready to battle her if she thought differently. Probably a defense mechanism or some weakness in her inner psyche.

She wanted to believe differently, but... She wasn't going to rehash her insecurities or her broken heart. She had work to do. And she needed Darby out of her world.

"Technicality," he said, slogging toward her in his own pair of waders. "But this is my land."

She didn't say anything further, merely watched as he approached.

"Why are you out here so early?" he asked, looking around.

"It's department business and doesn't concern the landowner." She turned away, scanning the area because she felt unsure. Maybe slightly unsafe. Darby's charming, good ol' boy demeanor had been replaced by the hard-nosed navy lawyer, and he looked plenty peeved. Gone was the smile, the flirty eyes, the rolling gait. In place was the hardened jaw, flinty eyes and erect posture. Here was a man who wasn't taking crap from anyone, much less her.

"Actually you here in this field does concern me."

"Fine. If you must know, the whooping crane's tracking device came off, so now we can't locate it. Hasn't happened on this project yet and we were hoping to keep tabs on the birds for longer than a few months. We need the data so that we can get more funding and bring more birds down to winter."

"You think it left the area?"

She shrugged. "Not sure. Could have met with a predator. In fact, I was combing the area looking for evidence of an attack."

"I'll help."

She shook her head. "It's not your concern."

"Everything about you is my concern. Legally, you're still my wife."

"Technicality," she said, echoing his words and not liking the possessive tone he'd taken.

He nodded. "But that's your decision, not mine."

Something twisted in her stomach. "Yeah, it *is* my decision. One that had to be made. I tired of pussyfooting around looking for a good place to land."

"Why are you doing this to us, Renny?"

Doing what? Protecting herself? Trying to gain back some measure of control over her life? How was it wrong to resist throwing all she was away just on a hunch? "I'm not doing anything you wouldn't have done in my same position, Darby."

"I don't follow."

"You have choices. You have options, options that you kept open, I might add. It was very simple for you to suggest rolling the dice on a relationship between us because if you got hurt or decided things weren't working, you'd be on the next flight out of Bayou Bridge. Clean slate, remember? You had a job, a wife and a new life all lined up waiting on you. But me? I'd still be here. Nothing new and wonderful for me."

"So you storm off and end all hope of us because you're chicken? Because you think I could cut my losses here and pick up with Shelby without a beat? That's what you truly think of me?"

She needed a moment to think about that accusation. He made her sound flighty and foolish for wanting to play it safe. "You're making it sound like I'm afraid, and I am. Last time you left me behind, it hurt, and I've been protecting myself ever since. It may be wrong—"

"Yeah, it is. The Renny I knew wouldn't hide behind past mistakes. She embraced life and lived it without reservations. You're right in saying that you've changed. And frankly, I don't much like the woman you've become."

"Good. Then leave me alone."

"Doesn't work like that, Renny. I'm not running from you. I'm not letting you fade back into some shadow of yourself because you might fall down and get a boo-boo." He moved toward her, crowding her space, forcing her to look up at him. "I love you too much to just give up on you."

Her heart sounded in her ears and she knew that if this were a movie, this was the moment she surrendered to Darby, giving herself to him, claiming their happy ever after.

But this wasn't a Lifetime Original movie.

And she wasn't going to fall into his arms just because he'd made up his mind to love her.

He stared at her, awaiting her answer. She stepped back from him, giving herself some space, realizing at that moment space had been what she'd been lacking all along.

"Are you going to say anything?" he asked.

She held up a hand and closed her eyes. "Part of me wants to jump into your arms and tell you I love you too."

Darby stretched his arms out and arched an eyebrow. For a moment, she almost smiled. He looked so good, freshly shaven, so solid, so delicious. But she shrugged that inclination off and shook her head. "Part of me does, but the other part needs some time."

"Time?"

"You came back into my life the way you first entered it—blazing across a field, cocky and confident about what you want. You use your charm like a weapon, disarming anyone in your path. And then you push. You push and push and push past any barriers anyone throws up against you."

"You make me sound like the Nazis. Blitzkrieg." His words were dry. Sarcastic.

Renny shrugged. "Not evil, just determined. You don't take no for an answer, and that's how it's always been between us. You don't ask, you do, cajoling and applying pressure until I roll over and give in."

"But you benefit when you roll over and give in to me. You can't pretend you don't derive pleasure from—" His words sounded silky.

"Really? We're in the middle of a bog and your girlfriend is less than a mile that way." She pointed toward Beau Soleil.

He blinked. "Sorry. She's not my girlfriend. Besides, she flew out this morning. And there's always fire between us no matter where we are."

She pressed her lips together and gave him her own eyebrow arch. "Sure. We're tip-top full-on passion, but here's the deal, you don't get to decide. I do."

"Decide what?"

"Decide whether or not we go forward. You want me? Great. You love me? Spectacular. But maybe I don't want you."

For a moment his sharky-attorney facade cracked, but he pulled it right back in place. "So you don't want me? You don't feel anything toward me but what, pity?"

"No, that's not what I meant. Do I love you? Probably. I don't think I ever stopped, but the chief question that's been floating around since I climbed into your pickup truck twelve years ago—are you good for me?"

He opened his mouth just as she jabbed a finger at him. He closed it.

"I decide."

"You decide," he stated, narrowing his eyes and shaking his head. She realized not many people ever told Darby Dufrene no. He probably didn't understand the concept, but at that moment she wanted him to give her space and not force a decision about their future.

"And honestly, the way I feel right now, you should forget about good ol' comfy pants Renny Latioles. I don't want to be your consolation prize or your safety net. I don't want to be your faithful companion who will heel when you tell her to heel, or fetch when you tell her to fetch or sit—" Renny sighed. "That's it. Done. You can go now and stop bulldozing yourself into my life like you know what's best for me. Because you don't."

"You don't mean that."

"Don't tell me what I mean. For once in my life, Darby, let me decide who I will love without coercion. Without using those damn blue eyes and your sneaky sexy smile to color my judgment."

"God, Renny." He stepped back with his hands turned out. No longer did he have that hard lawyerly look. He looked like she'd conked him in the head with a crowbar. Like he'd never imagined Renny Latioles would tell him no.

"Right now I can't have you in my life. Not until I'm

sure of a few things, and one of those things is who I need to be. Two people in a relationship should be equals. I've never had that with you because you never let me choose you."

"That doesn't make sense. We've always been good together. We've—"

"But always on your terms. You made all the decisions. You chose me, like you graced me with good fortune. And for the past week, it's felt the same. You strung me along all week, pushing past my armor, worming your way back into my heart, and then a girlfriend shows up. I felt like I was on *The Bachelor*. I thought maybe Picou had a hot tub installed out back."

"You make me sound dastardly for falling back in love with you. Like I did it to complicate your life. I didn't want to love you again."

Renny closed her eyes. A full ten seconds ticked by before she opened her eyes and took him in again. "Right now, I can't choose you, Darby. You have to give me room to breathe. Room to make decisions about what is right for me. It may sound foolish to you, but that's where I am. If we enter a relationship, it's going to be that fresh, clean slate you wanted—a new start between two adults who choose each other. Not some polluted dirty-laundry relationship where you run roughshod over me. You may choose me, Darby, but I'm not choosing you. Not now."

He looked shell-shocked. "I don't get it."

"Well, give yourself time to think about it. Maybe with some distance and some intentional thought, you'll see what I mean."

"So this is it? You're telling me to get lost?"

"Maybe getting lost is not a bad thing. Maybe you don't have to hop on a road, determined to walk it no matter the consequences. Perhaps you should let go and just be."

Darby propped his hands on his hips and glanced at the world breathing around him. Birds swooped and squirrels scrabbled up and down the bark of the trees behind him. Life went on even if she'd released him back into the wide world—hopefully with a different outlook on their relationship, or lack of one at the moment. "Guess there's not much left to say, Renny, other than I wish you luck in finding the whooping crane." His blue eyes were so sad that her heart wavered, but she smacked it back in line. She had to get herself straight, examine her priorities and make the best choice for her life, which meant she needed Darby to leave.

At least for a little while.

They both needed space.

She was sure her brown eyes mirrored his. "Me, too."

And then Darby walked out of her life again—a week after he'd walked back into it.

CHAPTER EIGHTEEN

One month later

DARBY WATCHED THE STREETCAR toodle by from the window of the bar on St. Charles Street as he took another sip of scotch and soda. Didn't really taste good, but he figured he needed nerves of steel for what he was about to face.

Just as he'd done nearly eleven years ago this upcoming spring, he'd placed his future in Renny's hands. Just like she wanted.

Last time he hadn't fared so well. He'd waited for over three hours before allowing hope to slip away on a rare breeze blowing through the heart of the French Quarter. He'd walked down Decatur, ignoring the people calling out for him to come in for fluorescent shots of potent crap and the titillating beads and shirts hanging in the shop windows. He'd passed by the French Market with its piles of Creole tomatoes and shiny silver bracelets and walked until he was in a rough neighborhood. He'd turned around, walked back to the Quarter, strolled into a random bar and drank until he'd puked in a back alley. No, it had not ended well.

And he had no clue if this go-around would be much better.

But he'd had to try.

He'd left it up to her.

When he'd walked away from her that warm September day, he felt like someone had pulled a rug out from under him and left him on his ass.

Renny had told him to get lost.

Take a hike.

Sent him packing.

And don't let the door hit you on the ass on the way out, buster.

It had seemed inconceivable she didn't want him. She loved him. He could see it in her eyes; in fact, she'd said as much herself. But then she'd also implied he wasn't good for her, another tidbit he couldn't wrap his mind around.

Pissed him off well and good.

He'd spent much of the weekend faking happiness, then on Sunday, he'd climbed into his little rental car, cranked up the volume on some random metal music, and done his damnedest to slake his anger on the looping curves and straightaways of the Louisiana back roads. He hadn't driven that fast since the wreck, but he didn't care. Fury burned inside him.

How dare she?

He'd finally thought he'd found his way in life then Renny nailed up a Bridge Out Ahead sign and blew up the damn road in front of him.

She would decide?

Not *we?*

Anger lashed him and he muttered all sorts of dirty words about women, Louisiana and his own dumbassery for coming home.

When the anger faded, the pain began.

Something tore inside him, rattling around his chest, out of control. Maybe that something was also armed with razor blades, because his heart felt sliced to ribbons. If he coughed, he might have spit out blood. That's what it felt like. After a near miss with a speed limit sign, Darby had pulled the car over, banged his head on the steering wheel and pretended the moistness on his face was sweat from the abnormally hot day.

God damn it all. It hurt. Again.

Renny had torn him to shreds.

And he hadn't seen it coming.

Because he'd never intended to fall back in love with her.

Once he'd driven back to Beau Soleil, he'd calmed down and entered some sort of acceptance phase. Fine. He'd go to Seattle. It was a big town and even if he had no future with Shelby, there were other women. Other women who weren't complicated and wanted some simplicity in a relationship. But then again, maybe he wouldn't bother with a woman for a while. He had a career to launch. Just like before, he would throw himself into work and allow time to heal his wounds.

But as he'd climbed the front porch of the place where he'd grown into an almost man, greeted by his smiling sister and one of Picou's famous pralines—the best thing his mom made in the kitchen—he realized he didn't want to leave Louisiana.

Renny had dumped him, but with reluctance. In fact, it seemed as if she'd pushed him away because she thought it was the right thing to do—not because she'd rejected him.

So he'd sunk into the rocker beside his sister with a big sigh.

"Well, that says a lot," Della said, drawing her long legs up and clasping them with her bare arms.

"Yeah, sums up my life for the last week."

"Never easy coming home, is it?"

He watched the wind catch the leaves on the oak trees sprawling lazily in front of the house, bordering the broad expanse of still green grass. "You would know."

"Abram and Lou left earlier. Abram wants you to call him about whatever y'all talked about. He said you'd know. I, for one, didn't bother asking. Our mother, however, pinned Abram down like a linebacker and dropped water on his forehead for a whole hour."

Darby managed a smile but said nothing.

"Don't worry. He didn't cave. So whatever he's cooking up for you is still a mysterious secret." Della stretched her hands out and wiggled her fingers.

"It's about a job in Baton Rouge. He has a lot of connections in that area, so I thought I'd look around for a firm that might need an attorney specializing in International law."

"Wow, so when Shelby left, she really left." She pushed her hair back. "You're not moving to Seattle?"

"I don't think so. I thought I'd be happy there, and who knows, maybe I would have, but I don't think it's the place for me. Coming home made me realize that."

"So you're going to live here? In Bayou Bridge."

He shook his head. "I don't know yet, but I want to be closer than Washington State. What about you?"

"Me?"

"Are you staying in Galliano?"

She stared out at the yard, popped another praline in her mouth and chewed thoughtfully. "I don't know. I love my little town and the school where I teach, but one of Grandmère's greatest wishes for me was I explore the world and not relegate myself to, as she put it, 'this backwater hellhole.' Enola started fishing when she was twelve years old, had her first baby at sixteen, and never saw beyond Lafayette. I think she only went to New Orleans once. Wanderlust was hidden beneath that tough bayou skin."

"So you want to travel?"

"Did you like living abroad?"

He shrugged. "In a way. I've never been one much for dragging a suitcase behind me. I've lived on the East Coast and overseas. Guess I got my fill—it's the main reason I left the navy. I wanted to put down roots somewhere."

"I talked to Shelby and she gave me some info on the teacher program she was part of. I may do some checking around on that, but I have time. I'll stay in Galliano to finish out the year. I still have loose ends to tie up with the Cheramie homestead. Grandmère willed it to me, and somehow that doesn't seem right. I have uncles and cousins who are blood relation who didn't get squat from Enola. Of course, some of them don't deserve squat. Just many decisions to make."

"But you will stay part of this family?"

"I changed my driver's license to my legal name."

He jerked his eyes toward her. "Big step."

"But it's time. I'm not Sally Cheramie. She was my great-aunt, a baby Enola lost when Sally was but a year old. She gave me her daughter's name and social security number, but she couldn't make me the daughter she'd lost because I already had a mama. I was already Della Dufrene, even when I didn't want to be."

Such insight from an unexpected source. Like his sister, he'd tried to deny who he was. After leaving Beau Soleil, he'd tried to erase the boy he'd been. No longer would he be the kid who trashed study guides or snuck bourbon from his daddy's liquor cabinet, but he'd be the kid who studied hard and ignored the boys tearing out of the academy on Saturday nights for a little fun. He'd chain himself to his desk, drive the speed limit, think rationally and repress the charming laissez-faire boy he'd once been. But thing was…he was still that boy. He had to own all parts of himself. He couldn't change the past, but he also didn't have to pretend he didn't love his home. That he didn't love the meandering bayou, the moss-bedecked trees and the sweet Louisiana girl he'd left behind.

Embrace who you are, Darby.

The wind whispered this message to him.

Or maybe it was Picou.

Because she was standing behind him uttering those very words.

"Mom," he said, spinning around. "How long have you been standing there?"

She shrugged. "Long enough to know you two are like cream cheese and pepper jelly. Put you two together and magic happens."

Della started laughing. "You're comparing us to an appetizer…an easy one at that?"

"Tell me you don't like dipping a cracker into cream cheese with pepper jelly poured over it. I could live on it myself. Plus it was an analogy. I didn't say it was a good one."

Another way he was like his mother. Darby pushed his rocker into motion. "I'm flying out tomorrow."

"What?" Picou stilled his rocker and held it firmly. "Don't tell me you're still trying to build a life in a place where they eat granola and make you wear Birkenstocks?"

"Mom, you have Birkenstocks."

"What does that have to do with anything?"

He had to actually think about that. "Well, if I wanted

to move to Seattle, I'd damn well go to Seattle, but as it were, I'm not moving there. Just getting my stuff sent here then taking a trip down the West Coast on my bike. After coming home and reevaluating things, I know it's not where I belong. Shelby knows it, too. We were both trying to shove our feet into shoes that weren't made for us."

His mother smiled. Big. She might as well have rubbed her hands together and drawled, *Just as I had planned.*

But she didn't. Thank God.

"So you're coming home? For good?"

"Don't get the *Star Wars* sheets out just yet."

"So does Renny know about this?" Picou asked, releasing his chair before leaning against the rail.

"Actually, this isn't about Renny."

"Renny's a touchy subject," Della said, eating another praline. "Good night, I gotta stop eating these things. I won't fit in my clothes."

Picou reached over and moved the plate closer to Della. "You could stand to gain a little."

He didn't want to talk anymore about Renny, but as he'd sat there, he felt oddly soothed by the women sitting with him on a porch over which he'd once rolled Matchbox cars. A warm sort of rightness seeped into his bones, as he thought about the way a person felt when he knew things were right.

When he found the person made for him, or in his case, rediscovered her. She never seemed to come along at the right time, but often it was in the nick of time.

Right when a man was about to make a big mistake and force something into his life not meant to be.

And a strange notion formed in his mind—a notion born from a classic movie about two people hoping love would work out, and meeting at the top of the Empire State Building. He'd fallen asleep to it playing on the TV last night. Two people caught up in circumstance, finding love and hoping it would pan out.

What if he and Renny weren't *An Affair to Remember* but were a love of a lifetime?

What if? He nearly snorted.

Nah.

They were.

Time to toss the ball into Renny's court and see if she would hit it back.

And so that's what he'd done. He'd sent her another letter—this time delivered certified because he wasn't taking a chance on his proposal not landing in her hands.

Then he'd set about recreating a new direction for himself—one that included looking for a place in between Bayou Bridge and Baton Rouge, procuring a job and winning back his wife.

The sound of two men arguing about football at the bar dragged him back to his present. He looked down at his watch. Nearly three o'clock. He should head to the Quarter or he'd be late.

He signaled for the check.

This was an appointment he didn't want to miss.

For better or worse.

DARBY STOOD BY A HUGE banana plant trying not to look like a stalker since there was a group of high school girls clad in plaid skirts and white oxfords shuffling around with a nun who kept giving him the evil eye. He pulled out his phone and pressed the ESPN app. At least he'd look like he had a purpose, rather than looking desperately at the iron gates that opened to the courtyard housing the statue of Andrew Jackson on his steed. The statue stood in the middle of the courtyard of St. Louis Cathedral, which rose magnificently from the swath of humanity milling below, an elegant testament to the toughness of the inhabitants of the Crescent City since 1720.

He struck thoughts of Louisiana history from his mind as he wondered for the hundredth time that day—would she come?

The question beat in his gut, pounding in his chest.

He scrolled through scores he'd never remember and then pocketed his phone with shaking hands.

Hell.

He couldn't believe how nervous he was. Almost anxiety-attack nervous. Of course, it felt a bit like going into battle again—when the last go-around hadn't gone so well.

He passed a woman who dragged a screaming toddler behind her. She kept saying, "Just one time for mommy? Please? Mommy wants a picture."

He knew about wanting something, too.

Hope they both got what they wanted.

Darby moved toward the statue, but it was a prime place for tourist photos so he moved away again, glancing beyond the iron gates to where horses and carriages stood awaiting fares and artists displayed their work, propped along the bricked walls and scrolled wrought iron. People moved past at fast clips with the occasional tourist poking along, head moving back and forth as he or she took in the eclectic city with its Old World crumbling buildings melded with high-tech capability.

Where was she?

He glanced at his watch. It was ten minutes past the time he'd given her in the letter he'd sent.

If you can.

Those words haunted him.

Should he have used the exact lines from the movie? Would she think it was stupid? Or desperate? Or… He had to stop overthinking everything. He glanced at his phone to see if she'd messaged him. Should he call? No. It was her decision.

Besides, just because she hadn't shown ten years before didn't mean she wouldn't come today.

An hour later, he wasn't so sure about that.

It looked pretty certain Renny had made her choice. And it wasn't him.

He'd milled around for so long, a fortune-teller took pity on him and offered him a beer out of her cooler. He'd declined, but presently wished he hadn't. He was tired, thirsty, but more than anything else, he was heartsick.

And he felt like a fool.

"You sure you don't wanna cold one, man?" The fortune-teller lifted a silver can and wiggled it. "I don't usually share, but I'll be damned if you don't look like a kicked pup."

Great. He was officially pathetic.

"Nah, I probably need something stronger."

"She stood you up, huh?"

He didn't know whether to admit his heartache or deny it. So he shrugged.

"Well, from where I'm standing that gal looks like a horse's ass. Or is it a fellow?"

"Uh, woman."

The fortune-teller nodded her head. She had curly red hair that streamed past her shoulders. Could've been a wig. She wore a black dress that had cutouts, revealing colorful tattoos. She had two small rings in her nose, and warm blue eyes that looked like they belonged to a grandmother, not a street performer. "Want me to give you a free reading? It's the least I can do."

"Oh, no thanks. Wouldn't be fair."

"Then you can pay me. Business has been slow today."

Hell. He didn't want to have his palm read, but the older woman had been nice to him—at a time where he needed someone to be nice to him.

So he walked toward her little folding table, sat down on the warped metal chair and stuck his hand out.

"Well, ain't you just a get-right-down-to-business sort of fella." She grinned, and he saw she was missing a couple of teeth, but still she had a nice smile.

She clasped his hand and he didn't feel anything.

He'd once heard there was supposed to be some kind of energy or something. But there was nothing. Maybe he was numb because Renny hadn't shown up.

Renny hadn't picked him.

The woman bent over his hand making a lot of "uh-huh" sounds along with a couple of grunts. "Well, you have a nice life line. See here?"

She dragged a red fingernail across his palm.

"This is your love line. It's very interesting."

He didn't bother looking down. He did one more sweep of the area, hoping Renny had gotten held up. Damn it, now he knew exactly how Cary Grant's character felt in the movie. He almost wished he were an artist himself, so he could lose himself angrily in his work. Pissed-off art. He and Cary Grant.

"Lots of misunderstanding in your love life. You aren't very forthcoming and that causes pain and mistrust."

"You need to tell me something good if you want a

tip," he muttered, giving her a sideways glare. Tell him something he didn't know.

"But I like the way the lines merge. Tells me there will be a long-lasting love in your future."

"You just want a good tip."

She dropped his hand. "The palm doesn't lie."

"Sure, it doesn't." He stood and dug into his back pocket for his wallet and drew out a twenty. At her "ahem" he added another twenty to it and dropped them on the red silk cloth.

"For another ten, I'll read the tarot cards for you."

He gave her the nun's evil eye and it made her laugh.

"Cheer up, sailor. May have been a rough voyage, but it was worth making."

"How did you know I'm a sailor?"

"You are?" She lifted painted-on brows in what should have been surprise, but her blue eyes probed him. "I see many things, and I'll tell you one you must heed."

He lifted a brow.

"Look to the past to find your future."

Great. He'd already done that—and the future hadn't shown up.

"Thanks." He pushed the metal chair in and gave her a nod. She gave him a secret smile and nodded back.

Then he started walking, heading around toward the cathedral and the museum next door—the Cabildo, which contained collections of Spanish and French artifacts from the days of early Louisiana. Darby had always adored history, loving that Beau Soleil held a little bit of it in the form of Indian mounds on the land.

A sixth sense compelled him into the foyer of the museum he hadn't visited in too many years. He hadn't seen the displays from Hurricane Katrina and wouldn't mind perusing a brochure on it, maybe even drop by tomorrow since they looked to be closing up.

"Darby!"

He'd been sliding a brochure from a slot on the docent's desk when he heard her voice. He froze, his heart dropping into his toes. He'd never thought that could happen— a heart plummeting that fast, but he was sure he'd felt it all the way down into his trail runners.

"Renny?"

He turned to find her sitting on a bench with her leg elevated on a stack of books, a bag of ice sitting on her ankle. "I can't believe you found me. My phone is dead—I forgot to charge it."

"What happened? Are you okay?"

She started laughing. "Yeah, but I can't walk. This damn leg buckled—" she motioned to her bad leg "—and I tripped, landed on a grate and twisted my ankle so badly I can't walk on it. Luckily a nice man helped me hobble into the foyer here."

He moved toward her, trying not to get his hopes up, but letting them fly anyway. "You came."

"That's what she said."

He laughed. "Oh, my Lord, woman. That's your response?"

She shrugged. "Sorry, but how's this for irony? It's like the movie, the one you quoted in your letter, though I didn't think another accident could happen. I mean, I was already crippled in the last one."

He shook his head and sat down on the end of the bench, sliding the ice bag off her ankle. Sure enough it was red and puffy. "Do you think we need to go to the hospital?"

"I don't know." She peered down at the ankle and

wiggled her toes. "I can't believe I did this. I can't believe you waited."

"I've been getting my fortune told."

Renny made a face. "Your fortune told?"

"Yeah, and you know what the last thing she said was?"

"What?"

"That I should look for my future in the past." He looked around. "I'm not sure if she meant literally or figuratively."

Renny raised her eyebrows. "Um, both?"

He took a moment to study Renny. Her face held the vestige of tears and she looked a little sweaty. Not exactly the romantic reunion of two destined hearts he'd intended. "Did you come here to say yes or just let me down gently?"

"What do you think?"

"I don't know. I only know what I hope."

A woman in a navy jacket interrupted. "Miss Latioles, I'm assuming this was the gentleman you wanted us to look for?"

Renny looked up and nodded. "Yes, thank goodness he hadn't left."

"Yes, well…" The woman looked at the guard standing inside the inner door to the museum. "We need to close up so…"

"We'll be out of your hair in just a minute," Darby said, readjusting the ice pack. He wasn't exactly sure how they'd manage, but they would. "Okay, Renny, I'm going to have to carry you."

"You can't do that. I'm too heavy."

"Come on, I work out, and you weigh maybe one-twenty."

She smiled. "I'll let you keep thinking that."

He laughed. Like he gave a good damn what she weighed. She could weigh 150 or 200 and he'd still be giddy that the woman he loved had shown up to claim a life with him. Of course, he probably wouldn't have been able to carry her very far. He didn't work out that hard.

"Hold the ice and your shoe," he said, handing them to her before scooping her up under her arms and knees.

"You want me to call a cab?" the docent asked, her silver head swiveling toward a phone on the desk.

"Nah," he said. "I have a better idea."

Darby walked out of the Cabildo, carrying Renny, who kept shouting her thanks over his shoulder, and strolled about seventy yards to where a horse and carriage sat.

"A buggy ride?"

"Why not? It's more romantic than a regular cab and probably just as fast considering the end-of-the-day traffic," he said, helping her onto the red leather seat that had seen better days. It didn't matter that the white paint was chipped or the horse pulling the buggy wore a ridiculous feather on her head—at that moment nothing else mattered but the woman sitting next to him.

The driver turned around and stated his route, and Darby slipped him an extra twenty to stop them at his hotel, which was right off Bourbon. The man clicked his tongue and set "Blanche DuBois" off at a steady clip. Darby pulled Renny's ankle into his lap, took the dripping ice bag from her hand and placed it on her ankle.

She hissed then unwound the scarf thing around her neck. "Here, wrap it in this."

"Won't it ruin your thingy?" he asked.

"At this point, I don't really care, though it's not

hurting as badly since the lady at the Cabildo gave me
a few pain relievers."

He wrapped the soggy bag in the wrap and gently replaced it on her ankle. She probably had a nasty sprain,
but it wouldn't hurt to get an X-ray. As soon as they got
back to his hotel, he'd send for his car and take her to
the closest emergency care clinic.

"So, you came."

She opened her mouth, but he stopped her from tossing out the snarky comeback with a kiss.

She sighed against his lips and he caught it, absorbed
it, became that sweet sigh of submission. Because he'd
submitted to her weeks ago. His heart belonged to
Renny Latioles.

He broke the relatively tame kiss and looked into her
eyes. "Thank you for choosing us, Renny."

She brushed his cheek and gave him another kiss.
"After we talk, you might not be as happy."

CHAPTER NINETEEN

RENNY STUDIED DARBY in the waning light of the day. It was a Saturday and business in the French Quarter had slowed to a lull with all the day-trippers heading home or to their hotels, and the night-birds awaiting the sinful cloak of darkness so they could haunt the old bricked sidewalks much like the ghosts of Lafitte or Marie Laveau—except with the notorious Bourbon Street hand grenades or Pat O'Brien's hurricanes in hand.

"What does that mean?" Darby asked, alarm shooting through those mesmerizing blue eyes. "I may not be happy after we talk about it?"

She patted his hand. "It's not bad. I promise. Just some more thoughts I had about where we go from here."

Darby shifted his eyes away with a confused frown. "But you came."

"Yes, I'm choosing us, but not the way you think I am." She sighed as the driver pointed out the first bar to serve a Sazerac and then swiftly launched into tales of slaves who'd been tortured and movies that had been filmed among the cobbled streets and wrought iron that garnished the Quarter.

Darby rolled his hand in an insistent "get the show on the road" manner.

"Let's talk later because I don't think he's going to stop with the tour script," she whispered as the driver turned around to make sure they were listening. After ten more minutes of history lesson, Darby interrupted the man's practiced monologue to point out his hotel.

"This is as far as you wanna go? I haven't even got to the gay section of town. It's got interesting history, too."

"That's okay," Darby said, pulling out some money. "Her ankle isn't up to snuff and we don't want to walk back."

"Your loss," the man said, taking the money.

"Here," Renny said, digging for the cash she'd tucked in her back pocket. "I'll get the tip."

She was relieved that Darby let her toss in some money for the ride and that suited her fine because she wasn't some damsel who had to be taken care of.

Equals.

That's what she wanted.

But Darby didn't let her hobble from the vehicle. He swept her up Scarlett O'Hara style and strolled into the marble lobby of the hotel as if it were quite natural to carry a woman in.

"Just married?" questioned the hotel clerk with a smirk.

"Nope, been married for eleven years," Darby said, not bothering to slow his pace.

"Awww, that's so sweet that y'all keep the romance alive," she called as he pushed the elevator button.

Renny smiled and then frowned. "Oops. I left my bag of ice in the buggy."

"I'll get more from the ice machine," he said, stepping inside and making room for an older couple who kept smiling at them.

"I used to be able to pick her up like that," the older man said, eyeing his wife. "Until she found that cupcake bakery down the road."

The woman hit him with her purse. "Shut up, you old goat. You're lucky I married you in the first place."

Then they both grinned good-naturedly like they'd revealed an inside joke.

"Well, I just fell and twisted my ankle," Renny said, trying to shift her weight so Darby's arms didn't get too tired.

The elevator dinged and Darby stepped out without giving the older couple a chance to acknowledge Renny's declaration. "Night."

"Have fun, you two," the man called out.

His wife giggled as the elevator closed.

"They didn't believe me," Renny said, counting the doors as Darby strolled toward…a suite. "Is that the honeymoon suite?"

He smiled.

"Sure of yourself much?"

"Not really, but I figured we didn't get one the first time."

He slid a key card from his pocket and she heard the door whir and then click open. Darby pushed them through the dark foyer and deposited her on an upholstered chair before clicking on a lamp. Dim light flooded the luxurious room.

"Wow," Renny breathed, looking around at the canopied bed, sitting area and glittering view of the Vieux Carré. Darby had spared no expense when he'd rolled the dice on her. All in.

"Yeah, but maybe a waste of money…if your words in the carriage are any indication."

She shrugged. "Beauty is never wasted, is it?"

"Maybe." He sank onto the adjacent chair. "We should get your ankle looked at by a professional."

Renny moved her ankle gingerly, trying to discern

if she needed to go to the hospital or not. It was still puffy but the ice had done its job. She knew it wasn't broken. "I'd rather wait and see. I'm pretty sure it's just sprained. I'll see how it feels tomorrow and if it hasn't improved, I'll go."

Darby made a face. "I'm not sure—"

"Darby," she warned. This was what she meant. The man would have to learn to walk the line between concern and control if he wanted this to work.

He snapped his mouth shut. "Sure, that sounds reasonable."

That made her smile. "It does, doesn't it?"

They sat there for a moment before he stood. "Let me get you some ice."

"Okay, and then we'll talk."

He hesitated, looking as if he'd like to say more before nodding and grabbing the ice bucket from the ornate cherry bar serving as the division between the sitting area and bedroom.

The door snicked closed and Renny took a deep breath.

So not the way she'd planned the afternoon. She'd envisioned a dramatic reunion, sweet wet kisses and some café au lait and beignets while they discussed where they went from here. Damn her bad leg. She'd not even seen the grate she was in such a hurry to get to Darby.

Which surprised her. Because a day ago, sitting on the flowered bedspread of her hotel, she hadn't been sure she had the guts to take what she wanted. For a good hour, she'd sat in that room wondering if the hotel room harbored bed bugs…and if she should go to Jackson Square or walk away?

It was the same question she'd asked herself many, many times over the past few weeks, all the while angry at herself for not knowing the answer. But it was the most important question she'd ever faced. She'd missed out on the opportunity to decide the answer over ten years before, and she wasn't going to pass on the chance to actually be in on the decision.

It was too important.

So it had occupied her mind most of the time.

Darby had given her the rarest of gifts—a choice.

Of course, she'd had a choice all along. She was, after all, a big girl who'd faced bigger battles than the one she'd waged with Darby over their relationship.

Getting her master's and doctorate hadn't been a cakewalk—she'd slogged plenty of hours in the nastiest places known to man and woman and had matched wits with the most chauvinistic of men. Not to mention she'd talked her mother out of a ridiculous peacock jacket. Renny could do battle despite what Darby had implied that day out in the field.

But she hadn't had to.

Because Darby had quite simply, and very romantically, laid out his gift.

Her choice to accept him as her future. Or not.

A great deal of thought had gotten her to where she now sat, even though there were times she wished he'd merely left Bayou Bridge behind and not given her a chance to change her mind. Maybe it would have been easier.

Still, distance from Darby had given her clarity.

And at the very least, she owed him an answer.

This time he wouldn't stand in the middle of New Orleans waiting for one. She would go to Jackson Square.

For better or for worse.

But what would be her answer?

It had come to her in the small hours just before

dawn, when she'd awoken that morning. The epiphany had jackknifed her to sitting, slamming her with truth.

She could live without Darby...but did she want to?

The mechanism on the door lock rotated, jarring her from her thoughts as Darby returned. Her ankle held a dull throb and she was a sweaty, soggy mess thanks to frustrated tears and a drippy ice bag. Her silky blouse was damp and crumpled, and her makeup was long gone.

Goodbye romance. Hello reality.

"Here we go," Darby said, breezing back into the room, knotting the plastic ice liner before wrapping the bag in a bar towel. "This should work."

"Thank you," she said, accepting the makeshift compress as she propped her ankle on the ottoman.

He assumed his former position on the chair beside her and looked at her expectantly.

Okay, time to do this.

"Well, the good news is I choose you, Darby. I do."

Relief pooled in his eyes. "But..."

"It's not really a but, just more of a how."

"How?"

"Let me explain," she said, leaning back into the plush silk pillows behind her. Her hands shook from the adrenaline rushing through her. This was so important and she didn't want to screw it up. "I think you know how I feel about your very nature. How I don't like the whole bulldozer approach, but I understand who you are, Darby. There's nothing wrong with going after what you want, and there's something attractive about your tenaciousness. As long as you can pull in the reins when necessary."

He nodded but didn't say anything. Renny liked how

serious his eyes were, how committed he was to hearing her out. This was important to him, too.

"And distance gave me clarity into why I hid from love for so long. I loved you, but I never felt I measured up to you. To being a Dufrene. All those years ago, I expected you to leave, not because you'd done anything to indicate that, but because I felt inferior. I believed your father not because of you, but because of me."

He shook his head, "Ah, Renny, being a Dufrene isn't always easy, but there isn't a blood test to qualify. We don't test you to see if you know how to set a table for twelve or force you to do a debutante bow. I've never seen you as less than what you are—a smart, beautiful woman."

Renny smiled. "I can see that now, and I'm sorry you had to be the brave one. I'm sorry I wasn't strong enough to see my own flaws, to see my own inadequacies."

"Apology accepted, and I don't blame you for feeling hunted. I couldn't seem to stay away from you. Maybe it wasn't me pushing, maybe it was fate."

Renny cocked her head. "Perhaps that's true, but if we are meant to be, we have to carve out the terms."

Leaning forward with his forearms on his knees, Darby nodded. "Go on."

"Our relationship has been like a line graph. We started the way love is supposed to start—dating, growing intimacy, sex, and, uh, marriage." She drew an imaginary line with her finger. "But then we did things backward—marriage, sex, dating. You see what I mean?"

Darby narrowed his eyes. "Kinda."

"So we're back where we started."

"With you in a berry patch?"

They both took a little head trip back in time. She smiled at that young girl with the trim stomach and bramble prickles embedded in her hands. And at that long-haired sun god in a pickup truck wearing no shirt and blaring Toby Keith. "In some small way."

He grinned. "Well, I loved you in that bikini top and cutoffs shorts, so not a bad thing."

"Not the way I was dressed, but more in the realm of the mystery of it all. You were right. There's a lot I don't know about you. We haven't been Renny and Darby for ten years, and both of us have changed. Even though our love has remained, as people we're different."

He clasped his hands between his knees. "But not so much we can't bridge that."

"You're right. Not too much, but enough that we need time to rediscover the other person, not as love-sick teenagers, but as—"

"Lovesick adults?"

"I can buy what you're sellin'."

He slid to his knees and took her hand. "Can you? 'Cause that's what I'm selling, Renny. Love. True love. The kind I won't walk away from. No more misunderstandings. No more allowing others to make us doubt what we have. Binding, forever kind of love."

She swallowed, begging tears not to spring to her eyes. "I do love you, Darby, and that's exactly what I want. But, I want us together as equals, being patient and allowing ourselves to grow into a lasting, mature love."

The tears fell despite her attempts. Darby reached up and caught them, brushing them on his jeans, as he leaned forward and kissed her.

A beautiful rightness encompassed her as she leaned

into his kiss, wrapping her arms around the man God had made for her.

She knew this as certain as she knew her heart beat or the sun rose in the east.

Renny Latioles and Darby Dufrene were meant to be. Forever. And ever.

He broke the kiss and leaned back to look at her. "I'm game for taking it slow and giving ourselves time to enjoy this new, yet old, love. I think you're a pretty smart woman."

Renny traced the scruffiness of his jaw before running a finger over his thick brows, before pressing a finger to the small cleft of his chin. "You think right."

He laughed and kissed her again.

She reveled in the kiss.

It was a kiss of freedom. No more guilt. No more concern over whether she should or shouldn't. No more worry over where it would take them.

It would take them into their future.

Back to Bayou Bridge.

Back to where they'd started.

PICOU DUFRENE ADJUSTED her flowing skirt so it didn't get caught in the rockers of the chair and stared out at her children gathered beneath the branches of the oaks that had tangled themselves in the soil of Beau Soleil for hundreds of years.

She couldn't stop smiling.

Her children.

All together.

All happy.

The thought expanded in her chest, filling her with an immeasurable sweetness.

Nate chased after Paxton, who'd recently started

toddling around, shoving anything he could grab into his mouth. Currently, it looked like Nate was working an acorn from the baby's mouth. His wife, Annie, slid the occasional worried glance his way as she unfolded newspapers and handed them to Lou, who promptly taped them to the two large folding tables sitting on a level part of the lawn. Abram lifted a huge sack of shrimp from the bed of Nate's truck, and after slapping Lou on the butt and getting the requisite squeal, headed toward Darby, who stood staring at the huge pot sitting on a burner as if he could conjure magic from the depths of the boiling water. Renny stood at a separate small table cutting up onions and lemons. She couldn't seem to take her eyes off Darby, which seemed dangerous considering she held a knife in hand.

And then there was Della, who looked as if she were in charge of the whole production. Picou's daughter wore an old apron made of flour sacks that she'd dug from the bottom of Lucille's apron drawer. Declaring it just like the ones her *grand-mère* had sewed for her as a child, she'd donned it and started purging the shrimp with a box of salt,and ordering everyone around.

When Della had decided to be Della, she'd jumped in with both feet. Which had tickled Picou. How easy it seemed the girl had slipped back into being a sister. A daughter. A Dufrene.

The boys were just as amused by their sister's bossiness, sliding each other funny little glances and doing aggravating stuff to tease Della, which earned them good-natured scoldings from Annie, Lou and Renny.

Picou relished every second of her family's...well, being a family.

"Are you gonna come help, Mom, or just play mistress of the manor?" Nate called, scooping up Paxton and swiping a finger in his mouth. He pulled something out and made a face. "Oh, God, I think he just ate a bug, Annie."

His wife dropped the tape and took the baby, who'd started wailing and kicking his little feet.

"What do you need me to do?" Picou called, not bothering to get up. If they couldn't figure out how to do a simple shrimp boil between the seven of them, there were bigger problems at hand. She'd stay right where she was, sipping hot tea, watching the world she'd created play out in front of her. Plus, she was tired.

She'd made pralines that morning, completed an extra-challenging session of yoga, and trudged out to the rice field to retrieve the plastic storage bin she'd abandoned last month. After a threat of a federal charge for obstruction that she was pretty sure Renny made up, Picou had stopped donning the white makeshift biologist costume and a puppet and put a stop to feeding grapes to the whooping crane. It seemed her son's soon-to-be ex-wife and current girlfriend didn't see eye-to-eye with Picou on keeping the bird on the land until the prophecy played out.

She'd had to formally apologize to Renny and she'd taken her one of Lucille's pies to sweeten the deal, especially since the bird had disappeared. It made Picou desperately sad to miss seeing the bird leave their tiny part of the world. She'd wanted to be a part of the prophecy concluding.

The sound of a car crunching up the driveway interrupted her thoughts and made her stomach flip over. She hadn't been sure he'd come.

"Who's that?" Darby called, taking a few steps and wrapping an arm around Renny, who smiled as his lips brushed her jawbone. "Did you invite Father Benoit to the boil?"

"No," Picou called, standing and smoothing down the ballet top over the waistband of her favorite orange broom skirt. She also brushed back the silver hair she'd left to fall past her shoulders. "Just an old friend."

A dark sedan pulled into view, and she walked down the steps of her home, waving toward the car in greeting. She could feel the stare of her children as she walked toward the gravel parking area.

Picou tried to calm herself, drawing on the strength of the land to center her, calling on her ancestors to give her patience, begging the universe to allow something to still be present between her and whoever would emerge from the car.

The driver's door opened and a young man climbed out, looking around uncertainly. He had shaggy brown hair and the scruffy five-o'clock beard so popular with the young men today. Jeans and a plaid shirt rolled up at the sleeves hung on a lean, fit frame, and Picou noted the laugh lines around the man's eyes and kindness shadowing his mouth.

A very good-looking man, indeed.

Then the passenger door opened, and Gerald Greer stepped out.

"Hi, Gerry," she said, taking in the man turning toward her, studying her with those emerald-green eyes. He looked good—still trim with massive shoulders, and though he'd aged, he'd done so like a fine antique, the beauty still in the product despite a few dings and chips. "Welcome to Beau Soleil."

"Picou." He smiled, and his rich voice caused sheer pleasure to shimmy down her spine. "Aren't you a sight for these old eyes."

"Piddle, Gerry. Speak for yourself. I'm not old, just experienced."

His laughter swirled up through the trees, launching a few birds into flight, as he walked toward her.

Yes, this was a fine figure of a man, with more than a little interest in those luscious eyes. Picou's heart sped up as Gerald lifted her hand to his lips.

"Beautiful," he murmured, his eyes capturing her gaze, putting to rest those doubts about whether there was something still between them.

Ah, yes. Definitely sparks pinging around them as they spoke with a simple look.

Picou knew her cheeks were pink, but didn't give a good damn as she spun toward her boys and the women who loved them. They'd circled around her, looking positively bumfuzzled, except for Darby. Smiling, her youngest son shook his head and held out a hand. "Mr. Greer, I'm Darby Dufrene. These are my brothers, Nate and Abram."

Both of her other boys stuck out their hands, introducing Annie, Lou and Pax, while shooting her curious looks.

"And I'm Della, Picou's daughter," Della said, extending her own hand after having wiped it on her apron.

Then they all turned to look at Picou.

"Gerald was my first lover," Picou explained with a flourish of her hands. "But don't worry, he's single again, so…"

"Christ, Mom," Nate said, making the sort of face a son was supposed to make when confronted with seeing his mother as something more than the woman who'd birthed him.

Gerald laughed and wound an arm around her, pulling her into a brief hug. "See, that's what I've always loved about you, Picou. You do know how to kick pretense to the curb and get to the heart of things."

Picou felt that man's embrace all the way down to her glittery Toms, and something even more wonderful than she could have ever expected unwound within her, rising up and spreading its wings. Something portent, potent and good.

She held out her hands to a wiggling Pax, dropping a kiss onto her grandson's forehead before settling him on her hip. Gerald's arm fell away and he motioned the man who'd driven him to Beau Soleil to his side.

"Picou, this is my son, Connor."

The young man held out a hand and gave hers a brief shake, before offering it to each of her sons.

"Connor just completed his residency in pediatric surgery last month and is finally moving back to Louisiana."

Connor shot his father a long-suffering look, but it was tolerant. Really, didn't kids know it was part of a parent's job to brag on them?

"How fascinating," Picou said, pulling Della over. "Della works with children, too. She teaches second grade."

Della's eyes widened. "Not quite the same thing. The only surgery I'm required to perform is untangling ponytail holders from Emma Badeaux's hair. She has really curly hair."

Picou didn't miss Connor's eyes dipping to take in all of Della as he offered his hand to her. "But both bring tears, no doubt."

Connor smiled at Della, catching her gaze, and Picou swore she felt a small tremor vibrate through her daughter.

Well, then.

Picou turned to her children. "Someone better go check those shrimp. I don't want to serve overcooked food to our guests."

Nate jumped. "Oh, crap."

He and Abram took off for the pot, with Abram beating him by a good two strides while Annie and Lou ambled off behind them.

"Della, I'm taking Mr. Greer in to show him the house. Why don't you walk Connor down and show him Bayou Tete?"

"But, Mom—"

"Go on, dear. I can tell he's the sort of boy who needs to stretch his legs after a long drive." She didn't wait for her daughter's answer. Instead she turned and beckoned Gerald with her eyes, and like a good boy he followed her up the stairs.

Paxton sucked his fingers as he laid his little head on her shoulder, and Picou turned before entering the house.

Della shrugged at Connor apologetically with a sort of "oh, well" look as she untied the apron around her waist and tossed it on the stone pillar at the foot of the steps.

Oh, good girl.

Her daughter wore a tight spandex shirt of brilliant blue that hugged her small breasts and emphasized her tiny waist. The jeans were trim and hugged her cute little rump. Connor didn't look at all upset at being shuffled off to look at sluggish bayou water.

Gerald held the door open, but Picou didn't move.

At that moment, the golden glow of the sinking sun blanketed her family in a sweet gloriousness, laying over them in a warm bath of brilliance, streaming triumphantly through the ancient dark limbs of the giants that guarded her home.

And as that glowing orb sank toward the western horizon, a great white bird spread its wings and sailed above them, catching the wind and sailing high over the tree line.

Picou's mouth fell open as she watched the bird disappear into the southern sky.

Inside her body a low hum had started, vibrating all the way up to her heart, filling it with the wonder of something she couldn't begin to describe.

She jerked her eyes to Nate, Abram, Darby and Della—all of whom were still staring at the sky.

But it was Renny who caught her gaze and held it.

Simultaneously, both women smiled.

Then Picou Dufrene felt her heart sing as the prophecy was completed. And the sun dipped down, finally setting on Beau Soleil.

* * * * *

*Look for Liz Talley's next book
THE SPIRIT OF CHRISTMAS
Coming December 2012 from
Harlequin Superromance*

REQUEST YOUR FREE BOOKS!
2 FREE NOVELS PLUS 2 FREE GIFTS!

Exciting, emotional, unexpected!

YES! Please send me 2 FREE Harlequin® Superromance® novels and my 2 FREE gifts (gifts are worth about $10). After receiving them, if I don't wish to receive any more books, I can return the shipping statement marked "cancel." If I don't cancel, I will receive 6 brand-new novels every month and be billed just $4.69 per book in the U.S. or $5.24 per book in Canada. That's a saving of at least 15% off the cover price! It's quite a bargain! Shipping and handling is just 50¢ per book in the U.S. and 75¢ per book in Canada.* I understand that accepting the 2 free books and gifts places me under no obligation to buy anything. I can always return a shipment and cancel at any time. Even if I never buy another book, the two free books and gifts are mine to keep forever.

135/336 HDN FC6T

Name	(PLEASE PRINT)	
Address		Apt. #
City	State/Prov.	Zip/Postal Code

Signature (if under 18, a parent or guardian must sign)

Mail to the **Reader Service:**
IN U.S.A.: P.O. Box 1867, Buffalo, NY 14240-1867
IN CANADA: P.O. Box 609, Fort Erie, Ontario L2A 5X3

Not valid for current subscribers to Harlequin Superromance books.
**Are you a current subscriber to Harlequin Superromance books
and want to receive the larger-print edition?
Call 1-800-873-8635 or visit www.ReaderService.com.**

* Terms and prices subject to change without notice. Prices do not include applicable taxes. Sales tax applicable in N.Y. Canadian residents will be charged applicable taxes. Offer not valid in Quebec. This offer is limited to one order per household. All orders subject to credit approval. Credit or debit balances in a customer's account(s) may be offset by any other outstanding balance owed by or to the customer. Please allow 4 to 6 weeks for delivery. Offer available while quantities last.

*What happens when a Texas nanny learns she is
the biological daughter of a prince? Her rancher boss
steps in to help protect her from the paparazzi, but who
can protect her from her attraction to him?*

*Read on for an excerpt of
A HOME FOR NOBODY'S PRINCESS
by* USA TODAY *bestselling author Leanne Banks.*

Available October 2012

"This is out of control." Benjamin sighed. "Well, damn. I guess I'm gonna have to be your fiancé."

Coco's jaw dropped. "What?"

"It won't be real," he said quickly, as much for himself as for her. After the debacle of his relationship with Brooke, the idea of an engagement nearly gave him hives. "It's just for the sake of appearances until the insanity dies down. This way it won't look like you're all alone and ready to have someone take advantage of you. If someone approaches you, then they'll have to deal with me, too."

She frowned. "I'm stronger than I seem," she said.

"I know you're strong. After what you went through for your mom and helping Emma to settle down, I know you're strong. But it's gotta be damn tiring to feel like you've always got to be on guard."

Coco sighed and her shoulders slumped. "You're right about that." She met his gaze with a wince. "Are you sure you don't mind doing this?"

"It's just for a little while," he said. "You mentioned that a fiancé would fix things a few minutes ago. I had to run it through my brain. It seems like the right thing to do."

She gave a slow nod and bit her lip. "Hmm. But it would cut into your dating time."

Benjamin laughed. "That's not a big focus at the moment."

"It would be a huge relief for me," she admitted. "If you're sure you don't mind. And we'll break it off the second you feel inconvenienced."

"No problem," he said. "I'll spread the word. Should be all over the county by lunchtime. No one can know the truth. That's the only way this will work."

Coco took a deep breath and closed her eyes as if preparing to take a jump into deep water. "Okay" she said, and opened her eyes. "Let's do it."

Will Coco be able to carry out the charade?

Find out in Leanne Banks's new novel—
A HOME FOR NOBODY'S PRINCESS.

Available October 2012 from Harlequin® Special Edition®

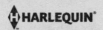

HARLEQUIN®

SPECIAL EDITION

Life, Love and Family

Sometimes love strikes in the most unexpected circumstances...

Soon-to-be single mom Antonia Wright isn't looking for romance, especially from a cowboy. But when rancher and single father Clayton Traub rents a room at Antonia's boardinghouse, Wright's Way, she isn't prepared for the attraction that instantly sizzles between them or the pain she sees in his big brown eyes. Can Clay and Antonia trust their hearts and build the family they've always dreamed of?

Don't miss

THE MAVERICK'S READY-MADE FAMILY

by Brenda Harlen

Available this October from Harlequin® Special Edition®

www.Harlequin.com

HSE65697

celebrating 15 YEARS

Love Inspired™

Another heartwarming installment of

— TEXAS TWINS —

Two sets of twins, torn apart by family secrets,
find their way home

When big-city cop Grayson Wallace visits an elementary
school for career day, he finds his heartstrings
unexpectedly tugged by a six-year-old fatherless boy and
his widowed mother, Elise Lopez. Now he can't get the
struggling Lopezes off his mind. All he can think about
is what family means—especially after discovering
the identical twin brother he hadn't known he had
in Grasslands. Maybe a trip to ranch country is just
what he, Elise and little Cory need.

Look-Alike Lawman
by Glynna Kaye

*Available October 2012
wherever books are sold.*

www.LoveInspiredBooks.com

LI87770

HARLEQUIN® Romance

At their grandmother's request, three estranged sisters return home for Christmas to the small town of Beckett's Run. Little do they know that this family reunion will reveal long-buried secrets... and new-found love.

Discover the magic of Christmas in a brand-new Harlequin® Romance miniseries.

In October 2012, find yourself
SNOWBOUND IN THE EARL'S CASTLE
by **Fiona Harper**

Be enchanted in November 2012 by a
SLEIGH RIDE WITH THE RANCHER
by **Donna Alward**

And be mesmerized in December 2012 by
MISTLETOE KISSES WITH THE BILLIONAIRE
by **Shirley Jump**

Available wherever books are sold.

SM B9

HARLEQUIN® *Blaze*™

red-hot reads

Two sizzling fairy tales with men straight from your wildest dreams...

Fan-favorite authors

Rhonda Nelson & Karen Foley

bring readers another installment of

Blazing Bedtime Stories, Volume IX

THE EQUALIZER

Modern-day righter of wrongs, Robin Sherwood is a man on a mission and will do everything necessary to see that through, especially when that means catching the eye of a fair maiden.

GOD'S GIFT TO WOMEN

Sculptor Lexi Adams decides there is no such thing as the perfect man, until she catches sight of Nikos Christakos, the sexy builder next door. She convinces herself that she only wants to sculpt him, but soon finds a cold stone statue is a poor substitute for the real deal.

Available October 2012 wherever books are sold.